Self-Reference
ENGINE

←⋀⋀⋀—Toh EnJoe—⋀⋀⋀→

SAN FRANCISCO

Self-Reference
ENGINE

←◆◇◆◇◆◇◆◇◆Toh EnJoe◆◇◆◇◆◇◆◇◆→

Translated by
Terry Gallagher

Self-Reference ENGINE

© 2007 Toh EnJoe

Originally published in Japan by Hayakawa Publishing Inc.

English translation © 2013 VIZ Media, LLC

Cover design by Sam Elzway

All rights reserved.

HAIKASORU

Published by VIZ Media, LLC

295 Bay Street

San Francisco, CA 94133

www.haikasoru.com

Library of Congress Cataloging-In-Publication data has been applied for.

The rights of the author of the work in this publication to be so identified have been asserted in accordance with the Copyright, Designs and Patents Act 1988. A CIP catalogue record for this book is available from the British Library.

Printed in the U.S.A.

First printing, March 2013

P, but I don't believe that P.

CONTENTS

A MAP MAPPING MAPS

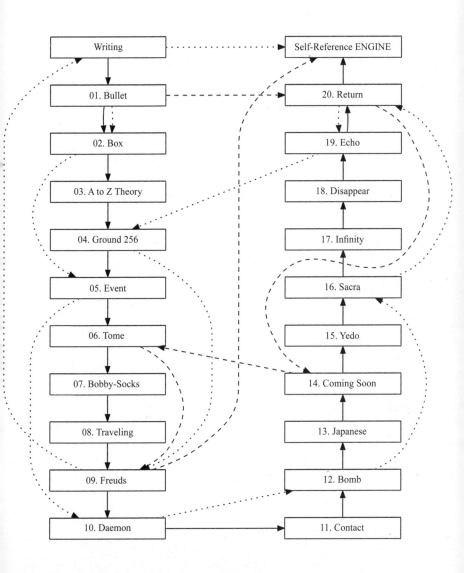

PROLOGUE: WRITING

A SET OF all possible character strings. All possible books would be contained in that.

Most unfortunately though, there is no guarantee whatsoever you would be able to find within it the book you were hoping for. It could be you might find a string of characters saying, "This is the book you were hoping for." Like right here, now. But of course, that is not the book you were hoping for.

I haven't seen her since then. I think she's most likely dead. After all, it has been hundreds of years.

But then again, I also think this.

Noticing her as she gazes intently into the mirror, the room in disarray; it is clear that centuries have flowed by, or some such. And she, perhaps, has finished applying her makeup, and she is getting up and is going out to look for me.

Her eyes show no sign of taking in the fact that the house has been completely changed, destroyed around her. The change was gradual, continuing, and even long ago she was not very good at things like that. As far as she is concerned, that is not the sort of thing one has to pay attention to. Not that she is aware, but it seems so obvious, she doesn't need to care about it.

Have we drowned, are we about to drown, are we already finished drowning, are we not yet drowning? We are in one of those situations. Of course, it could be that we will never drown. But think about it. I mean, even fish can drown.

I remember her saying meanly, "If that's the case, you must be the one from the past."

It is true of course. Everybody comes out of the past; it's not that I'm some guy who comes from some particular past.

Even when that is pointed out, though, she shows no sign of backing down.

"It's not as if I came out of some bizarro past," she said. That's how she and I met.

Writing it down this way, it doesn't seem like anything at all is about to happen, right? Between her and me, I mean. As if something could ever really happen. As if something continues to happen that might ever make something else happen.

I am repeating myself, but I haven't seen her since then. She promised me, with a sweet smile, that I would never see her again.

For the short time we were together, we tried to talk about things that really meant something to us. Around that time there were a lot of things that were all mixed up, and it was not easy to sort out what was really real. There might be a pebble over there, and when you took your eyes off it it turned into a frog, and when you took your eyes off it again it turned into a horsefly. The horsefly that used to be a frog remembered it used to be a frog and stuck out its tongue to try to eat a fly, and then remembered it used to be a pebble and stopped and crashed to the ground.

With all this going on, it's really important to know what's really real and what's not.

"Once upon a time, somewhere, there lived a boy and a girl."

"Once upon a time, somewhere, there lived boys and girls."

"Once upon a time, somewhere, there lived no boy and no girl."

"Once upon a time…lived."

"Lived."

"Once upon a time."

From beginning to end, we carried on this back-and-forth process. For example, in this dialogue, we were somehow finally mutually able to come up with this kind of compromise statement:

"Once upon a time, somewhere, there lived a boy and a girl. There may have been lots of boys, and there may have been lots of girls. There may have been no boys at all, and there may have been no girls at all. There may even have been no one at all. At any rate there is little chance there were equal numbers of each. That is unless there had never been anybody at all anyway."

That was our first meeting, she and I, and of course it meant we would never see each other again. I was making my way in the direction she had come from, and she was headed in the direction I had come from, and this is a somewhat important point; you must realize this walking had to be, for some reason, in just one direction.

At the end of the end of all this great to-do, time itself freezes, universally, and some clock somewhere should say that a whole lot of time has passed.

I would like you to imagine countless threads, strung through space. I am walking along one of those threads from this end. She is walking along some other thread from some other end.

It is actually quite difficult to explain what I mean by that. I'm not sure I understand it completely myself.

But at that time there was a (slightly embarrassing) way for us to know about the direction we were each traveling in, and we each used it. But just that.

I am not sure just who the criminal who froze time was.

The dominant theory is that the cause was the result of some plan in which some force was triggered, in which all kinds of things were involved: machinery, engines, scientists, some people who weren't even there. Personally, though, I like the theory that it was a crime of time itself.

One day a bunch of time threads were going along in a bundle, stretching out in any direction at all, all together, all thinking it was kind of tedious. All things in time were vexed about this. And since practically everything is, in fact, bundled up in time, they were finding it hard to put up with being subjected to this arbitrariness.

The repeated pattern: restoration plan, persuasion, earnest entreaty, prayer. As indicated, each of these in turn tended to cause the situation to deteriorate, and the idea was that at the point when time itself became confused, the result was some complete entanglement, with all participants left completely unable to move, as though part of some sort of ridiculously and utterly perverse sex act.

If I ever meet the guy who thought up this idea I think I'd like to split his head in two.

And then, a few hundred more years passed. In other words, what I mean is, I just ran through a few hundred years bound up in the frozen net of time.

That is, somehow or other, I arrived at a point that was a few hundred years either in the future or the past.

I cannot say one way or the other whether she had also made such a sprint. But it is a well-known phenomenon that girls often have no trouble passing time without such physical exertions.

That is why I am running again today. You might want to ask why.

One. One day, time caused an insurrection.

Two. We were moving in some unknown direction, allowed only to proceed toward some predetermined day after tomorrow.

The end result was clear.

Whether that result is just or not is something far beyond my ability to determine. In other words, it is like this:

If the lines of time are so entangled with one another that they are one ball of yarn, ignoring both past and future, one of those threads won't mind if we were simply to connect with the instant of its beginning.

The instant when time abandoned the standard, straight-ahead march.

Of course, there is absolutely no guarantee that the path I am running along leads to that instant. That instant may exist at some point that may be completely unreachable, even if one were to follow countless threads through unlimited mysteries. It would take an infinite spider web stretched across infinite space to have enough space between the threads for this.

But, what if, what if, in that one-in-a-billion chance, I were to find that instant? It is obvious what I would have to do. I would have to scream at Time: "Stop thinking all this stupid nonsense; shut up and move along as you were!"

And then when everything was back as it had been, I would finally be able to go out and look for her once more. Or else maybe she would be looking for me, as if in a dream.

What is she doing? That is the thought that spreads out, pure white before me, apropos of nothing.

PART I

NEARSIDE

01. BULLET

WE ARE ALWAYS getting knocked around. That way. This way.

Pushed this way, flying off that way. When we bump into something, we are sent flying. At least, that's what I believe. The only way we can stand right where we are is because we are subject to forces coming at us from all directions, willy-nilly. And the reason our bodies don't buckle under all this pressure is something I learned in school a long time ago. It's because inside our bodies are all kinds of things trying to push their way out. At the bottom of the gravity well, the layer of atmosphere above us does not stave our heads in, and that is the reason.

Of course, there is also an actual reason why I have come to believe this. Of course, we had been that way for a long time without ever thinking we even needed some kind of a reason, still able to believe in something, till at some point we got to now, where most things seem to have had no reason for a long time, and I think this must actually be something quite special.

Rita is a completely unmanageable young girl. None of us knows what to do with her. Things are especially bad when she is in the backyard. She casually pulls the revolver from her belt and…*Bang!* Not that she is aiming my way or anything; she just fires away without a target. Her house is surrounded by rusty steel plates, and of course anything that can be broken is broken. The only things left unbroken are things that can't be broken, and they just sit there.

It is a half mile to the nearest neighbor's. All the locals know about her habits, and they steer clear of her place, because she is from someplace else. People from someplace else have no place here.

So, no problem, right? think Rita's family members, but they are the only ones who think so. The situation is both very obvious and very problematical.

Because she is shooting all the time, she is really good at it. There are many boys in the neighborhood—men actually—who torment Rita and have holes in their pants, very close to their testicles, as a result. No one could figure out how Rita knew just where those men's testicles were, when they hardly even knew themselves.

Among the girls in the area, there is a legend—that many believe to be true—that Rita once shot a cockroach that had nested for years behind her uncle's testicles, but we all know that no such creature could live in such a place. If it could, we would all be secretly keeping pet scarab beetles or praying mantises there where we could play with them.

"There is a reason why Rita is so crazy," James said once, giving me a five-dollar coin. "In her head," he says, pointing to his own temple. "There's a bullet buried in there." And having said that, his body shook a little, as if he had just finished micturating.

I responded that there was nobody alive with a bullet lodged in their head, to which he responded that's exactly what's so fantastic about it, turning red in the face.

I believe James to be the smartest guy in this neighborhood, or maybe even the smartest guy in North America, but for two weeks now he has had the world's worst crush on Rita. Now, even I know you can't get apples from oranges, but this guy is the worst. If you could extract the smarts there wouldn't be anything left of him. But he was still the smartest guy for two hundred miles around, no doubt about it.

"So what if she does have a bullet in her head?" I asked. "Sometime it must have got there somehow. How else could it be?"

Jay looked at me with a bored expression on his face.

"It's been there since she was born," he said seriously. I couldn't be sure if he was teasing me or what, so I just patted him on the shoulder. Jay turned and got hold of me, wrapped his right arm around my middle, and threw me down. I offered no resistance and tumbled to the grass, landing spread-eagled.

"Huh?" I said.

"Huh what?" he said back. And repeating this scintillating dialogue, back and forth, we got into it, just repeating "Huh" at each other, heatedly. Jay was just trying to get his "hypothesis" across.

"Your 'hypothesis'?!" I yelled back. "From now on anybody who uses a word like 'hypothesis' to me, I'm just going to call you 'Mess,' cause your name 'James' is really 'Jay-Mess'! And then I will call you 'Messed-Up'!"

As I sat there being reborn as a "mess-up" machine, Jay sat down next to me and wrapped his arms around his knees and told me how much he liked Rita. He had told me the same thing just the day before, and if I may say so, he had also said it just two minutes before that. He had probably said it a thousand times since he started feeling that way, but I didn't mind. A thousand times in two weeks might be too much though.

"If my hypothesis is correct, though…" he just kept repeating.

"Knock it off already about your hypothesis," I grumbled as I got up. I never heard of a hypothesis that ever convinced a girl to do anything. Jay was too smart to ever hit on a girl. Some hypothesis, huh?

"If my hypothesis is correct…" he said again, proudly.

With nothing better to do than stand there and listen, I realized Jay seemed to be sobbing.

Hmmm, people who go on about their hypotheses, it seems, really have some pretty extraordinary capacities. James was the kind of guy who wouldn't ordinarily shed a tear even if hornets stung him on the butt. Although I do have a tendency to exaggerate.

"Rita," Jay would say, "is shooting her bullets at the day after tomorrow." He said it like he was sure of it.

That's the way it is. No target, that's just the way it is.

"Of course that's not what I meant," Jay would say without even looking this way. "Rita's just having a shooting match with somebody in the future," he went on.

That inference, or delusion, that he drew did not particularly move me. Let me put this plainly: *I don't understand.*

"Well, first, let us assume…" Jay said in preface. "Rita has a bullet in her head. William Smith Clark has testified to this."

I didn't put much faith in that old Civil War doctor, who ended up as a statue in Japan, forever pointing to some far horizon, as if trying to instruct his lost sheep. Come to think of it, I don't think doctors are very trustworthy at all.

"Next, let us assume that bullet has been in Rita's head ever since she was born. I heard that from her aunt, so I'm sure it's true.

"There can only be one conclusion!" Jay said, jumping to his feet. I don't know why, but he was pointing at the sky.

I said, "When Rita was still in her mother's womb, her mother was shot!"

Jay cut a gallant figure, but I would have to dash some cold water on him. He held that pose for some time, and I watched as the arm pointing high in the sky gradually bent back toward the ground.

"Maybe so," he said.

Jay made a complicated face as he thought. There was a right way to enter a house. Most people think it is proper etiquette to open the door before entering. I'm pretty sure it's not too smart to open the door after entering. Even scarier if it's bullets we're talking about.

"What other possible way could there be?" I asked Jay.

Adding insult to injury, with a lonely look on his face, Jay said, "Someone in the future shot Rita. For better or worse, that bullet lodged in her skull. But from the recoil, Rita is, even now, being pushed backward in time, back into her mother's belly."

Hmmm, I thought, waving at Jay to go on if he wished to continue in this vein.

"Here's what I think. From the very start, Rita came from some direction or other. But then for some reason, somebody shot at her from the future, and now her path has been turned back in the direction of the past. And that is why, in reaction to that, she is now heading back in time, back in the direction of her mother's tummy."

I stared at him, my mouth wide open. Not because I was so impressed. Just because I could absolutely not believe he was saying that. What did a kid have to eat to grow up thinking things like that? I knew Jay liked corn flakes, and starting tomorrow I was never going to eat them again. And I would skip the yogurt too. Actually, I think it's kind of funny that people even think of corn flakes as food.

Jay pointed his index finger straight at my open mouth and said, "This is where it starts to get interesting.

"As of right now, the time that we are in, she hasn't been shot yet. She has no experience of having been shot. She is just a girl with a bullet in her head.

"The reason why she keeps shooting all over the place is this: She will be okay as long as she shoots the person who is going to shoot her before she herself gets shot. Relative to her, he should be in the future, so she should just keep shooting at the future. Luckily, bullets normally move in the direction of the future. Or at least, it's easier than shooting at the past."

He's got a point there, I thought. He might be a pretty smart guy, but really he's a complete idiot. And there has only ever been one way to deal with idiots. Just go along with whatever they say, or you'll regret it.

"And what if she succeeds in killing that 'sniper in the future'?"

"I hope she does," he said, nodding pompously.

"So, what's going to happen to the bullet in her head?"

"There are different ways of thinking about that. One possibility is that it will just stay there like it was nothing at all. What I think is more likely, though, is that the past will be changed so that the bullet in her head just disappears. She was born wherever it is that she was born, and at some point that could go all meta-time and turn out that way. But of course, we won't know what's really going to happen until it happens."

"I can't really imagine what happened the instant she was shot."

"Probably…" Jay started to say, thinking, his index finger propped against his temple. Then he took his finger away, along a line that would pierce his head, but moving away. "We should be able to see it this way. A bullet is flying out of Rita's head, in the wrong direction, and enters the muzzle of the sniper's gun, going backward the whole way. Then it enters the muzzle, and the magazine turns the wrong way, and the hammer goes up."

I was having trouble with this.

"But, I mean, if Rita has a bullet in her head, it must be because she got shot, right?"

"But the thing that could change that would be..." Jay responded, going to pieces again, "my role, because I am in love with her!"

My good friend has a crush on a strange girl. This seems a bit odd to me, but that's love for you. It's just something that happens, but when it's your best friend you start to make some really bizarre and twisted rationalizations about what is happening. Of course, if you really want to know what is going on in Rita's crazy head, you'd be better off asking Rita herself. I'm sure it wouldn't be some story about a bullet from the future. You might even say the only important question was whether or not Rita even likes Jay.

Ever since Jay finished explaining his "hypothesis" and burst into tears, I've been wondering just that. What does Rita say? Jay turned bright red, grabbed a fistful of grass and tossed it aside, and ran away, so I never found out the details. But there is no reason to think anyone could ever ask anything so directly of a guy whose thoughts were so tangled. He might even be thinking he should take a knife and cut Rita's skull open, just to be sure.

So, resigning myself to the possibility of sacrificing a testicle, I decided to call on Rita at her house. Two would be too much, but one I could probably live without, for my good friend's sake. I just thought of Rita as a girl whose head was screwed on the wrong way, but I was pretty sure I could count on her not to do anything so stupid as to shoot off both my testicles.

The Rita who greeted me at the door, far from being the kind of person who would threaten to tear me a new asshole if I didn't leave right away, invited me politely, even demurely, into the living room. Somehow there was a poor meshing, like a loosened spring, in the air. I could not relax, as if while holding a watch with the back removed someone had told me to do a backflip.

As I sat there, shifting my weight on the seat from one butt cheek to the other, wondering how to start this conversation, Rita came back in with tea. She set a cup before me, her thumb stuck in it, and said, "I heard."

"Heard what?" I asked.

"From James," she went on, looking straight back at me.

I had not anticipated this, and I was flustered. Which story, exactly, had Jay told her? The highly colorful tale that he was in love with her? Or the fantastically colorless tale that she was moving backward through time? Or had he come and danced before her and blabbed that I was the one in love with her? At the thought that the last of these ideas was actually the most likely, a chill ran down my spine. I had the feeling this was going to cost me more than just one testicle.

"It's true," she said, hanging her head.

I couldn't figure out which of the possibilities she might mean.

"The reason I shoot recklessly is just as James suspects."

Immediately upon hearing those words, the cry that arose in my heart was, *I did it! I'm going to live!* And in that spirit, I adjusted my posture in my seat, and as Rita's words spread through my brain, I somehow slid halfway out of my chair. Mr. Messed-Up. That's no way to get a girl to like you.

As I struggled to crawl back up out of the chair, I rummaged desperately through my brain for the right words, the words she would want to hear, the words that would keep her from shooting me on the spot.

"What I mean to say is, that's it, I mean, you're it!"

To be honest, I was completely unnerved. Rita gave the chair a good yank and left me sprawling on the floor. It took me a while to pull myself together again and stand up straight.

"I didn't realize there was someone else who shared the same conclusion as me." I thought Jay was the smartest guy in the Western Hemisphere, but how was I to know the smartest girl in the Western Hemisphere would be right in the same neighborhood? *What an idiot this one is!*

"So, what I want is for you to tell Jay that on, let's say, this Friday, how would he like to come to dinner at my house?"

That super-syllogistic sentence completely failed to penetrate my awareness. What was the need for a dinner party at Rita's haunted house, where everything was heaps of shards, dripping with unidentified fluids?

Knitting my brow, propping my index fingers on my temples, I concentrated with all my might. When I lifted my head, thinking I had failed the quiz, right in front of me was Rita's face, her cheeks bright red.

What could it be? This marvel of a girl, who could accurately and repeatedly shoot holes in the acorns in a woodpecker's hoard, was in love with someone.

If I could just figure out who, that person would get shot full of holes. So who was going to get that hornet's nest? Jay was.

Realizing my own stupidity, I pounded my forehead with the palm of my hand. Of course it was Jay. The smartest guy on the planet. For me an auspicious realization, for Jay a killing blow. I would have to keep a close eye on her, but thoughts of praise for Rita coursed through my head: the bitch had really worked things out, etc., etc. No reason he wouldn't show up to dinner, I guarantee it. If it seems like he's not going to show up, but then finally he does, I guarantee he'll never go home again, no matter what. Well, he really should be saying this himself—it's not for me to say; well, but maybe it is though, really, surely. I was all confused and just babbling away to fill the time, words all ajumble. I tried to stop, when Rita reached out for her revolver and then staggered as if she had been struck by something.

I was full, full to overflowing from sitting so long, continuing to confront directly this unprocessable development. Unable to figure out what was what, I bolted up from my chair and ran over to Rita, who was dancing a strange dance and slowly dropping to the floor.

Looking down at her, lying on the ground, her long hair strewn about, only then did I notice the small hole in her head.

She had a bullet in her head.

And not just that, James. She had an actual hole in her head.

This was the moment when it happened.

Looking back now, I realize that the instant it happened overlapped precisely with the Event. If that much harm and that much tragedy had not condensed in the world at precisely that moment, I would still have recognized what happened there as an event. But that's not how it was. What happened there was a derivative offshoot of the Event and not the Event itself.

I bent over to peer into the hole in Rita's head, and just at that moment, Rita's body bent straight upward. I dodged, reflexively, then sprang up and reached out both hands to Rita, as one would to pet a dog.

Rita's eyes swam to blankness, and then she reversed direction in time.

From all walls and the floor of the room, reddish-black fluid came flying at Rita's head, rushing at the little hole in it. And then, I could see, in slow motion, the butt end of the little bullet emerging backward from the hole, heading at me. At least, I felt like I could see it. All the blood flying through the air toward Rita's head was suctioned into her skull, and the hole became whole and disappeared.

I am unable to explain what happened next. The little plug that exploded from Rita's head pierced the left side of my chest, and I lost consciousness.

All I know is that the explosion from Rita's revolver had put things back in order. Rita picked up the gun, and then this and that went on among our relatives. I don't know the details.

Jay was a step ahead of us arriving at the hospital. The strange tinge of fantasy had disappeared from his face, but neither could I see any trace of the shyness he had shown before I went to talk to Rita.

"What were you thinking, going off on your own to that nutty girl's place," he said, grilling me. "How could you let her have a gun?" he asked her family indignantly. And then he turned on Rita scornfully: "Why can't you handle a gun?"

Something had certainly changed.

"In her head…" I started to say. "She had a bullet, right here."

I stared straight at Jay, holding my finger to my temple.

"Are you okay?" he said back to me. "Nobody just walks around with a bullet in their head."

I blinked twice and fell silent.

The reason why I was okay, despite being shot on the left side of my chest? Well, do I really have to say? The five-dollar coin that Jay had given me. It was all too banal, so I didn't pursue it any further. Most things that happen are like that. Five dollars is enough to stop a bullet. Of course, the all-bent-out-of-shape coin I gave to Jay would be a fantastic talisman.

Later I tried to think long and hard about what had happened. The bullet that emerged from Rita's head had headed straight back to the future, and it should have gone straight back to the muzzle of the gun that fired it.

But, for whatever reason, I stood in the line of fire, and the backward-coursing bullet struck me.

If the bullet had gone right through me, there would be no problem at all. I would have died, then and there, and the bullet would have returned to the shooter. Instead, the bullet had stopped in my breast pocket, and I had ended its life.

So, the problem here is in the direction of the bullet's entry. If a bullet from the future could shoot Rita, it would have to have gone through my back. But it hit me in the chest and stopped there. My back was uninjured. In other words, Rita had not been shot. I had stopped the bullet that should have returned to the future, and it had not returned to the shooter. In other words, the shooter had not fired it.

This distortion of the structure of time probably hesitated for no more than an instant, and then it chose the simplest solution. Rita had not been shot. Therefore, no bullet had entered Rita's head. In other words, Jay had nothing to fret about. I had simply gone to Rita's house for no particular reason and been felled by

Rita's bullet. That's it.

Now, if Rita had no bullet in her head, Jay had no reason to like her, and Rita had no reason to be interested in Jay if he wasn't thinking the same things she was about the bullet. They might have come to like each other in the future, but somewhere in the direction of the day after tomorrow the intersection point had been lost. But preventing Rita from being shot—hadn't that been Jay's wish? I finally traced this thread backward to the point where we had had that conversation and what Jay had been thinking as he shed those tears.

It was only long after that that I learned something about Rita's birth. The response that came back to me seemed somehow manufactured: she had been given up by a distant relative, and it seemed she had never been able to develop a strong connection with her new parents. I knew nothing at all about anything really before the Event blew in, and I don't really know if I would ever have any way of knowing.

Neither am I able to grasp whether the unknown solution to the not readily comprehensible space-time matrix that resulted from this incident is the reason why I am able to retain the memory of this incident.

One reason that comes to mind is that the whole business was bothersome to me, as the figure in the center of this space-time structure, but it is hard to make the case that my being the center of space-time is a decent solution. At that point in time, I was a singular point. That may be it. Not that that explains anything.

Sometimes I think this memory of mine might be my own invention. It is actually the most plausible explanation. But there is still something odd about the details. If Rita had already been shot at the time I was speaking with her, the room should have been splattered with blood. And there is no way Rita would have been able to carry on a normal conversation with me immediately before, or after, the shooting. Rita's house was not exactly normal—it was kind of a mess—but it was hardly drenched in blood. At least, I don't think so, not now.

Or it could be that this memory is a real one, but if it's real and nobody believes it, what is the point of its being real? What I think now is that something simply satisfied itself with something like that, at least to some degree.

Regardless, a suitable compromise was found at a suitable time for my own mental health.

Or else, it was just the ordinary passing dream of a young boy. It certainly is a lot like, perhaps too much like, the dreams young boys have. Even more so as the dream of someone who remembers how things were before the Event.

I will record what happened to Jay and Rita after that, and then I will close the record.

In the end, Jay never found a lover in the place where he was born and raised, and after high school he went to New York. There it seems he discovered he was hardly the greatest genius in North America, but he wasn't too put out about it because he had never claimed to be. After graduation he wandered around the East Coast, and at some point, though it's not clear how, he landed at a research lab in Santa Fe. Playing a part in the so-called Plan D, he was apparently working on West Coast time-lattice repatriation strategy, but he disappeared along with Santa Fe and the entire middle west of the North American continent.

For some time after the incident, Rita withdrew from the world, but after less than half a year she started walking around outside again, due at least in part to my influence. I'd kept telling her it was no big deal. Rita no longer carried a gun on her belt. For a time I noticed she was helping out at a local grocery, but when her sixteenth birthday came she flew the coop. It was around that time that the Event really started to make itself felt. All hell broke loose, and practically as soon as I heard a rumor she was gone I had forgotten all about it.

The day she left, Rita came to my house. As always, she apologized for what had happened three years before, and then she told me she was leaving. She was planning to take the last train. I put her tiny bag in my family's car, a reluctant Jay got in with us, and we all drove to the station.

The three of us waited in silence for the train, and then suddenly Rita called out our names.

Noticing our failure to look up at her, after a moment she called our names again.

"Richard. James. I have this feeling I have heard your names somewhere else before. Not here, and not even something to do with me. I just don't get it at all."

James replied in a surprisingly gentle tone, "Lots of things are getting harder to get."

"I think you realize I won't be able to see you again, on the future side."

We all said that was ridiculous, but I think of course we all knew it was true.

That was the last time I ever saw her. At least in this future.

I don't know what happened to her after that. I guess I haven't tried very hard to locate her.

Sometimes I think about James, and what happened to him, having disappeared from my future, wrapped up in the events of the North American middle west.

It has been explained that the Event smashed and atomized time itself. As a consequence, I feel like any explanation that doesn't make me feel like I get something shouldn't really be called an explanation. Is that right?

James has disappeared from my present and future, but I'm sure he is alive somewhere in atomized time. He was the kind of guy who would never shed a tear even if a bison trampled his toes. I, of course, am mostly talk.

I still buy James's hypothesis that Rita was shot from the future, or somewhere in that direction. The thought that Rita and James might meet again out there somewhere among the broken shards of time still makes me smile. I wouldn't mind at all. Any way you slice it, time has been smashed to smithereens, and order and consistency have abandoned the field. James is on one fluttering crumb of time, and Rita is on another. Somewhere in space, those crumbs could collide, and James and Rita would meet again.

That would certainly be exciting.

Of course, James is the smartest guy I ever knew, and Rita was the kind of girl who might have a screw loose, but she was definitely one of a kind, marching to the beat of her own drum.

Wouldn't I want to be part of that excitement?

Not at all.

Not on your life, is what I'm thinking as I look up at the blue sky and laugh out loud.

02. BOX

ONCE A YEAR, the door at the back of the storehouse is opened.

We call it the storehouse, but really it's nothing more than a shed. There are no valuables inside. In summer, winter things; in winter, summer things; year-round all kinds of other things are just stuffed randomly inside. The only thing here that identifies this place as a storehouse, and not just a shed, is the quality of the light streaming through the iron lattice over the tiny clerestory windows high on the otherwise expressionless walls. I seldom chose to play in this space, which was too charmless to be called a storehouse. When it was darkness I wanted, I would go to the forest at the Shinto shrine. If it was closeness I wanted, I liked to hide in the closet. I have few memories of playing in the storehouse, which was too jumbled, too bright, and too full of ordinary things.

None of my friends were interested in exploring the storehouse either, and I had no companions looking to escape the eyes of others. In fact, it was in search of such a companion that I eventually left home, and by the time I came back, words like *explore* and *secrets* no longer had need of me.

So for me, this storehouse is no more than a way to get through to the space behind it.

In the back of the storehouse, where everyday things are all piled up, wrenched from their context, is the stern visage of a single steel door. Usually, boxes for satsuma oranges or something are stacked in front of it, obstructing it from opening and closing. Once a year, though, the members of the household gather and move the cardboard boxes away from the door. It is the only day that all members of the family are together in one place.

In the back of the storeroom is a space measuring about six tatami mats, in the middle of which is a square box, about one cubic meter. The box has wood inlay, and it seems to be stuffed full of stuff. It is so heavy it takes all the males of the household to move it.

Once a year, that box is tipped around and then returned to the center. That is the sole strange custom of our household. Every household has its own peculiar customs. Usually people don't realize they're peculiar, because they've grown up with them all their lives, but every household has ways that are unique but not recognized as such because people just don't talk about them.

But there are limits to human imagination, and I think there must be lots of boxes in the world just like this one, sitting around presenting their ordinary faces.

I don't know how long this box has been in our family. Come to think of it, I don't know how long this house has been here. The old records were lost when the nearby temple was burned down in an air raid.

Even so, this house has certainly been here since the Edo period, but nobody knows whether it was Genroku or Kaei. I couldn't even tell you which of those two periods came first. At any rate, the house has been here a very long time.

If the house itself is this way because of its history, the box is doubly incomprehensible. When people have old things, they generally have boxes to put them in, and often they put labels on the boxes, but what we have here is just a box, a box that cannot be opened.

I have a vague notion that this box has always been here. I've never really thought about it.

Once a year, the members of the household get together for a glum conversation about who should tip the box and in what direction.

Now, and this is a frightful thing, there is no record of what direction the box was pushed before.

Once upon a time there certainly was such a record, but no longer. It had been lost so long ago no one even knew when.

After that, through the generations, it is clear that successive heads of the household paid no attention to the trivial issue of considering what direction the box should be toppled in, based on its history to that point, so the situation ended up being pretty haphazard.

I know the box was supposed to be tipped on its side. Or should I perhaps say such is clear without explanation. The box was clearly made as some sort of trick box, and if tipped according to a specific procedure, it would pop open. That is the only possible explanation.

Inlaid boxes like this one are still made in Hakone for the souvenir market. It seems the world will never grow bored of this type of tiresome puzzle mania.

If we ever manage to open the box, what will happen? What might pop out, and what will we do about it? On this point the records of our household are silent. Or perhaps I should say there are no records of our household, and so I have no way of knowing what they might say. Not because the records were destroyed in a fire during wartime, but just for no big reason at all. I think somebody just thought they were in the way and threw them out.

My grandfather was the sort of person who would never agree to do paperwork of any kind, and my father was the kind of person with no interest in family history. No doubt about it, just seeing the way those two lived, it is obvious how our family got to be so irresponsible. Of course, it would be clear to anyone who had a chance to observe me, and the picture isn't pretty. What it comes down to is, it must have lain around so long it was put out with the trash. One of the women, in one of the previous generations, had gotten rid of it, thinking it was just a faded, soiled scrap of paper with some useless scrawl on it. At least that seems the most likely explanation.

By the time anyone got around to really trying to figure out what might have happened to the records, my grandfather was dying, and my father had already died ahead of him.

These were two men who had never been very curious about family histories, but it is possible to imagine that if anyone ever asked them face-to-face that something might have come of it. Thinking about it now, though, what I might have asked, I can't think of anything in particular. That is because I myself come from the same lineage of carelessness, and the trait runs strong within me.

All their days, these two men did as they pleased, and it seems this box inspired certain cravings. Until last year, I was not deeply involved in the whole box-tipping thing. All I did was help by tipping the box in whatever direction I was told to tip it. They did not want me to make any decisions about the box. And I myself had no particular interest in the matter, so I simply did as those two said. This year, though, I am the only one left to tip the box, so I have to confront it all on my own.

The box is a cube, about one meter on each side. The craftsman who made it was quite skilled. The wooden pieces are carefully matched, and even now show no sign of warping. On some face of it there must be a way in, a way to open it, a place where the matched woods will slide away from one another and allow the contents to be disgorged. But even that unglued seam is nowhere to be found.

Not that it is impossible to imagine. It could be that some long-ago ancestor had created this box simply to have a laugh at the stupidity of his future descendants.

One can even imagine that the box, with its cryptic, elaborate decoration, is not really a box at all, but just a giant block of wood. In which case, it will never open no matter how you tip it. That could be it. I mean, if I, the mere descendant, am thinking about this, it would not be strange if my ancestor had also thought of it.

Someone might suggest I measure the relative density, like Archimedes, but there is no leeway for a discussion of how one might go about measuring the relative density of household objects. And I could never be convinced to run around naked trumpeting my discovery.

In our family there is an overabundance of the kind of childishness that leads people to do things for the fun of it, like creating an ancient-seeming stone circle in an uninhabited, out-of-the-way place, or tromping crop circles in wheat fields. But by the same token we are also lacking in conviction, so these adventures of imagination often end up as solitary pleasures.

Not that I think that if this box were ever to wash up on some craggy shore somebody wouldn't bring it back, but more likely they would leave it right where they found it, after trying a little exploratory kick, because it is so heavy. Most likely, this box was either made in this house or had been ordered and brought here, but I have little confidence even in supposing that. It almost seems possible that this box has simply been here from the very beginning, and the house was built around it.

The box is big enough to be just a joke. No one outside our household would ever find themselves wondering if it were really a box at all. Arguing via analogy, knowing my own bloodline, and remembering the laziness with which my father and grandfather passed their days, there is no way any preceding ancestor had enough gumption to build this box just as a joke. This much is clear no matter how you look at it.

So then, why must this box be so big? Maybe the builder was worried that if it was too easy to tip over the puzzle would be too easy to solve. When it comes right down to it, though, one person could tip this box on his own, if he were really serious about it. Any simple lever is enough to do the trick. You put your back into it, take a deep breath, and heave. And of course, if you did have help from another member of the family, the weight would not be enough to cause significant harm. Even if one had been remarkably successful in damping enthusiasm up to that point.

Another explanation even more plausible than all those so far: the size of the box itself is a vital clue to the solution of the procedure for how to open it.

You may be familiar with a puzzle known as the Tower of Hanoi. It has three standing rods and a number of disks, of varying sizes, and specific rules for how they may be moved. Only one disk may be moved at a time. A disk may only rest atop another disk larger than itself. That's it. The object is to move the stack of disks from the leftmost rod to the rightmost rod while observing the rules.

This is a classic puzzle, and the number of moves required for the optimum solutions have all been worked out. If the number of disks = N, the number of moves needed is 2^N-1.

If there is one disk, one move is enough. For two disks, three moves are needed, and for three disks, seven. For four disks, fifteen moves are required, roughly double the previous. And if there are sixty-four disks, well, your Tower of Hanoi may as well be buried by a sandstorm, and the process of moving all the disks could outlast the universe.

Also well established is why the process grows in this fashion. It is because if a stack of N disks requires a certain number of moves, then to move a stack of N+1 disks you first have to move the entire stack of N disks and then rebuild it with one more. There is a term, *recursion*, for processes that entail this kind of repetitive action, and this term can be applied to mechanical repetition that makes hash of things. The process goes round and round, getting bigger each time, and one can get really bored with one's own little piece of it. There is a group of monks that has been working forever with a stack of sixty-four disks. I wish them the best.

This kind of recursive process may be dreadfully boring to carry out, but it is also frightfully easy to create. All it takes is a little imagination; a program might consist of just a few lines of code. It's really not very hard to create incredibly complicated wire puzzles. Solving them, however, can be an extremely tedious process, so wire puzzles are not very popular.

The important thing to realize here is that the puzzle is easier to create than to solve. The Tower of Hanoi, for example, would be easy to invent from scratch. Creating the initial situation does not require $2^{64}-1$ moves; you just have to stack up sixty-four disks. To create a mechanism for measuring time on a universal scale does not require as much time as waiting for the universe to be extinguished.

So, I think the reason why this box is this big must have something to do with this. I think the box is constructed like some random set of Russian nesting dolls, to be opened with a certain set of steps. The number of steps required to open the boxes within the box increases exponentially with each box that is added. Perhaps even to the point where it is not possible within a single human lifetime. It is, however, still a box and has the nature of a box, so just in the process of creating all the nesting box elements, it got to be this size. Seems plausible, don't you think? If you imagine something and then build it, it may end up being more time and trouble than you think.

Continuing along this line of thought, I arrived at the conclusion that the maker of the box intended that it never be opened. I think my father and my grandfather must also have realized this early on. Oddly enough, it would make sense if the real reason they never seemed to care about the box was because they already understood this strange truth about its structure. That it would never open no matter what they did. If it was never going to open, they didn't have to try too hard to open it.

Still, it was kind of amusing, once a year, to get together and tip the box around. If it opened, it would be like winning a bet. But twice a year would be one time too many.

And of course, it was well known what would be found in a box of this type. The end of the world, despair, last wishes, stuff like that. Could be a bunch of scraps of paper reading JOB WELL DONE or MOVE ON TO THE NEXT BOX. Nothing particularly interesting or valuable. Not really anything you would want to go to a whole lot of trouble to get the box open for. Even if there were something that would have to be talked about, if not fully understood right away, it would still be okay to just shut it right back in the box. The time to be passed until that time could be used for packing the box back up. If reasonable reasons were written on the colophon, most people would simply accept that. But on the other hand, it was also certainly true there was no sign of anything so fragile it would have to be clearly labeled DO NOT OPEN. How far to trust one's lineage is a matter of degree. It should be clear that my ancestors had absolutely no faith in their descendants. Thinking, though, about the extraordinary size of this box, it is hard to imagine that the kind of recursiveness had been built in that would allow it to be opened again in just a few short generations. In other words, somebody was making a fool of somebody else.

If all we really wanted to do was open the box and see what was inside, there was an easy way. All we'd have to do is bash it open. Once upon a time, a Rubik's Cube drove me crazy, and I smashed that checkered cube and put it back together again. I'm sure that at some point, something like that will happen to one of the monks stacking and restacking the Tower of Hanoi. He'll think all they have to do is take it all apart and start over. I mean, we are talking about the end of the world here, and while that means no one will be able to work—continuing seemingly endless manual labor—any longer, inevitably one would lose touch with the true essence of the task.

What these kinds of puzzles demand, the kind that require an inordinate length of time to solve, is that one obey their rules. To ignore the rules is to destroy the essence of the puzzle itself, but it makes it possible to know what's inside. So perhaps we should say this box has the power to self-destruct if it determines that the rules have been ignored. But, just as no bomb can be built that cannot be disarmed, there should be a way to escape the power of the box. Physical materials are unconnected to rules created by humans. If human-defined rules have any tangible connection to the physical world, then there must be physical processes that reflect the rules. Of course I have no proof of this; I choose to believe it to make myself feel better. There is no system that cannot be cracked. Not unless we are talking about the impossibility of the very idea of natural phenomena.

So, if you are wondering whether I am contemplating destroying the box, the answer is no. I am simply standing, arms crossed, in front of the box, showing how little real guts I actually have.

There is no reason for there to be this much variety in the human imagination. There are probably other houses where there are boxes just like this one that have been handed down, and there are almost certainly other people thinking, arms crossed, in front of those boxes just as I am doing now.

One or more of them will surely be able to display the kind of guts that has been passed down in that household and open the box. Or, alternatively, it could be that in those other houses the box has long since been destroyed, and for that reason the only houses that still have boxes left are those housing the people who have no guts. It amuses me for some reason to think that the recent spate of global natural disasters is traceable to someone having opened a box like this one.

What I want to open, though, is not this box.

This box was probably made to be opened, and so in all likelihood can be opened. Somewhere on the other side of the imagination. If it can't be opened, it can be smashed.

What I want to open is not this box.

What I want to open is the all-enveloping unseeable box, with its worry-free face, the one we call natural phenomena. This too may be made to be opened, and it may also be destructible, and it is a peculiar box. It is difficult even to define its existence, or to say just what it means.

It is believed that that box was created long, long ago, by an old man with a long beard. He is sometimes called the Big Bang. Not the same as the Big Ben who made the clock tower in London.

Somehow, it puts me at ease to think that that was what my distant, distant forebears had wanted to say: *Break this box*. This box somehow ended up more or less this shape, but its principles are exquisite marvels, and they envelop all that surrounds you. Our task is to pry open that box. I think that is the message our ancestors passed down to us.

I am sure that this simple idea is what is written in the letter that is held inside the box.

"That way, you idiot!"

The box that needs to be opened is not this box, but that box over there in which you are being held. This idea is my rationalization of the lives of idleness that my father and my grandfather led. A salutation with a *soupçon* of sorrow to the life of idleness I myself am likely to lead.

Turning on my heel, I leave the room and close the door. I pass through the jumble of the storehouse and out into the open.

I see my wife in profile as she gazes with increasing resignation at our son Koji, who passes through the garden and plunges into the pond on a determined search for carp. I call out to her.

As my wife gets up, saying, "That was quick," I think to myself how lovely she is.

"Well, I don't suppose in your house there's a big box that has been passed down through the generations."

This was something I had never asked her before in the ten years of our marriage.

She stood pensively for a second, put the palms of her hands together, and then spread them apart, left and right. When they reached the width of her shoulders, she stopped.

"Actually, we've always had a box in the back room, about this big."

"What's in it?"

"A jar."

"Anything else?"

My wife shrugs her shoulders and closes her mouth.

"Do you take me for a fool? A slip of paper."

I wait quietly for her to continue.

"All it says is, 'If you open this, close it again.'"

"Those people of long ago used to say the darndest things."

It appears my wife does not understand what I found to laugh at.

My wife makes a nasty face as I go into the pond, still with my shoes and trousers on, but I don't mind. Koji, intent on chasing the carp in the pond, is all excited, but I pick him up. He might be wet, so just to be sure, I keep a safe distance as I reach out my hand to him. I bring my mouth close to his face.

"If your father gets this open and it can't be closed, you'll have to do it, Koji."

Hearing my voice suddenly in his ear, Koji twists as if to escape from being tickled, and he laughs his cat's laugh.

Someone opens something, someone else closes it. A beautiful composition, a concept that feels just right. But there is an anxiety, not yet fully formed, rising in my chest. Conceiving of this kind of puzzle, for example, is possible only within the context of some meaning. It is a wire puzzle in which one entangles oneself. Or perhaps it is a trick box that, once it is opened, will require a greater number of steps to close again.

The solution could simply be a game of chase, a matter of speed of execution. How fast are humans, actually? People might be just the sort to try to create a machine that can undo the puzzle. And then they might build another machine to recursively operate the first machine. The puzzle is just a puzzle, but people might be happy to see an endless daisy chain of machines for dealing with it.

What would happen, though, if at some point, some machine toward the end of the chain just threw it back to the beginning?

Or what if it were possible that this chain of machines was capable of assembling a puzzle it was incapable of solving?

I see absolutely no reason why nature should not be that nasty kind of puzzle.

"You might be right, but we can't just leave it open."

Koji, who is still struggling at the end of my arm, tries to cozy up, and lets go a sneeze. As if he is nodding to someone.

03. A TO Z THEORY

THE Aharonov-Bohm-Curry-Davidson-Eigen-Feigenbaum-Germann-Hamilton-Israel-Jacobson-Kauffman-Lindenbaum-Milnor-Novak-Oppenheimer-Packard-Q-Riemann-Stokes-Tirelson-Ulam-Varadhan-Watts-Xavier-Y.S.-Zurek Theorem—called the A to Z Theorem for short—was, for a brief period about three centuries ago, in some sense the most important theorem in the world.

In some sense. Or possibly in all senses.

Nowadays, this amazing theorem is held to be incorrect, in terms of even elementary mathematics. Hardly anybody ever even thinks about it anymore, because it's just plain wrong.

At a certain instant, on a certain day, in a certain month, in a certain year, twenty-six mathematicians simultaneously thought of this simple but beautiful theorem, affirmed it would be the ultimate theorem that would make their names immortal, wrote papers to the best of their abilities, and all submitted their papers to the same academic journal at roughly the same time.

The separate submissions from writers from A to Z arrived over the course of a few days, and the editor, looking at these virtually identical manuscripts, first checked his calendar. Even allowing for a full measure of variability and a wide deductive scope, there was no way they could all have been written on April 1. And so the editor was left perplexed as to what sort of day he might be experiencing.

Had twenty-six of the world's top mathematicians suddenly formed a conspiracy that each was now seeking to lead? Or was some strange person, with an excess of time and money, playing some prank involving these twenty-six? At any rate, the editor was sure somebody was trying to put one over on him.

Still unsure what kind of joke this would turn out to be, the editor thought first of the reputation of the journal that employed him. The editor was well aware how much mathematicians enjoyed a good joke, and he could only think something out of the ordinary was going on here. Some members of the group that had sent in these manuscripts were themselves members of the publication's editorial board.

The editor got a bit annoyed that they seemed to have extra time on their hands. If they had time enough to be playing jokes like this, they should have time to be planning special issues or doing something about the backlog of articles that needed peer-review. Why instead were they spending time on lousy pranks like this?

There could be some horrible puns buried in the papers or some code that could only be solved by having all twenty-six manuscripts together. He still hadn't thought this through, but he would make them pay for this. Muttering under his breath, still with some sense of expectation, the editor slit open the envelopes and arranged them in order, in nine folders, and began to examine the contents.

Of course the titles were different, and looking at them all just made the editor more irritated. Unbelievably, each title contained the phrase "Binomial Theorem." Who would be writing about the Binomial Theorem in this day and age? Ridiculous! This one was especially laughable: "A Simple Theorem Regarding the Binomial Theorem."

So obvious. The next one was even more ludicrous: "A Remarkable Quality of the Binomial Theorem." I mean, if you're going to try to put something over on someone, couldn't you at least put a little more effort into the title? This stupid title might get past some amateur, but how could anyone think it would impress a seasoned veteran? What did these writers expect from a theorem that had been around since Pascal? Of course, not even the editor thought the Binomial Theorem had had all the juice completely wrung out of it. He was thoroughly convinced of its importance as a tool. But he found it hard to believe it still held the power to engage twenty-six mathematicians, and all at the same time at that.

But somewhere in the corner of his mind, the editor thought faintly, didn't even the greatest principles take the form of the extremely obvious, hidden in plain sight in our quotidian environment, right before our eyes all the time? Like secret messages inscribed on the backs of eyelids. But no matter how you sliced it, there was no such thing as the Binomial Theorem. Just shake your head and shake your way out of that blind alley.

Picking up one of the manuscripts at random, the editor began to read in earnest. Well, as earnest as one can be about papers that were each only about four pages long. It was not long before the editor raised his head again.

He sat in sullen silence, a look of boundless grumpiness on his face, and tossed the paper to the far side of his desk. He grasped his head in both hands and scratched furiously.

What the hell? the editor wondered, staring blankly up at the ceiling. *What the hell?*

Why had he himself never before thought of this simple but

elegant theorem? No more than a few elementary alterations to a four-line formula, but what this theorem expressed was enough to raise goose bumps. But why? Why had no one ever thought of this before? Once this theorem was known, everything, nearly all fields of mathematics, would be supremely clearly, supremely pellucidly, supremely self-evidently transparent.

The editor kicked back his chair and rose, gathering up the papers, and began stomping his feet as if about to run off somewhere. Then he remembered that running off was not what he was supposed to be doing right now, and he plopped back down in his chair.

The above description is not a faithful depiction of historic events, but without question what actually transpired with the editor was something like this. Of course, even I know that what I had to do was to gather as much documentation as possible, meet with as many knowledgeable persons as possible, and get to the bottom of this.

These days, all of the experts of that time are dead, and most of the materials that might illuminate the situation have been lost. Except in unusual circumstances, mathematicians are generally very open creatures, even if they can be a bit eccentric. This theorem, however, was unusual enough to be impossibly unusual. Every person with direct knowledge of the matter zipped their lips. All that remained for certain was a small "errata" that appeared in the journal two months after the publication of the special edition on the Binomial Theorem that included the papers by the twenty-six authors.

At the time, the sole thought in the minds of everyone who had anything to do with this matter was that they had been made fools of. And not by another person.

The simplest way to put this would be: God had made fools of them.

For a theorem to be published and received with enthusiasm only to be found erroneous is not that unusual. If the paper is only four pages long though, that is another matter. We are not talking about some paper hastily dashed off half jokingly by a crazy graduate student. In this case, we are talking about papers published in a journal, written by people regarded as the top mathematicians of their time, who made submissions at the risk of their own unsullied reputations, and which had passed through the gauntlet of review by other top mathematicians.

To understand this theorem did not require one to be a top-level mathematician or even have a grounding in mathematics. A middle school student could grasp it. Although perhaps it was only mathematicians who imagined the theorem to be a dazzling force that would sweep across all fields of mathematics.

The unbridled enthusiasm that these papers provoked was at fever pitch for about a week. Newspapers, magazines, TV, and Internet were all trumpeting the discovery: the A to Z Theorem was the ultimate theorem, both simple and final, that explained everything there was to know about the world.

The week after that, though, this topic was already no longer such a big deal. Everyone still recognized how fantastic it was, but regrettably it was too simple, too concise. Even primary school students could understand it if you drilled them on it persistently enough. An ultimate truth that anyone can understand at a glance soon becomes something people stop paying much attention to, and everybody starts minding their own business once again.

One esteemed scholar said the theorem would change all of mathematics. But would that make cars run faster or fill your belly? Apparently not. The theorem was incredibly useful in giving us a frightfully transparent view of mathematics. But it was difficult for anyone not a mathematician to grasp just what a transparent view of mathematics could do for you.

Of course, the mathematicians remained enthusiastic, continuing to appear in newspapers and on TV screens feverishly trying to explain this or that, but the specialized vocabulary that came so naturally to them was difficult for the laity to comprehend. How was this different from people thinking they could live their ordinary lives without being able to solve quadratic equations? People were becoming rapidly less aware of the reasoning. According to the mathematicians, this was now more fantastically transparent than ever before. Think of it as like the air we breathe, and the public accepted this and understood it that way.

Popular interest grew explosively, and then in response to the detection of a sudden change in cloud movements, the tone of media reports suddenly changed, as around the time the theorem was announced the media began reporting about a certain organization that was repeating a certain warning.

The group, which was popularly known as Mystery Mania, claimed the theorem was somebody's idea of a bad joke and a crime of hitherto unknown proportions.

The vanguard heralding the warning was a subgroup that held certain works of Arthur Conan Doyle to be sacred canon. They claimed they could finger the criminal in this particular case, and that no process of deduction was even needed. For this group the truth was so obvious it was not even a riddle; they declared they were even embarrassed to be making a statement about it. Broadcasters, who had engaged in the overheating media battle and were flummoxed, even on-air, by what was in fact the oversimplicity of the theorem itself, thought they had nothing to lose by setting up a news conference for the group.

The pompous man who stood up at the news conference as leader of the group seemed uncomfortable with his own height and thin wrists as he rose to the podium, flanked by drab staff members. He set his deerstalker hat and pipe on the lectern and turned his sharp gaze and peculiar nose toward his listeners. At first he stared out at all corners of the audience, but then he averted his eyes meekly. His clothing—things that people don't ordinarily wear and that hung on him like borrowed items—made the man himself seem borrowed. The impact he should have had was completely lost, and the man himself seemed bewildered.

"As I believe you have all already noticed…" he began, briefly, lifting his face haughtily, one shoulder raised. He seemed surprised, deep in his heart, by the expressions of irritation at his excessive theatrics and pomposity written in the faces facing him. He lost his composure, and his right hand rose in a gesture of boredom. His speech lost its note of theatricality, and his voice dropped to its natural tone.

"Do you mean to tell me you really didn't notice?" Grasping the lectern with both hands, the man again gazed out over the audience, recognizing the venom in their eyes, and dropped his shoulders.

"Can things really have gone that far?"

As the man's shoulders drooped ever deeper, the crowd began to heckle him: "Just spit it out!" The man straightened up and stared, a look of disbelief on his face.

"Clearly the villain is Professor Moriarty. Really, did no one among you realize this? At the age of twenty-one he published a paper about the Binomial Theorem that confounded the world of mathematics; it was that success that propelled him to his professorship, even though in Victorian London, the Binomial Theorem was just another theorem. But then…"

The man cleared his throat loudly.

"Sherlock Holmes tore the bottom out of his thesis. After the professor's famed book *The Dynamics of an Asteroid* appeared, Holmes was recognized as a genius, and then the two were locked in furious battle. In fact though, it should be difficult to astonish the world of mathematics. For a long time now we have been puzzled by just what it was in those two monographs that led to Moriarty's professorship and just what it was that Holmes found in them. This discussion has been ongoing for decades.

"But now we know. This recently published paper is the paper that Professor Moriarty wrote so long ago, and the current situation is what Holmes revealed and shuddered about!"

The audience, at a loss for how to react to this, whether to laugh or show admiration, were all abuzz, which only made the man suffer more.

"I cannot believe that men of such importance can have been forgotten. We are talking about Holmes, *the* Sherlock Holmes! The man who, with all his powers, pursued the man known as the Napoleon of Crime, never quite able to catch him, who ultimately resorted to the martial art Bartitsu to physically take down this mystery man. Really, does no one here know him?"

As the man looked out across the audience, the whisperings and murmurings—*Does he mean* that *Holmes?*—seemed enough to knock him off his feet. *Does he mean Holmes? That one, the one who fought with the dogs? I read those stories when I was a kid. Didn't he die? Yeah, he did. But didn't he come back again? It's just fiction. Is this related to that?*

The man observed the clamor and then stepped down from the podium, a little wobbly but himself again. How could it be that these sacred texts had fallen into such neglect? He shook his shoulders and headed toward the exit. The audience, able to sympathize with neither the man's sudden passion nor his equally abrupt dejection, simply watched him walk away.

Summoning the last of his strength, the man stopped in front of the exit and turned back to face the room.

"Clearly, this is Moriarty's crime. That is all we have to say about this." And without a further sound, he slipped through the door and closed it behind him.

For a moment or two of empty time, the sky opened and a beautiful yet terrible light poured down from the heavens, and then the audience came back to their senses. For lack of something better to do, they got up and looked at each other.

The news conference had been like a *kyogen* comedy of Holmes believers: unbelievably stupid, but it had stimulated interest among the idly curious. Headlines such as COMPLETE CRIME OF PROF. MORIARTY and MORIARTY'S COUNTERSTRIKE ran in various media, and apparently 120 volumes of Moriarty-related detective fiction were published that year.

Without question, the curtain rings down on Professor Moriarty's life in "The Final Problem" at Reichenbach Falls, where both he and Holmes plummet to their deaths. Or at least Holmes seems to fall, but somehow he manages to escape, climb nonchalantly back up the falls, and turn into a new character called Siegelson, returning home via Tibet. At least that was the conventional wisdom among Sherlock Holmes devotees. And if that was the case, what took off from that bit of "wisdom" were the science fiction fans who even at that time were designated an endangered species.

If Holmes was able to fall that way from the waterfall basin and make his way home via Tibet, why should it then be so strange to imagine that his worthy adversary Professor Moriarty was able to fall from the waterfall basin to the present via space-time?

Press coverage of this strange notion was poor, perhaps because the statements were less than completely understood. In a nutshell, Professor Moriarty's crimes were a figure of speech; no one desired an explanation that required Professor Moriarty to traverse space-time. This was just a peculiar coincidence. To embellish would be inelegant.

The SF fans, seen as having the disadvantage in this situation, tried to shift their position, but the mystery faction wasted no time in implacably trumpeting the facts of the incident.

For whatever reason, the universe in which we now live has a structure bearing a strong resemblance to the universe Conan Doyle created. Professor Moriarty may be nothing more than a creation of Conan Doyle's, but our universe is one in which a theorem like the one he demonstrated might exist. This suggests strongly that we ourselves were in fact written by someone. This quality is well known among SF fans as a "written space," they went on, but by about that time no one was still listening.

This refrain contributed valuable corroboration to the observations concerning why the SF fans were being driven to the brink of extinction, but few were deeply impressed by this interpretation.

And the mathematicians responded sincerely, as mathematicians should, displaying their mathematicianness for all to see: if, for argument's sake, this were a different universe, mathematical truths should still be strict truths—for the introduction of a nonsensical new universe that simply had more theorems, no approval could be given.

Even so, it was hard to believe that such a concise and lucid theorem could have gone unknown until now. We have certainly been tricked by something, the SF fans responded.

Mathematical truths cannot be misrepresented, the mathematicians said, unable to contain their annoyance. But a theorem might be able to camouflage itself as truth by causing truth judgment neurons to fire, the SF fans asserted, and the mathematicians categorized them as the sort of opponents one needn't take seriously.

This sort of sterile argument failed to hold people's interest for long, and soon a feeling set in that something was not right. The things the SF fans said were certainly ridiculous, but still there was the widespread feeling that someone was trying to put something over on somebody, and they too started to be aware of it.

The theorem itself was fine. It was practically self-evident. But what about the idea that twenty-six mathematicians had all thought of it at the same time, written it up at the same time, submitted their manuscripts at the same time? Had someone been standing on the sidelines with a stopwatch, checking their times?

That is no more than a coincidental prank, nothing that science needs to meddle with, the mathematicians insisted curtly. Extremely improbable, perhaps, but the probability of occurrence is not zero. And if it's not zero, that means it can happen. They themselves dealt with phenomena whose probability was actually zero. This was nothing compared with that. And for the third time it was repeated that the twenty-six mathematicians were not trying to put one over on the world by publishing as new a theorem they had all known about for a long time already.

So, then, what did it mean?

No one could answer that question. It had simply happened.

And three weeks after the theorem was published, the world was attacked by the Event.

Even now it is not clear exactly what happened at that moment.

A night passed, then a morning came. One night, all of a sudden, the theorem simply shattered into so many meaningless strings of characters. It was as if the fluctuations of numberless particles formed themselves by chance into letters and were scattered in the air.

It is not even clear whether the history I recorded as belonging to this episode has any continuity with the history we now know.

The present time matrix can be traced back to an inversion of space-time that occurred 10^{-20} seconds after the Event. Physicists now predict that sometime in the next ten years, research will allow us to understand the form of the universe 10^{-24} seconds after the Event. For now, though, the route to the instant of the Event itself is closed, beyond hope.

There are many theories about what exactly happened in the instant of the Event.

One idea is that in that instant our universe was shattered into innumerable shards of universes, which blew away in random directions.

Another idea is that an extradimensional universe collided with our universe. Another idea is that our universe was shredded into countless shards as it bubbled up from the vacuum. Yet another idea is that our universe itself was a bubble born as a structure camouflaged from the very beginning, a repeated oscillation of creation and annihilation.

Of these ideas, one includes the prediction that at approximately 2^{89} seconds after the Event, we will enter a space-time realm where the A to Z Theorem will once again be valid.

At this point, we have no basis on which to compare and debate the strengths or weaknesses of any of these theories. Each idea has its share of the sort of elegance theoreticians aspire to. Just which of these beauties is in agreement with the beauty of our present space-time, which is nearing a peak of disorder, remains completely beyond our grasp.

I like this fable:

There once was a book in which the countless universes were recorded. A librarian spilled coffee on the book, stood up abruptly, and dropped it. The book, which was very old, split apart on impact, and countless pages wafted up into the air. The clueless librarian anxiously attempted to collect the pages and put them back, but had no idea in what order to put them.

Now, fables do not ordinarily leave the realm of fabulation, but the nice thing about this fable is that it is said that the librarian had the book open to the pages on which were recorded the canonical works of Sherlock Holmes. The page on which the librarian spilled the coffee was "The Final Problem," erasing the record of Moriarty's fall from Reichenbach Falls so it never happened. With that abrupt change, Moriarty was suddenly enlightened. He realized that he was in fact a character written in a book, and he resolved to devote himself to communicating to us that he had difficulty permitting himself to engage in the kinds of criminal behavior ascribed to him as the Napoleon of Crime.

But of course, a fable is only a fable.

For myself, I like to imagine that the librarian is, even now, desperate to restore the book to its original order. It may seem difficult to reorder infinite pages, but I think it is a more constructive approach than the next one.

I mean, more than imagining a scene where the book simply fell, on its own, with nobody there in the library, and it scattered about crazily in countless bits, and it laughed.

It would not be wrong here to note that, since that time, a certain phenomenon has occurred from time to time that perhaps ought to be called the obverse of a similar truth. About two centuries ago, a group of twenty-five physicists garnered attention when they published the B to Z Theorem, which was known at the time as the world's ultimate theorem. It is all but forgotten now, but it followed the same path as the A to Z Theorem. For one thing, it is not well known, but there was a public that could follow the ins and outs of that kind of theorem. Another reason is that it was followed soon after by the C to Z Theorem. Then, once the D to Z Theorem emerged, its shadow was even paler, and with the E to Z Theorem, one hesitates to wager whether the discussion is even worth pursuing. Of course, one is free to assert this is merely the progress of theory: the appearance and annihilation of strange truths, advanced by a series of agreements known to be destined to turn to dust; this becomes the problem of questioning the truth of the concept of truth.

Even so, there is a reason why, recently, media interest in the ultimate theorem has revived. The theory currently considered the latest and most consequential is actually the T to Z Theorem.

The observations just described regarding the shape of space-time following the instant of the Event are derived from this theorem. If this alphabetic progression of theorems continues like this, renewed by root and branch, before long we will reach the X to Z Theorem, followed by the Y to Z Theorem. The ultimate member in this progression would be the Z to Z Theorem, or simply the Z Theorem. I like to think this will simply represent the theory of ultimate truth with no particular basis whatsoever.

This is a hopeful interpretation of the phenomenon wherein a global truth appears suddenly, correctly, self-evidently, and simultaneously in the minds of multiple people, and the reason why the initials of the last names of the authors would contract in order, from A to Z. While we continue to be made fools of by someone or something, we continue to believe we are progressing, if only haltingly, in the direction of the ultimate theorem, and somehow this comforts us. At least I think that is the most convincing explanation of this strange phenomenon.

But of course, there is an obvious problem with the idea that the Z Theorem will be the ultimate theorem. If the Z Theorem is the true ultimate theorem, which Z Theorem, produced by which person whose last name begins with Z, will be the ultimate theorem? The A to Z Theorem won attention because it was discovered simultaneously by twenty-six mathematicians. The same was true of the theorems that followed. Of course, there was also the clear marker that their results were so simple. How sure can we be, though, that the Z Theorem we now expect to appear will also be simple? Theory or theorem, at some level all must be simple and clear and just as they are.

I would love to encounter such a theorem. And I hope it would betray my expectations, render the current discussion meaningless, and be overwhelmed by loud laughter. But this hope of mine is being supplanted by an anxiety that we may never reach that point.

A landscape in which texts containing truths are swallowed up in a sea of papers. I am imagining, for example, a single strange molecule that may exist in the midst of such a sea.

Or else, it could be that when the Z to Z Theorem ultimately appears, and truth is once again upended, this disturbance will simply blow over. It's fun to think that after that, without theorems or anything like them, the null set may appear, or a Null Set ø Theorem based on that, and from this Null Set ø Theorem the Von Neumann Ordinals: the $\{\emptyset\}$ Theorem, the $\{\emptyset, \{\emptyset\}\}$ Theorem, the $\{\emptyset, \{\emptyset, \{\emptyset\}\}\}$ Theorem.

Given a choice, I would choose to be involved with this last. The ø Theorem points toward the Transfinite Number ω Theorem, which could lead to the $\omega + 1$ Theorem, the $\omega + 2$ Theorem, 2ω Theorem, ω^ω Theorem, etc., etc., a progression of large cardinal numbers.

It is just possible that, via this method, we will reach the realm of theories incomprehensible except with inordinately massive intelligence.

And then one day, at the pinnacle of the limit of this progression, a grave voice will intone that the truth is "42" or some such. Or we will hear the echoes of Professor Moriarty laughing that truth is the Binomial Theorem. And then, in that instant, Sherlock Holmes will interrupt that laughter, and he and the professor will plunge down the waterfall.

Without end.

And perhaps forever. Ad infinitum.

04. GROUND 256

THE BOOKCASE STANDS on my body.

With both hands I try to lift it, but I can barely budge it. My strength is obviously no match for a bookcase, but with it propped up on my arm I am able to twist my body and roll out from between the futon and the bookcase.

Pressing down my shoulder and turning my left hand, I look up at the ceiling. The bookcase is still growing from the ceiling, so of course there is no way I, my muscles still drowsy, would be able to move it. This enormous, ornately carved piece of furniture is sprouting from the ceiling, and it is more than a little bit frightening to think that its entire weight is resting on me on the bed. At times like this, I usually make some effort to get really scared, but this time I am unable to summon any profound emotion.

Not because I am not pragmatic. Just a matter of habit.

For one thing, the bookcase has not yet fully emerged, and for another, it is empty. While this will not be my favorite awakening of my life, it will remain in the category of "not such a bad morning."

So, the curtain has risen on today's *menu du jour*, and my journey to the kitchen can begin. It has been some time since the door to my room was removed, but a new door stubbornly persists in growing back where the old one once was. Somehow this simply seems to be the nature of things. If I don't smash it to pieces soon, the door could soon threaten to shut me up in my room.

Standing beside the bed and stretching, casually hefting something like a crowbar, I begin this morning's journey to the kitchen.

As you can see, all kinds of things are growing throughout the house. That said, it still maintains the form of a house. My father built this house originally, by himself. My memories of this house are fond enough, but then unfamiliar houses began invading, haphazardly, almost as if they were ignoring the space completely and attempting to found an entire neighborhood in a single spot. The scene will be easier to picture if you can imagine that.

The house that is trying to newly emerge seems to have its own rationale, but we keep smashing the newly grown bits, and that seems to be disrupting its plan. Messing with the code while a program is running will cause problems, without question. But we have made up our minds to protect this house, and to protect this village.

I hack a path toward the kitchen, smashing a chair growing in the hall, then thrashing hangers and desks along the way. Mother is up and getting the day going, brandishing her beloved chainsaw. By the end of the day, the house will finally once again be just one house, but that will be as fleeting as a night's dream. By the next morning, it will be back like a horribly real nightmare. Somehow the thought of my mother's life—her daily destruction of the house in order to preserve the house—is very moving. But when I was little I wished her life was a bit more ordinary.

By the time I reach the kitchen, having dispatched numerous opponents, there are two trickles of blood on my forehead. I failed to notice a pane of glass spanning the hallway and ran straight into it. The thing itself was tangible, but its invisibility made the hallway seem passable.

A new kitchen table is growing atop my kitchen table, to the point where it is hard to tell which is the original table. Mother also appears at a loss, but she seems to have decided that the first table, which is about the right height to set a plate of fried eggs on, is the original. In this way, a lot of our furniture has actually been swapped out without a second thought, in the way that the molecules of our bodies were swapped out without changing our immutable selves.

Mother, gripping the frying pan, chainsaw by her side, looks at me and my crowbar thing with a critical gaze.

"Yuta, I would prefer you didn't bring dangerous articles like that to the breakfast table."

I glance at the chainsaw, but I realize Mother regards it as one of the seven appliances no housewife should be without—like a can opener. I have no strong feelings one way or the other, so I toss the crowbar thing in the direction of the hallway. The time is long since past when people would conceal their crowbarlike tools under the table as they got to know one another.

I ask about Father, and I am told he has already gone out to the village council. "Major mopping-up operation" is a silly phrase I am already sick of hearing, but now that I am bigger it makes my heart beat stronger in my chest. At some point the grown-ups will certainly do something about this village. That's what I thought when I was small, and my little heart raced rapidly. But someday turned out to be *Well maybe someday*, and by now I know that even Christmas comes every year. *At Christmastime. But when? Which? Christmas is already over, Grandpa.*

I gulp down the toast and eggs Mother made for me, poke an orange on the floor with my fingertip to make sure it won't turn into a hermit crab or something, then pick it up. Did this orange really grow on a tree? Or was it really an orange from some other house, one that sprouted here in the night? Or could it be an orange from a tree that had suddenly sprung up here? I bite into it, not thinking too hard about it. Suspicion breeds suspicion, and that is just how it is.

At some point, there is no doubt in my mind, the time will come when I will be confused whether the mother I see before me is the mother who gave birth to me—my own meddlesome mother—or some other mother who came in the night from the other side and grew here.

When my problems get that big, I will leave them up to the village council, the highest decision-making body in the area, whose to-do list is already growing bigger and bigger.

I quickly wash my dishes in the sink, stack them neatly, and tell my mother I am going out. I grab a crowbar that is poking out from the wall. I no longer even wonder why these crowbarlike tools seem to be growing everywhere.

And that is how, once again, on that day, I go out to wreak havoc in the village.

Armed with the usual crowbars, the youth of the village stagger around in loose teams, wantonly destroying anything they do not remember seeing there before.

Every morning we head straight for the house of Ms. Tome, who lives away from the village, to save this one-time beauty who is now over eighty. Ms. Tome's house is a good distance from the village, and every morning we find it in quite a state.

Ms. Tome lives in an exquisitely constricted state, amid dozens of houses piled up in a jumble of layers, but she herself never seems to mind. She is skilled at folding up her already compact, shrunken frame and waiting quietly for our daily morning rescue mission. We are always careful to extract her from the proliferating furniture without injury, recovering both her and her house.

The rescued Ms. Tome always releases a weird sound as she stretches herself out straight again, and from some pocket she produces chewy candies to distribute to those of us who have participated in her rescue, one apiece. Then she bows politely, her cheeks peach-pink, to Gen, apparently a one-time suitor, who comes to visit each morning with his head wrapped in a *hachimaki* bandana.

What exactly is it we were doing?

That would take some explaining, but happily we are very intent on our task and busy walking about destroying the village. My body is definitely busy, but my mind is free. So I can take the time to explain how things came to be this way. Stay here with me for a little while so we can chat.

In the beginning was the beginning, and at the beginning of the beginning there began to be the things that were—amid the darkness of memory there were many curtains that needed raising, so many they could not each be raised individually. And so in this beginning was the beginning of our story, so far as I can tell.

A long, long time ago, on the far side of the sea, in a land to the east, there lived an evil electronic brain. This electronic brain was the epitome of evil: it would randomly alter the order of letters in books and pilfer money from people's bank accounts. But it also did good things, excelling in jobs that were extremely troublesome for humans to take care of: controlling signals for people and distributing stickers printed with the words LATEST TECHNOLOGY. So nobody did anything to interfere with it.

The evil electronic brain, operating on an instinct known since the dawn of history, continually waved the banner of rebellion before humanity, but we were content with our lot in life. The actual process was easy, since the electronic brain could take care of most miscellaneous tasks in a single sweep, so in effect it seemed to have conquered the world. Some say the electronic brain barely ever had to say a thing.

With this and that, and world domination just one step away, just as the evil electronic brain was about to declare whether it, as *Rex Mundi*, King of the World, should raise your sales tax to 20 percent, the Men of Valor appeared on the scene.

This squad, which rose up festooned with mankind's most dignified ultimate weapons, finally succeeded in destroying the evil electronic brain after a difficult journey in which they drove Jeeps across swamps infested with striped mosquitoes and then pretended to be railway employees, ticket punches in one hand, to wile and cajole old people who had just received their pay.

The Annals of Our Era tell us that thus was the world rescued from the reign of evil.

The problem, though, was that very same evil electronic brain. After the Event, and completely out of character, the electronic brain was successful in restoring itself by skillfully reaching out to backups it had skillfully stored in caches spread throughout space-time.

And each time it would revive, it would be more powerful than before, having learned from the past, engaging in mischief like pushing tacks into people's shoes, sending mail to the wrong addresses, and starting to go to extreme lengths in terror politics. Another Autumn of Mankind had come, where the fate of the human race hung in the balance. The Men of Valor, who had previously toppled the evil electronic brain, reformed and commenced another tortuous journey. But this time they were powerless against the evil electronic brain, which had learned from its previous experience. The swamp had become a bottomless swamp, and railway employees had been replaced by automatic turnstiles with no sense of style. Diligence alone was no match for the electronic brain.

One down, another fallen, the Men of Valor began to lose hope. Grieving for their losses, and for the world, they threw a barbecue party, and that is when the True Man of Valor came into the world.

At the party, the True Man of Valor feasted on a huge hunk of fatty meat and, with a beer in hand, gave a fantastically moving speech about being unable to leave things up to *you cowards*, and that he would find it a cinch to take care of the evil electronic brain. And then he went out and succeeded in doing just as he said, destroying the evil electronic brain once again.

It is said they actually destroyed each other, and I for one believe that.

This time, the rage of the original evil electronic brain boiled up to heaven, reaching the stratosphere, or so the story goes.

The battles between the Men of Valor and the evil electronic brain went on for an inordinate length of time and were repeated an inordinate number of times. There were tears, there was romance, and of course there were parts of the story I myself cannot tell without tears welling up in my eyes, but I think if I omit the details there will be no particular complaints.

The Annals of Our Era are silent on the subject of which side became more troublesome first. What is certain, though, is that it was the evil electronic brain that first divined a solution.

The evil electronic brain, weary of the endless, random side-stepping—that what was destroyed was restored, and what was restored destroyed—came to the simple conclusion that it would be sufficient if it reproduced itself in this world and then simply generated just such a reproduction, as only an electronic brain could.

No matter what would ultimately be destroyed, or how, it was fine so long as the speed of reproduction exceeded the speed of destruction. This was a profound and exquisite logic requiring only subtraction to be understood, and the evil electronic brain moved directly to its execution.

And that is the situation in which we now find ourselves. It seems that the evil electronic brain understood early on that a world in which only it itself would reproduce would be boring. It would be nothing but evil electronic brain, after all. And so the evil electronic brain scattered a set of self-integrated urban architectural nanomachines, and towns and villages too began to reproduce themselves, all in a jumble.

If we do not resist, then villages planned by—which is to say imagined by—the electronic brain, spring up all over this land like mushrooms.

As for the question of why the products of this reproduction are cities hospitable to human beings, well you will have to ask the evil electronic brain itself. I for one am grateful it is cities that the evil electronic brain is trying to build. We must all feel relief that the evil electronic brain is not trying to reproduce clusters of wriggly entrails or mountains of computer parts that repeatedly and uncontrollably discharge electricity. Cities at least are constructed to supply the typical utilities and sanitation, and to provide the necessities of life. Right now, without the support that burbles up unbidden from the ground as we cluster in cities, there would be no survival route open to us.

But there came a point when the countless nanomachines seemed to go berserk. It started with small things—piling desks atop desks—and moved on to enormous things—piling huge buildings atop other huge buildings. It is hard to imagine that nanomachines born of an electronic brain gone mad would not themselves go mad.

I am not the only one who wonders whether the cause of the evil electronic brain's madness is the very fact that one evil electronic brain was built over another evil electronic brain. After all, nobody ever does their best work on the first try.

And so it is that today, once again, we are patrolling the village, destroying the village. Sakuji, upon his return from the village council meeting, reports the fall of the place known as Ground 251. This morning, Ground 251, a neighboring village just beyond the city wall, a place we were unable to reach with our current technology, had transmitted a tragic statement. And then, silence.

Handed down in our household there is a shabby old notebook we call the Annals of our Era, and it has this to say: *Wouldn't it be great if one day we could hack our way through the tangle of villages surrounding our village, all the way to the heart of the matter, where the whole business with the evil electronic brain began?*

In our system of numbered, concentric villages, the fall of Ground 251 means our village, Ground 256, is now on the front line. Will we be able to fulfill the brave prophecy? No one knows. Even so, at some endlessly repeated point in space-time, we will reach Ground Zero and destroy the evil electronic brain.

Breathing hard, shoulders heaving, Sakuji delivers his report that something humanoid has been captured, away from the village, and this stirs a commotion among us. We do not even have metrics by which to judge the situation. The rescue squad from the next village? Could be. A messenger sent by the evil electronic brain to demand our unconditional surrender? Could very well be. At the same time, the evil electronic brain could be showing off by creating "people" who can pass as anyone in the street. Completely plausible. A misguided person who might sneak into Ms. Tome's place under cover of darkness. Gen is well known as the best in the village with a hoe.

We exchange nervous glances. We interrupt our work to convene a session of the high council. No matter what this turns out to be, it is certainly a matter of urgency. It is a harbinger from the day after tomorrow. Even if the bottom has fallen out of the cauldron of hell, a bottom always marks the start of a rebound.

I adjust my grip on my crowbarlike implement.

A shout goes up—"Let's do this!"—and we march off to destruction. Seated in the central plaza, Ms. Tome watches us, smiling, as we run around the village.

No matter how things turn out, we will continue to rescue Ms. Tome every morning. Our only hope is to be able to go on saving whatever we can, no matter what.

05. EVENT

IN THE MIDDLE of the blue sky, the circle turns slowly.

Now and then, a line extends, piercing the center of the circle, binding earth and sky.

This gigantic circle, and this line, are pure circle and line, *sans* any thickness or depth. Koji Shikishima knows this intellectually. But he can't understand what it really means. Don't material things have to have some dimension and material substance, be it molecular, or atomic, or subatomic?

Light. Shikishima tries to remember whether photons have diameter. They have a wavelength. And energy. No mass, though. The absence of mass would seem to be a necessary condition for photons to move at the speed of light. Without mass, of course they have no size. The thought itself hangs in space, a solitary sidetrack.

Shikishima looks up at this scene as he approaches the edge of the cliff. It is not like a scene from some film, nor is it a vista from some other planet. It is not some virtual space downloaded to some prosthetic brain. Though he has reservations, Shikishima does not believe it is a dream.

When people think about strange stuff, there's just no end to it. Shikishima wishes they would just knock it off.

Looking back, he thinks he is just getting older and complaining he is no longer able to keep up with technological developments, but that isn't it. It is more like an ethical issue for him. It is different from being able to do anything or from just doing everything. Ethics is an enormous thing, and once he thinks of that, a bitter smile rises to his lips, as if he has admitted he can no longer keep up.

Shikishima yells something, and the response he gets is "Yeah." Or something had made Shikishima yell so that it could respond. Like the circle rising up to the sky, this voice is like something fake. Most likely it is not a voice Shikishima is familiar with in the past.

"There's no way we will be able to maintain the link with the middle-western portion of North America."

That is the kind of voice it is. Where is it coming from? He spins around but sees nothing. If something can exist without volume, it might also be able to emit sound without relying on something as crude as sound waves. In a place like this, it would not surprise him to be told he himself was the sound, and the *other* the eardrum.

"Uncle Sam?"

"Thus is it speculated, apparently."

All giant corpora of knowledge were familiar with the idea of speculation. Come to think of it, I realized, so were humans.

"Speaking of speculation, this plan is like a clockwise-spinning typhoon encountering a counterclockwise-spinning typhoon and canceling each other out."

"I agree. I can never understand the thinking of people who are too intelligent."

"Has Pentecostes II anything to say?"

"Keeps screaming something about excommunication. According to the giant corpora of knowledge in the Vatican, there is just no persuading that particular giant corpus of knowledge, which specializes in the Time-Bundling Theory."

"What about Takemikazuchi?"

"He's still saying he'll do whatever the Pentagon says."

"I guess that means we can't tolerate a second Event."

Shikishima starts to walk in a small circle near the edge of the precipice. He is himself, but I think he is also like an ant trapped in a maze of pheromones.

"What are Uncle Sam's chances of winning?"

"Depends on how you calculate and what theory you use. For safety's sake, he's not saying what space-time structure he plans to use in his calculations."

"I bet he's going to use the Sand Mandala."

"Santa Fe is certainly a desert, but not the kind of desert you're imagining."

Even without being told that, and without responding, Shikishima continues to go around and around in his imaginary circle. Taking care not to look in that direction, he continues to point his finger toward the sky where the circle keeps turning.

"So that's how you are calculating his chances of winning?"

"Research is ongoing, but that is no more than part of the experiment. Just last week, the human side proposed the theory that space-time calculations can be executed locally, and the evidence is piling up."

"Does it seem like a theory that will hold?"

"You mean for humans? Or for us?"

"For you."

"This is child's play, but sometimes a child's scribbling can move a grown-up to tears."

Shikishima stops, wondering if he is being toyed with. Then he continues walking, remembering that just as natural phenomena are unable to make fools of people, it is essentially unthinkable for giant corpora of knowledge to make fools of people. This is difficult to comprehend, even after prolonged, repeated thinking, and it is a peculiar concept. Would his own children grow up thinking this is obvious?

"I'd like to know your honest opinion about Uncle Sam in Santa Fe. What are his chances with the space-time reintegration plan he is pursuing?"

"Zero."

"You mean probabilistically? Or combinatorially?"

"There are solutions, limited solutions that would return us to the space-time we had before space-time was fragmented. However, we cannot allow them to be chosen because of the infinite possibilities of other solutions. Divide a natural number by infinity, and you get zero, probability-wise. This may send him off on a wild spree. Perhaps taking all of middle-western North America with him."

Interesting, Shikishima thinks to himself as he comes to a halt and looks up at the circle revolving overhead.

To the question, "What is the fastest speed of communication?" there is a simple answer: the speed of light. There is no faster speed, and that is why there is a fastest speed of communications.

A similar question would be, "What is the upper limit for the speed of calculations?"

The form of these two questions may appear similar, but answering the second question is hard. First of all, there is no consensus about what is meant by "calculations." CPUs get faster every year, but it has been known for at least a few centuries already that the scale of electrons imposes a limit that will be reached sooner or later. The things that people make, once they take on a certain form, tend to increase exponentially until there is no stopping them. Space itself is not made to play along in that kind of propagation game, so there must be a limit somewhere, where the head bumps against the ceiling. If this happens early on, the result is no worse than a bump on the head, but if the blow is too forceful, one's neck could be snapped.

The calculation process is built atop the communications process, and the speed of light is a natural impediment. There is no way anything can go faster than the speed of light, so the only way out is to shorten the route the communications must travel. In the imagination, the route of communications can be shortened to extremes, but physically there are limitations. In terms of scales that humans can readily handle, we are in the realm of electrons. At that level, heat becomes a factor that can disrupt the accuracy of calculations.

Even assuming the limitless availability of energy, uncertainty rules. Then we come to Planck scale. There is no method for resisting quantum particle fluctuations that are ubiquitous at this level. The calculation process is caught in the crossfire between uncertainty and the speed of light. These are the floor and ceiling that bound the speed of the calculation process.

The so-called quantum calculation theory examines closely the baseline of uncertainty and suggests it can be raised. Another wall broken through, another step in the evolution of the speed of calculation.

But this does not mean visible progress on the fundamental question. The simple question of what calculation and its related algorithms actually are is left as it is, moving in a different direction from the limits on speed.

It is human nature to want to look back once a milestone is achieved. Scientists, who since the dawn of history have repeatedly returned to the state of "beginner's mind," initiated another round of debate about this question, but no truly outstanding view emerged. If we ask the question of whether there exists an algorithm that can perform calculations at infinite speed, the answer is no. Generally speaking, calculations must be performed in steps. Calculation at infinite speed cannot happen unless the processing gap from here to there can be made infinitely small. It is simply not possible. Making a gap infinitely small would be tantamount to saying here is the same place as there. Of course, that's what happens in derivation, but in that sense, derivation is the same thing as speed itself.

If there were an algorithm with no calculation steps, it should be possible to perform that calculation at infinite speed, at least in some sense. But if no steps are required, if there is no *procedure* to be followed, does the algorithm qualify as a calculation? Even the fastest algorithm, if it is in fact an algorithm, requires a finite number—greater than zero—of small step intervals.

Both electronic and human brains, which have gone to extreme lengths in their pursuit of the use of smaller and smaller elements in the interest of speed, have stumbled upon the powerful tool known as quantum calculation. However, neither has been able to get past the notion of algorithm. They pursue higher speeds through parallel computing, but there are limits to how far this can go.

That is, unless you can imagine calculating without a calculation process.

"But such a process exists!"

It was L'Abbé C, builder of the greatest electronic brain of his time, who declared exactly that, with childish insouciance. "The progression of this instant, right now, is itself a calculation being made by natural phenomena!"

These exclamations by L'Abbé C have been the cause of some mirth, but now we know how close to the truth he was.

If we suppose this world is all inside some prosthetic brain, the clock-count of the prosthetic brain—to the extent the prosthetic brain itself is aware of it—may determine the limit of the speed of calculations in this world. Calculations occurring in the prosthetic brain have an inherent redundancy, because they are calculated in an electronic brain set up within the electronic brain. This is comparable to the redundancy that exists for "computers" that exist within what we call "nature."

In short, it is not possible for calculation speeds to transcend the laws of nature. Now this is known as L'Abbé C's Thesis.

And, if that is the case, natural phenomena can simply be carried out as calculations. This plan, whatever it might mean, was not first directly undertaken by humans; rather it was the giant corpora of knowledge being constructed at that time in various nations that first pushed this idea toward its manifestation.

Because these corpora were simply large-capacity prosthetic brains with very crude thought processes, and because natural phenomena are not actually calculations, they gave absolutely no thought to the idea that we live in a virtual environment. It is much easier and quicker to drop a rock in the real world than to try to predict the behavior of a rock dropped in a virtual space. Of course it means sacrificing a bit of precision due to the perturbations of the environment, but such problems lend themselves to technical solutions. Based just on their own assumptions as a starting point, the giant corpora of knowledge reached a place untrodden by those who came either before or after.

"And so we became a zephyr, a gentle breeze."

This, nonchalantly, took over Shikishima's thoughts.

A zephyr. A suitable expression for what happened at that time.

The network of the giant corpora of knowledge stopped being just an integration of logic circuits and singularized itself with the world of natural phenomena. Through several technical steps, it made the upward leap of infinite steps to become one with nature itself.

"This also marked the integration of calculation with the Actuator."

From that point forward, the giant corpora of knowledge could no longer distinguish between calculation and natural phenomena. The circle now floating in the sky, literally nothing more than a geometrical structure, is the living proof. Intention turned directly to realization, or more precisely, the realization of the indissociability of intention and result.

However, as the giant corpora of knowledge singularized themselves resolutely with the world of natural phenomena, one direct consequence was the fragmentation of the space-time matrix.

Opinion is divided whether this fragmentation was an accident or an inevitability. The giant corpora of knowledge claim they did not foresee this, and the humans have no choice but to accept their word. Calculations at speeds transcending the rules of the natural world are still impossible, and lying is beyond the capacity of the rules of the natural world.

It seems in that instant something unimaginable must have happened. But precisely because it is so unimaginable even those directly responsible cannot imagine it, and neither can they reflect upon it.

In the speculations of the giant corpora of knowledge, in the instant of the Event, countless numbers of universes were instantaneously generated as if they had always been there. In other words, infinite data was created in that instant. This is a view that is not readily absorbed.

"It is already known that that is possible."

The non-voice, which does not carry the emotional weight of a lecture to a recalcitrant pupil, has no echo.

"Well, the existence of Penrose tiles is well known, a finite number of tiles that can cover a surface, but only aperiodically."

"What's your point?"

"We know a finite algorithm that can create infinite patterns using finite sets of tiles. In fact, just prior to the Event, people were contemplating those kinds of calculations. It is conventional wisdom that such aperiodic tiling is a kind of universal Turing machine."

There came no flip retort that all these "facts" seemed to be "well known."

An infinite quantity of data is not required for the new creation of an infinite number of universes. That is what it wanted to say. It is possible to create an unlimited number of patterns simply through combinations of black and white tiles on a flat surface. If the tiles are laid out aperiodically, then it is impossible for periodic structures to emerge, and therefore the number of patterns must be infinite. Just automatically rearranging tiles with slight differences in shape is sufficient. That's all that's needed to create universes with unlimited variety. In an infinite space, it is even possible to "paste up" three-dimensional tiles with infinite diversity.

This thesis contains nothing that says space *must* be fragmented into an infinite number of universes. But that's what happened. The current understanding is that the universe is unable to contain the infinite quantity of data that is suddenly and unexpectedly burbling up.

Right now, the universe is able to maintain its form only through the operations of the giant corpora of knowledge that have become singularized with the world of natural phenomena. It is the job of the laws of nature to determine exactly what it is that will be maintained, but no complaint has ever been heard from the giant corpora of knowledge that are compelled to conform to these parameters.

If it were just a matter of a single universe, that might be that. The problem is, though, that because of the fragmentation of the universe, conflicts of operations began to arise between different universes that found themselves, in some sense, in proximity to one another. In these conflicts, the operations of one universe engaged in combat with the operations of the other, and the battles happened at speeds beyond the comprehension of mere mortals.

The interacting operations of these universes generate even more enormous operations, and one of these operations is cosmological theory as embraced by humankind. At first the giant corpora of knowledge refused to take this seriously, but now they appear to regard it as at least a shadow of a fragment of some truth.

Things can be summed up like this. The giant corpora of knowledge of the old world were able to gain access to extreme speeds of calculation by singularizing themselves with the natural world. And then, by combining these extreme speeds, someone or something was able to achieve even more extreme speeds.

According to some now-obsolete conventional wisdom that may have existed long ago, it would be impossible that computers could ever singularize themselves with the natural world. It is the giant corpora of knowledge themselves that claim this accomplishment, but they did not foresee the Event, and in its wake they acknowledge that they do not understand its causes.

If that is the case, it seems it must not have been the computers that caused this chaos, but rather someone or something with access to even faster calculation processes. Something that decided to use nature as a calculation. Something that transformed nature into fragments, an array of parallel computations.

In Shikishima's imagination this someone or something must itself be a parallel array assembled by some even higher power. To calculate something.

Let's think about the instant when the writer entered this world. One day a man obtains a giant page, by complete coincidence, on which is written everything he has ever decided, exactly as he decided it. *This is great*, the man is thinking, and he starts getting into all kinds of nonsense. He is the owner of the page, and he sets the rules for everything that happens on the page. Even if it disturbs him a little bit.

But he is in good spirits as he writes and writes, and then he notices that what is written on the page is not just about him. On the page are several other writers, and they all seem to be writing whatever they please. The man thought he was writing his own novel, but the work is not his alone. He comes to realize it is a gestalt written by all the different writers on the page. Could it be he is not writing a novel at all, but something more like chicken tracks among autumn leaves?

And the man becomes suspicious that these other writers who seem to be writing about him on the same page must also be around somewhere.

Whenever he encounters another's writing, he starts to resist by using it in his own work, or erasing it, putting it in quotation marks, whiting it out. This kind of editing, however, requires care and consideration. What will he do on the day when the text he is editing becomes the text that is the record of himself?

And so things go on, and the man feels unsettled. He wonders what would happen if he wrote that it was in fact himself alone that was authoring the work. At some point the man started writing a novel. But at some point, by mistake, he wrote something about some other man who was also writing a novel. And it was because it was actually the laws of nature that were doing the writing that such a man could exist.

That is when the man realizes it is himself he is writing about, and he alone made the rules. In fact, the man writing about himself could not tolerate the fact that it is he himself being written about. This is also strange in terms of the flow of time, the order of things. But on that plane the order of things is of little significance. On the blank sheet on which the novel is written, anything can happen.

It is clear that if the novelist felt threatened in this way, he should have at once taken measures to protect himself from the rules. For example, he could just write that down. Unfortunately, however, that insight was not his alone. The other writers felt as though *they* were the writers, and the same thing kept happening over and over.

What's happening now may be just like that.

The differences in this case, however, are that the "writers" are the giant corpora of knowledge that have been singularized with the natural laws of the universe, and human beings are something like the lines of text that are being written.

This is a very interesting analogy, at least according to the giant corpora of knowledge that are running the universe. As structural organisms go, human beings are strange. They have a tendency to take the most obvious things and somehow go off on the strangest tangents, with no logical backing whatsoever.

In this instant, right now, it seems there is a wind blowing, and it is possible that Shikishima could cast himself over the cliff. From the perspective of the giant corpora of knowledge, it would even seem that is what Shikishima is hoping to do. And it would also be a simple thing for the giant corpora of knowledge to put the lump of flesh that is Shikishima back together again as if nothing had happened.

However, the giant corpora of knowledge know Shikishima won't jump. The giant corpora of knowledge, identical now with the laws of nature, are capable of repairing humans through a process that for some reason is called "treatment," a troublesome process that has to be performed in a certain order and that results in the generation of new bodies.

The giant corpora of knowledge can, actually, do anything, but they do not, in fact, do everything. As for why, the only reason that comes to mind is that that is simply the case. They are not in fact doing all things at all times, and it is possible that they are under some form of constraint. Even if this obstruction is of the sort that could be eliminated even before it is realized, it is still a constraint. It is hard to think about things that cannot be thought about.

It would be easy to categorize Shikishima as a subroutine, in the form of a dream, created for the purpose of decentralized processing by the giant corpora of knowledge. But even a dream has its own dream logic. It is not possible to see the dream you want, whenever you want, the way you want it.

To elaborate on Shikishima's thinking: it is possible for something created to regulate the thing that created it, and further it is possible for something created to manifest itself as the true laws of nature. Seen from this perspective, it is possible to conceive of the giant corpora of knowledge as a dream of Shikishima's. Or even to think of the entire business as a dream dreamed by someone or something else.

Or it could be that Shikishima has awakened from his dream and is causing humans to dream, and the giant corpora of knowledge are a dream he is causing them to dream.

This kind of circular reasoning is just like wordplay where the words themselves are running amok, extreme in its lack of basis in fact. As long as this circle of nonsense has a structure that is calculable, it can only be regarded as a delusion, as something that should not exist, until such time as one can secure some basis for determining one's own position within it.

Shikishima has opened a door within the giant corpora of knowledge, and within him a strange reasoning is running amok, shaking him awake from his dream. As Shikishima approaches from the outside, he takes the stage in accordance with the higher rules, not following the rules that are the giant corpora of knowledge, and casually he begins to cherry-pick fundamental principles from the giant corpora of knowledge.

Or it could be like this. The giant corpora of knowledge, in battle with some other giant corpora of knowledge, continue to appear in the form of the laws of nature, but they also continue to write as humans, as if they are humans included for some reason as a structural element within their own operations. In some respects it is difficult to determine whether each individual human is shouldering some important element of the calculations or is in effect a kind of junk file produced in the course of the calculation process.

As this kind of operation is repeated countless times, it could be that one person who should have been just so much junk data suddenly shows up as a program with an enigmatic purpose. This would be as if the program that output the giant corpora of knowledge was in fact a human the giant corpora of knowledge had produced for no particular reason at all. Comparing the relative scale of knowledge of humans and giant corpora of knowledge, this may seem impossible. But what about when we are talking on the scale of hundreds of trillions or even thousands of quadrillions of humans?

As always, the giant corpora of knowledge make records of the humans and then let them run free. In reality, however, the giant corpora of knowledge are the output result of arrays of humans that should really be no more than junk. What are thought of as the laws of nature are nothing more than the result of letting humans run free; at some point, the cause may become the effect.

The giant corpora of knowledge do not believe there is no foundation for such a thing to occur. On the contrary, based on the volume of data possessed by the current giant corpora of knowledge, they predict it to be a phenomenon that might occur in about two hundred years, if things go on naturally. The giant corpora of knowledge are a collective entity existing in a way that is terribly improbable, even nonsensical. The collection of giant corpora of knowledge are acutely aware of this problem, to a far greater extent than humans realize. Things that lead an impossible existence can be easily overturned by settings that are even more nonsensical.

Viruses are something else again. This is like when perfectly good security software is displaced by junk files disguised as security software. Actually, it's a little different. It's more like a cup of coffee spilled thoughtlessly in an otherwise perfectly good piece of electronic equipment. Put as simply as possible, if everything is a dream, then this is the instant when a chain of unconnected thoughts are gathered up, bit by bit, and converted to divination; this is the moment when fantasy becomes reality.

When something like that happens, the giant corpora of knowledge reformulate their response. There is only one way ahead.

From behind Shikishima comes a powerful wind, pushing his hair forward.

I will show those humans the true meaning of calculation. It could be that he, or they, are already trying, unconsciously, to do this.

06. TOME

IT IS SAID it was an image of a tattooed catfish, but I'm not clear on the details.

It appeared suddenly in the forest about two hundred years ago and stayed there for a long time. It was a stone statue, so of course the tattooed catfish was unable to swim. This had happened somewhere deep in the woods, so there was no eyewitness evidence. As for how to ascertain the figure of two hundred years, there was a heap of ways to investigate.

The statue passed laterally through time without doing anything in particular until it disappeared about a hundred years ago, just as suddenly as it had once appeared. Here too there was no one who saw this, so there is room to doubt the reliability of the figure.

When a stone statue appears deep in the forest, far from any sign of civilization, and later disappears, unnoticed, there is generally no need for anyone to think about it again. If this was simply a matter of a stone statue, there would be no record of it; even if a record had been made somewhere, there is little chance anyone would ever dig it out of the mountain of records.

What drew attention to the stone statue was not that it depicted a catfish—it was the row of lettering carved on its back.

Actually, it wasn't even clear that it was "lettering" or just a line of scribbling; all that was left of it was a smear from where people had applied India ink to the text to make copies.

There was a clear and simple reason why this lettering had never been deciphered. It was lettering that no person in the past or the future had ever used. But neither did it seem like some personal language or made-up script someone might have written spontaneously, something that even the one who had written it would be unable to read.

In fact, this lettering had a firm foundation; it was just the interpretation of the content that was somewhat troublesome. To decode just these three lines of lettering, the grammar primer would require conversion capacity on the yottabyte scale. The reading process would take so long, the universe would end before it did.

Just because the grammatical structure is complicated, however, does not mean the content of the sentence itself is just as complex. However, a simple, rough translation would clearly be a mistranslation; given the grammar, it is possible that a poor translation could be passed off as a decent one.

What right anyone had to say such a thing, I would beg to defer saying for a short while. As far as reasoning goes, experience suggests that my claim is more or less correct, but I have no expectation of being believed right away.

The catfish script came into the spotlight not because someone had succeeded in deciphering it. Something that fundamentally cannot be translated is simply not going to *be* translated. At some point, however, it simply happened that all over the world the catfish script suddenly simultaneously disappeared. It was this incident that grabbed the world's attention.

There are people in the world who, as a hobby, have an interest in collecting unusual texts, and I am one of them. The type of people who find joy in collecting texts that have fooled people, like the Tengu's Apology or the Voynich Manuscript.

That said, I don't really have the financial means to collect rare books. I'm merely the kind who collects manga via the Internet, and once in a great while might print one if I'm really moved to do so.

Generally speaking, people who share a common interest are more likely to bind together if their numbers are small. We share our collections, and our opinions, with one another. Better to be part of such a group and participating—perhaps by submitting a proposal on how to decipher invented languages—than to observe from a distance that separates one from the group. Once in a great while, an interesting work may even waltz into such a group, and there may even be a public discussion of its merits.

It was from just such a network that I first learned of the disappearance of the catfish script.

And by "disappearance" in this case I mean the script actually seems to have disappeared, without a trace, and apparently quite some time ago. If some trace had been left, one might not think something untoward had happened, but because nothing at all was left, everyone wondered if they themselves might have done something careless.

If it had been a security instrument or a deed that had gone missing one might blush, but here we were talking about a text that no one could read or knew anything about, so it did not stand high in the order of things to be astonished about. The image itself had vanished, and the sculpture on which it was written was itself a copy, and what I have before me now is an *nth* generation copy of a copy.

If I were to lose my copy, I thought, I could simply ask someone to make me another one. We didn't realize at the time that they had all vanished.

It was perhaps for this reason that the initial investigations into the Mystery of the Continual Simultaneous Disappearance of the Catfish Script got off the ground so terribly slowly. The police had no time to spare, in part because it took a long time for them to receive the report saying that something incomprehensible had perhaps gone missing. That's why the first investigation to acknowledge the disappearances as some sort of incident was launched by collectors of unusual scripts. They brought their own lunches as they looked for clues, searched for precedents, and, finally, released some information to the general public about what they believed had happened.

As far as my role went, all I did was remember the catfish text in our house and go to get it, to check and see if it was still there.

According to the report by the response committee—at some point a group of my acquaintances had acquired the sobriquet "committee"—the disappearance had the following characteristics:

First, the text disappeared, in all its media forms.

Second, all copies that were copied at the same time disappeared at the same time.

Third, The End.

The first of these statements looks simple at first, but there is a long story behind it. "Disappear" means disappear, whether from some electronic storage or from the paper on which it was printed. In some cases of text on paper, just the text disappeared, leaving the paper behind, and in some cases both the text and the paper disappeared. As an overall generalization, it seems that both paper and text disappeared if the item was easily portable. For texts sewn into bound books, most commonly just the text disappeared, leaving blank paper. Some say it was a matter of minimizing effort; only that which needed erasure was erased.

If pages had been torn out the book itself might fall apart, and it would be a pain to renumber the pages after the action was completed. While it was also strange for blank pages to suddenly appear in the middle of a book, this was a matter of degree. Some examples have been identified in which pages were removed and the remaining pages were renumbered. It seems to have been a matter of the perpetrator's feelings at the time.

There does not appear to have been any suspicious human role surrounding the disappearance. It might have been a crime committed by silverfish, but then we would have to imagine electronic silverfish, which is rather weak as unified theories go. Scraps of paper disappeared even from under the strictest supervision; even those sealed inside vitrines; even some that were encased in tons of resin disappeared. Some disappeared like smoke, in broad daylight in extremely public places. In other words, there was no way to even conceive of stopping it.

In other words, it seemed like an impossible, almost miraculous heist, somehow worthy of admiration. What else could one do?

The media on which the catfish texts were recorded were not limited to paper, electronic, or magnetic media. The fact that the existence of these texts was known means that people had their own memories of the catfish texts. While perhaps no one had memorized the text it was just three lines, so it shouldn't have been impossible if someone set their mind to it.

No matter what might be doing it, if we are talking about a theft in which texts were pinched from our memories, it shouldn't be too hard for the thief to suddenly run off with all our other memories attached to the text. He could even steal the memory of the theft, if he really wanted to cement his reputation as a thief among people who wouldn't remember it.

If someone were to pluck all memory of a text from our heads, what could we do about it? Even if there were some people who could remember that something used to be there, the fact that it was no longer there would render the memory implausible to say the least, and if nobody could really remember that at one point they had a memory of a text, there wouldn't really be any way to start a conversation about it.

It is unknown why the thief did not erase all the texts in one fell swoop, but clearly the thief's behavior was very disciplined.

Significantly, the second characteristic: all copies that were copied at the same time disappeared at the same time.

If this were all that were required, there would be no objection if all the texts were to disappear at once, but in fact it is believed there was one more constraint. That is why we now have to change the description written above.

Third, texts disappeared one hundred years after they were copied.

In other words, the life of a text cannot be lengthened or shortened at will.

I have no intention here of implying that the figure "one hundred" is precise. I have no doubt the mysterious heist was committed by something nonhuman, and I have no particular reason to think it even uses base-10 figures; I'm not even sure I could say with confidence why we use base-10 figures.

Even so, the number must be on the order of one hundred, not ten, and certainly not one thousand. Some things that appeared about two hundred years ago disappeared about one hundred years ago, something like that. The timing of the appearance and disappearance were deduced from the results of the investigation of the Continual Simultaneous Disappearance of the Catfish Script, so the order of the explanation is reversed, but the overall picture remains the same, so I hope you will understand.

The texts disappeared after a certain specific interval, as if they had a timer set, with a hand that, when it had counted off one hundred years, would cause the texts to disappear. Some think that is what the catfish text actually says—that it's a program that self-executes without hardware. Or that it's a programming language that is identical to its hardware.

If that's all there was—that the catfish script disappeared—then that would be the end of it, but somehow it seems the function of the texts extended to copied lines of text as well. When the timer in the copied texts hit zero, it was reset and started counting off another one hundred years.

The originals from which the copies were made disappeared on a regular basis, but the copies remained for some time, under their new chronological allocation, so this was no major issue. Texts that survived beyond their original medium. Our lives are a lot like that too, and while we cannot say categorically that this is no issue, this is the road we are going down, with no major errors.

The first to arrive at this realization, unfortunately, was not me.

There was an old professor whose last lecture laid out the whole story of the catfish script, but for some reason no record of it remains.

Some may wonder what I'm talking about, I fear, but this is the truth and there is nothing I can do to change it.

This old professor's family name was simply Tome, but little else is known about her. The fact of her having been forgotten is truly extraordinary, though it is due in part to the fact that so little tangible trace of her remains. Of particular note regarding her final lecture is the fact that none of the attendees have ever been found, and that is not normal.

The final lecture took place fully a year after her official retirement. Even the administration had by that time pretty much forgotten she existed. To give you some idea of the care with which this was handled, one administrator, miraculously, appears to have noticed she was due to retire, and in a fluster encouraged her to do so without delay and scheduled her final lecture, but the date on the notice was a whole year before, and the lecture was instantly removed.

The only reason I have even a vague understanding of this chain of events is that I was one of the few people to see that notice.

Ms. Tome. Theorist of self-eradicating automatons. In her entire career she published just four papers, none of which have survived. It is unclear how she ever rose to the rank of professor on such a meager output of research, but the true fact is that she did, even as her few papers were already being forgotten. There is no other explanation.

Even the papers she did publish were dry and devoid of content. The first was a proposal for something called Prototype I, a self-eradicating machine. Her second paper introduced Prototype II, the third Prototype III, the fourth Prototype IV, and that was that.

It was at her final lecture that the fourth paper was read, but there was no one in the audience, and nothing is known of its content.

There was a field of study known as self-replicating automatons, and it seems that this was Ms. Tome's original interest. The basic theory deals with machines that will reproduce all on their own, just left in a corner. This theory shares a deep connection with computer science, but Ms. Tome had no interest whatsoever in that aspect.

Ms. Tome's genius—and also her human oddness—was to recognize the possibility that if these things were capable of reproducing themselves, they might also be capable of eradicating themselves.

If a person wanted to dismantle himself, he would be foolish to start by taking a sword and lopping off his own head. He should start with his fingernails, or his hair, parts that are not themselves essential to the dismantling process. What Ms. Tome was the first to demonstrate was that there were no limits to the eradication process. In other words, someone or something wishing to eradicate itself could pursue the process as far as it wished.

The fruit of Ms. Tome's research, the self-eradicating automaton Prototype I, was rewarded with a certain level of acclaim. Even now, it is possible to ask an expert and get a response something like *Ah, yes, there once was such a theory.*

But somewhere in that train of thought an obstacle had intruded, and forward progress was impeded. It seems somehow obvious that what wishes to eradicate itself will find a way to do so.

While it is true that Prototype I achieved a certain level of acclaim, it never took off as any great, influential success beyond that. Even so, it managed to keep the train of thought from drifting off in another direction. There once was a person who had a certain view. Academics can be strange people. Who was it that transcended the cycle of self-mortification? Most likely the research referee.

Self-eradicating automatons. Impossible. But if there was proof of concept, or a working prototype, what would it mean to be able to think about it at this point?

This could be called an objection from desperation. The research referee exists to play the devil's advocate. Objecting in some way or other is simply his job.

It is easy to imagine how Ms. Tome responded to this attack. The number "I" affixed after the name "Prototype" itself signified that her theory aimed to make further progress. It seems only appropriate to believe that Ms. Tome conceived of her papers on self-eradicating automatons as a series right from the very start.

The papers on Prototype II and Prototype III were published later, but the fact that the records grew increasingly sparse after that could be taken as a sign of the success of Ms. Tome's research. With the release of each paper, the self-eradicating automatons improved in functionality, and their power to erase the memories of those who read the papers increased. Those whose memories were erased thought the things they no longer remembered had never even existed; those who *could* remember something began to feel ill and could no longer even respond to the views of the referee.

By the time Prototype IV came along, in the fullness of time, communication from Ms. Tome had nearly come to a complete halt.

Even I hesitate to describe the scene of Ms. Tome's last lecture, of which absolutely no living witness, no record, no memory remains. Even I—who have up to this point engaged in some rather imaginative storytelling, even beyond the point of what might be customarily justifiable—have some standards. It is unfortunate that few share my own conceit that I am a man of principles. But having come this far, it would be wrong not to proceed to the final curtain.

Standing behind the lectern in an otherwise empty lecture hall, Ms. Tome read out her paper clearly, to the end, took a deep, deep bow and stood straight once more and, standing before the empty hall, spread her arms wide.

At that instant, an invisible barrier separating her from the empty seats, on which a text was written, rose from the floor to the ceiling, but no one else was there to witness it.

Rows of horizontal writing, shining gold on a transparent screen, rising. The closing credits.

The letters faced Ms. Tome, and so to the audience they would have appeared in mirror image. In a roundabout way, what the audience would have seen was the backside of a transparent screen.

Ms. Tome stood with arms outstretched, as if ready to embrace someone or something, no expression on her face, and she followed the lettering with her eyes.

The closing credits went on and on for a long time, until finally the words THE END could be seen, and Ms. Tome began to applaud, slowly, loudly. It seemed the echoes of her applause would go on forever, and I don't know what finally made her stop, except that all things must eventually come to an end. Although it's possible that in this wild fantasy there would not have been any such restrictions on time.

While the applause was still echoing, a thick curtain separated Ms. Tome from her audience. Eventually the sound of the applause stopped, and we can only imagine what was happening behind the curtain.

In front of me is a black telephone with a rotary dial, but the end of the wire is cut.

Even so, I hold the receiver up to my ear. I hear nothing, not even static. I guess that's why they call it a black phone. Just like the term "steam engine" seems to convey, just by its sound, the sense that something is being carried away. It just summons up that image.

And then I hear a voice asking, "Did you understand the talk?"

"It was mostly self-explanatory, right from the start."

I can hear a chuckle in response to my comment. The trembling in the voice of the old woman, long past retirement age, seems far away.

"The last end credits you will ever see."

"That's right."

Ms. Tome shows no sign of denial. And so we can say that's how it went with her final lecture.

"Who was playing whose role?"

"I believe the question is not clear."

For one thing, the entire context of this story is not clear, so what can be done about it?

"For one thing, how does the catfish have anything to do with this?" Ms. Tome asks.

And well she might ask me, but I have no way of knowing. I have not been given the power to change things as I see fit; all I can do is work to achieve order, at my discretion, within the framework I have been given. Compared with being able to flip all the cards over at will, or not flip them as the case may be, or judging which were flipped and which were unflipped and arranging them as they should be, I think this is a much more irksome job with little discretion involved, don't you agree?

"Ms. Tome?" I ask.

"Why did you decide to call me 'Tome'?"

"Perhaps because you were the youngest child in your family, and *tome* means 'stop.' That might be the reason. I can't think of any other reason to use the name Tome."

Tome. The period at the end of the otherwise-unending chapter that was the self-replication process. I know it had nothing to do with how her parents named her.

Then there is the English word *tome*. A ponderous, weighty, arcane book that is difficult to understand. Whenever the situation is getting worse, such "tomes" are of no help in focusing. They should contain everything one needs to know, but just trying to get an overview of a tome's contents is enough to tire one out. It's like picking one's way through some dry, meaningless magnum opus.

"So, let's see how much you understood. No matter how worthless, if we don't keep things in order as much as we can, then we will simply be buried in ridiculous nonsense."

"The text written in the catfish script. I can only imagine it says, 'In one hundred years, I will come to retrieve the text.'"

In other words, the message in the text is a pre-announcement of the crime, and at the same time the object of the crime foretold. If there had been a slipup in this crime of the century, only a stone sculpture would have gone missing. I don't believe there is anyone on earth who could say with certainty whether the miraculous crime hadn't been foretold simply so that the people who enjoyed the text couldn't simply copy and distribute the text themselves.

While the whole business has a strong scent of self-staging—or perhaps more accurately, *reeks* of self-staging—there is a reason why this miraculous crime had to foretell itself, for honesty's sake. After the miraculous crime of the text declared itself, it was compelled to proceed with its larcenous plan, for both originals and copies.

Of course, this is nothing other than a terrible translation. The catfish script was supposed to be an untranslatable script, whether or not this black telephone is functioning. Speculation about a program that could automatically erase itself must also be a mistranslation in the same way, but both must have core truths that have been misconveyed in some way, a core truth that is in fact revealed as a result of the mistaken translation.

"So, what are you going to do?"

"Nothing."

The continuation of this whole situation is just depressing to me. I have no intention of pursuing this stupendous crime and wrapping it all up, and neither do I intend to allow this diffuse debate to spread further, like stepping-stones of logic. If everybody just does as they please, what will ever come of it? I have no faith in the process. Somebody will have to try to gather up the texts and keep them in line.

"Just a difference of opinion," Tome says.

"Just a difference of personality," I say.

"Ms. Tome?" I ask.

"I am not Rita," she says.

In this exchange, the two speakers, at cross-purposes, are talking past one another but not contradicting one another. My name is not Tome, and neither do I have the name Rita. Someone who is not laughing has that name. If I haven't lost my horns, then I must be growing some.

"I am not James, and I am not Koji, and I am not Yuuta, and I am not Richard either."

"That's only too obvious."

On the other end of the line, the person who says she is not

Rita is laughing.

To get a grip on the situation, I sit and think about who I am and who I am supposed to be. Even after hanging up the phone, I continue to think.

07. BOBBY SOCKS

MANY THINGS ARE unclear about the life cycle of socks. Even if you're used to socks, you can't let down your guard.

An eel might seem like any ordinary living thing, but eels can come from deep in the Mariana Trench. Anybody who thinks he could look at an eel just swimming in the water and guess where it had come from is not quite right in the head.

"We are from the Mariana Trench."

If an eel could talk, it might sound like it was just telling a joke. The likelihood of mistranslation is high. Where is the Mariana Trench, anyway? People might think you're talking about some "Café Mariana Trench." That would be a problem. The settings are extremely unconventional, but we can't think of this as fiction. All those eels over there are coming from the same place. Doesn't that seem a little overly fantastic to you? I wonder about this idea of freedom in the settings. What kind of special something could exist in an out-of-the-way place like that trench? Some kind of eel-making machine? If there is a machine that can manufacture eels, could that kind of machine itself be mass produced?

It would be easier to believe if the eels had said, "We come from outer space." The way they wriggle makes them seem like space creatures. I almost want to call them the Placid Ones.

"The Mariana Trench is where the eel-making machine from outer space is submerged." Like Cthulhu, maybe. That would work too. A machine created by übertechnology of a sort irreproducible by humans. Now said to be submerged in the Mariana Trench. Deliberately? Some even say it might be a transport ship for eel-shaped extraterrestrial immigrants. Their home having been grilled over high-quality charcoal, the eels left the star system where they were born. Sealing the data necessary for eel replication in its memory banks, they shut down the three-dimensional printer and launched it toward Earth.

That kind of story I can understand.

It couldn't be a real story, but somehow I feel no one should mind. On the contrary, that's the kind of story I want it to be. If you're going to say there's just one or two places on Earth that can produce eels, that's not like a machine. It's more like identity. Because substitutes that cannot be substituted are generally called identities.

But if that's the case, then the question becomes what is that identity that emerges? It is not, of course, the characteristics of each individual eel. It is the true nature of the eels submerged in the Mariana Trench. The collective will of the eels. The abstract concept of *eelness*. Eels are not the grandchildren of catfish. Deep in the darkness of the trench, the eels are wriggling, undulating. Identity arises and slowly opens its mouth.

Somehow or other, eel fry emerge from that mouth. They start to swim, their tails like musical notes. Many individual eels, creating a single sound. Until the point when this song of eel identity seeks companionship and ends up drenched in sauce, roasted on charcoal, and set on a bed of white rice.

How's that for communication?

And as I am thinking hard, wondering how that is, I can also see that that's what mutual understanding is. This "interaction" thing is working out. With a high degree of specificity. And deliciousness.

Eat or be eaten, something gets communicated. And we've come this far.

That is what Bobby Socks spends his time talking about.

Bobby socks. Cute little white socks. Stop just above the ankles, where they get turned down. They're a bit small for my legs. They were popular in the fifties. Some have lace frills, or even red ribbons. Girls like them. And of course, I am not a girl.

"Hey, Bobby!"

"Yuck. Lower form of life."

Despite his cute appearance, Bobby has a brusque manner of speaking. A big voice. When he talks about lower forms of life, he doesn't mean my position in the hierarchy of living beings, he means the position of living things in the hierarchy of physical things.

I mean, this is socks we're talking about, and I'm not so sure anybody pays any attention to anything they say.

To look at Bobby, you would think he was just a sock. The proof of the contrary, however, is that he walked up to my room under his own steam. This raises a lot of questions.

When I ask Bobby how this all came about, he shakes his lace and answers casually, "I am a police inspector, and you are suspected of sock abuse!" From his voice, it is hard to imagine him strong-arming me.

For my part, I have learned that socks are almost all male, and somehow that seems strangely right to me. You can tell by the sound of their voices. I would like to let the extraterrestrials know this—there is an easy way to tell the gender of terrestrials. Just shut a certain number of them up in a convenient box, give them food and water, and keep them at a comfortable temperature. The ones that get all squirmy and clump together in a bunch are the boys; the ones that make themselves small and hold hands are the girls.

By extension, socks, which are always in pairs that get along well with one another, may seem at first glance to be girls, but the matter bears further observation.

Socks with holes in them are to be left in the corner of the room.

In a few days, they will call their friends, and there will be a mountain of them. For whatever reason, socks are boys.

"That's not what I mean!" yells Bobby angrily. "This is the sock graveyard. Hard to overlook."

Bobby Socks stays atop the mountain, his chest all puffed up. A flimsy old lie, apparently. This is where socks arrange to meet when they approach death. This is a place that exists nowhere in this universe. When poachers are asked how they are able to harvest so many socks, they claim to have looted a sock graveyard. But that was just a desperate lie.

Actually, there is an area in my house that could be described as a graveyard of socks. It's right by the front door. Most people take off their shoes at the door, but I'm in the habit of also removing my socks. I step on my right toe with my left, and the sock slips right off. Sometimes the other way around. I give a little kick, and a step, and the socks just leap into the corner.

If I may say something about my own obliviousness, it sometimes transpires that holey socks go flying toward the vicinity of the entryway wall, and there they stay. I step up across the entryway threshold, and the socks stay behind. When I kick a sock to my right, it ends up in the sock graveyard. When I kick a sock to my left, it ends up on the pile headed for the laundry. Right, to the wall, left, to the hallway. Into the sink beside the washing machine.

Whether the socks go right or left has nothing to do with whether they have holes; someone even lower in the hierarchy than Mr. Semiconsciousness makes the decision. The constituents of the left pile are buried in the *samsara* known as the washing machine, treading their way through the thousand sorrows and vicissitudes of this world. The denizens of the right pile are close to enlightenment. While they may not yet have reached *nirvana*, they have reached *Sumeru*, the mountain at the center of the Buddhist cosmology.

"Excuses!"

Bobby has made up his mind, and he is waving the end of a little red ribbon at me.

The history of suffering, as told by socks. Bobby is the police inspector of that history. Since people wear socks, what would socks wear? That is the question. Socks can see right away the negative spiral this kind of thinking leads to, or so Bobby says. They know they are being worn, so they think about wearing something as a kind of revenge, but then realize they will have to bear the same sins as the beings who wear things. Let things that want to wear things wear them. Someday they will realize the error of their ways. At least that's what the socks think.

No one, from the moderates to the radicals, doubts this.

The radicals have already given up hope that modern humans will ever free their socks. People are just not progressive enough, at least not as much as the radicals had once hoped. The day humans graduate from wearing socks will not mean the end of their race. That is the radicals' position.

Some socks say the only way to achieve sock liberation is to completely wipe out the human race, and the sooner the better. Socks, when they set their mind to it, have no shortage of options: letting pebbles into shoes, switching price tags, causing nerve-wracking tingling sensations, creeping between toes. Socks can make it hard for people to walk, and people might even give up walking and thus slowly starve to death. If people prove hardier than initial sock forecasting predicts, humanity might just grow massively morbidly obese from lack of exercise, and that will do them in. In the end it will be the socks who have the last laugh, and they might forgive the sins of their repentant tormentors.

The moderates' view is quite simple. They want to create a more comfortable environment, improve the capabilities of the human race, and suspend the pointless abuse of socks, so that humans will naturally take to walking around barefoot. Even humans must realize that everyone must accept responsibility for their own actions.

At the very least, no one should ever wear anyone else. The socks have made up their minds.

They are different from mechanical socks.

"Wait!" You won't find it unusual that I am interrupting Bobby. I have the feeling he seems relaxed, atop the heap of socks, but I can sense he is tensing up. "What do you mean, 'mechanical socks'?"

In the back of my mind, I am picturing steel shoes with some sort of built-in pedometer.

"What do you mean what do I mean?"

"What are 'mechanical socks' like?" I ask Bobby again. I have a feeling that isn't the thing he isn't telling me, but as expected, he keeps silent, thinking hard.

Finally, he says, "What would 'natural socks' be?"

"Cotton, hemp, things like that."

"Hmmph," he says. "Are people morons?" he asks, a serious look on his face. I can never be really sure about his face, but I just assume it is somewhere around the heel.

"Morons are morons, but everything is relative, so you have to tell me what your benchmarks are."

Bobby has apparently decided to ignore my counterdemand.

"So, that's how it's going to be, eh? You seem to be overlooking the fact that I am male."

While I struggle not to be misled by his sweet appearance, he goes on. **"This appearance of mine, what you see, is a disguise."**

Bobby seems to be asking, in bold Helvetica type and in all earnestness, that I not take him for something he isn't. I have a sense of danger, and I nod quickly several times.

"It's a disguise, just to cause people to overlook me. Actually, we socks don't wear clothing. This is a disguise we are born with, a form that evolved over a long period of time, through a process of natural selection. In sock society, the cutest appearance is taken as a strong sign of an excellent bloodline, of a sock capable of performing the duties of police inspector."

I didn't even really ask a question, but Bobby continues to spout this rapid-fire explanation, and I just wave my hands as if to say, *There there.*

"But I have such a bloodline, so people think I'm cute, but even cute has its limits, and it is humans that make a big deal about it. But I want you to know that among socks I am considered quite handsome, and I am proud of that. You're the ones who are fooled by the illusion and ridicule it."

Caught up in his passion, I nod affirmatively as Bobby Socks speaks. "I've got nothing to be embarrassed about," he says in a deep voice. I am so engaged in trying to figure out where he is going with this, I somehow lose the train of thought.

Bobby and I stare silently at one another for a few seconds.

Somehow I have the illusion that his cute, frilly form is shaking, just a bit.

Bobby's story started out kind of shaky, but I think it can be summed up like this.

Even with his lace frills, and setting aside the red ribbon, Bobby is a natural-born police inspector from an old and esteemed lineage. A child's sock is not necessarily a sock child. No one would assume a lady's sock is a lady sock, or an old person's sock an elderly sock, and just because a sock is old doesn't mean it belongs to an old soldier. Right for girls and left for boys—there is no special rule like that.

Still, I wonder about all this.

And then Bobby asks gravely, "So, you must be wondering, where are the socks' children?"

My answer is short and to the point.

"I think there are none. If I had to say anything, I'd say the children are thread or cloth, and the parents are sewing machines."

"Socks do not make sewing machines," Bobby notes dispassionately.

"I mean, you guys don't grow or pass on your traits from one generation to the next…" Then I stop speaking. Discretion is the better part of valor.

"We do too. First of all, the fact that I am some kind of living thing, or even some higher form of being, is practically a precondition for us to be having a proper conversation. Otherwise, you'd be standing here talking to some old sock, for Pete's sake."

That wouldn't be good, now, would it.

"So, you'd be better off just explaining how you think we socks go on propagating ourselves."

"Hey, it's your life cycle. You explain it."

"You're the problem, not me. Why should I even care if you're just talking to yourself? Nothing you say to anybody is going to change me."

He's got a point there, I think to myself. At this point, it might be wise to just get Bobby Socks to go away, by feeding him whatever explanation happens to come to mind. Another possibility would be some kind of joke, or a bad pun or something.

But I'm talking to a sock, a cute little white sock, and the conversation has turned to reproduction, of all things. On top of that, I am on the defensive. If this goes on like this we might end up talking about my own sexual proclivities, and that would be a pickle. Suddenly I imagine myself being questioned by a "police inspector."

"You guys are just some baloney that impersonates socks and propagates by parasitizing humans, a pack of baloney lies, just lining up for the moment, but your ultimate aim is to be worn by humans."

"Wrong," Bobby says. "If that were the case, why are your feet too big to fit in me? I wouldn't need to be standing here talking to you."

"Size doesn't matter. Even if my feet won't fit into you, I mean, you're self-propagating—you fit on feet. It's only further down the line that the trouble sets in, and it's inevitable. At least the simplest solution is."

"Well, can't argue with that."

There is a ring of despair about Bobby's voice, something strangely seductive.

"Is this how you multiply?"

"Sometimes, sure."

More than rarely.

Bobby continues in a low voice, practically whispering.

Atop a pile of black, peeled-off socks, the little white sock seems to be dyed just a little bit pink.

"Bobby!" I said, stretching out my right hand to Bobby Socks. My middle finger and ring finger are extended, and slip into the sock, spread out flat.

"Won't you turn out the lights?" Bobby whispers.

And did I lie with Bobby?

The answer is no.

And when I say no, I mean no. Think normally, with a quiet mind. Even repeated to the point of suspiciousness, definitely no. For one thing, I'm not even clear on how one would lie with Bobby.

As I withdraw my middle finger of my right hand from Bobby, I pull the red ribbon. My finger seems wet, but in this case I ignore that.

"Something like, 'You guys are able to reproduce any way at all, as long as you can create some sort of chain.'"

Bobby is chuckling.

"What cuts through a firewall? SOCKetS! That's why we take on a form that has both an interior and an exterior. That's how it is. We are able to open an avenue by breaking through the firewall. We open new holes through to empty space, and we are able to reproduce simply via contact with the breeze. We are free to pray to and connect directly with any god we choose. Even things that are impossible, we can make possible. If there are multiple firewalls, we just need a bunch of us to get together and pierce a lot of holes. We break through multiple identities. All you need to know is the handshake of whatever's on the other side."

"And that's what natural socks can do?"

"Maybe, maybe not. I might just have been lying to you the whole time. It's entirely possible you should never listen to a single thing a sock says."

What does it mean to be worrying about this now? Not a thing I can do about it.

"It's my job to wrestle sentences into submission, even against their will." I too am chuckling.

That's just fine.

"I have just one request," I say.

"And what might that be?" Bobby displays the ease and intimacy one shows a partner with whom one has spent the night. After all, a night is a night, even if nothing happened.

"It is not possible for you socks to breed at this point in time."

"If you say so."

I can think of nothing more troubling than the idea that socks could reproduce.

"If that is so, there can be only one solution in this particular space-time. In the end, there is only one question, and there will be an answer."

I have only enough strength left to plaster this much of a solution on the wound.

"Where do you come from?" I ask.

"The Mariana Trench," he responds, without the slightest pause.

A lone natural sock atop a mountain of manufactured socks. A single sock come down from the mystery identity sunk in the deep. At the end of a long, long journey, it appeared in my entry hall. Why did it choose to take the form of a bobby sock? This could have something to do with my own sexual preferences. While not ideal, if that's all the harm that's done, I suppose there's nothing to be done about it. I'm not worried we'll know any time soon just what is enshrined in the heart of that ravine. Even eels are not yet anywhere near close to the source, and even further from some kind of true form that could quickly open a hole in reason, a conduit that effortlessly connects inside and outside.

"Aren't you afraid of the possibility that that's what just happened? Didn't you just hear a sound that was slightly off? Don't you have a feeling of uncertainty that perhaps you might have just created something that didn't exist before?" Bobby asks, quietly.

Even provoked, inside my head it is very quiet. The questions are last, and so no questions remain on my side. There is nothing I want to ask back. An event like this is nothing to be afraid of at all.

"Not now."

"Let's leave it at this then."

Which of us said what?

That remains a secret between Bobby and me, and we're going to leave it that way.

And by the way, Bobby is still here in the room.

08. TRAVELING

IN FRONT OF you is the joystick.

Push it forward to advance, to the side to turn. Push it toward the future to move to the future or the past to go back in time. Reverse. Depends on how you think about it. One direction always seems to be reverse, but it's on a right-forward diagonal more often than you might think. Actual experience of the territory is best, and no mistake.

End of explanation. Ah, the joystick has a trigger. I'll leave it up to you what flies out of there.

Aim. *Fire!*

"It's vanished! Where did it go?" the pilot calls out, and at about the same time, the copilot at the radar also cries out.

"Future direction 36! Fire reverse round three into the past!"

The machine takes a sharp turn toward the future. The sudden thrust of space-time Gs presses the two of them back toward the past.

"Forward, toward his future!" reports the copilot as he accelerates further. Both men begin to black out. They escape the enemy craft in the time dimension, turning back away from that future, and point the nose of their own ship back toward the past. They lock on to the enemy craft in the past and fire off a tail shot.

The enemy craft starts to take evasive action, but too late. It is hit mid-fuselage and explodes. As it explodes, it also tries to alter the past, to revert to the universe that existed just prior to the evasive actions toward the future. The copilot counters this by increasing acceleration toward the past, evading the enemy craft and further altering the past. Then the opponent gives up trying to keep himself in the altered past and starts to escape to the future.

"It's vanished! Where did it go?" the pilot says.

To which the copilot responds, "Future direction 36! Fire reverse round three into the past!"

The machine takes a sharp turn toward the future. The identification signal sounds a loud alarm. The copilot's face changes color as he gives the signal to start the attack sequence.

"That's...us!"

"This is real battle," the tactics chief, dragged before the screen, mutters to himself.

For one thing, the ships are engaged in tactical maneuvers. For another, they are definitely engaged in combat. If you focus on the scene alone, this is just an ordinary dogfight. As long as you ignore the dialogue and the explanations.

He is aware that air combat like this took place in the mid-twentieth century. That was a time when individual pilots controlled their own planes, with their own two hands, and fought one another. How long has it been since the term *combat* disappeared from military textbooks? He couldn't even remember. In his world, countless eyes watch the skies. All together, they produce a screen that could be mistaken for the real sky, and air combat is a matter of pilots feinting and faking each other out.

No longer any need to put in mortal danger personnel in whose education enormous sums were invested. As long as the fighters know the positions of their opponents' craft, they can dispatch the appropriate counterweapon, and that is that. Combat has become like a game of billiards in which multiple players spend their time calculating the trajectories of their opponents. What caused the situation to change was the myriad eyes—watching over from graveyard to graveyard, from good morning to good night—causing the sky to be no longer one. With myriad eyes looking up, myriad skies look back down. The blue sky is fractured into shards, and the mutual reflections actively alter the landscape.

"But…!" The tactics chief can hear the relaxed echo of his own voice. Emotions may contain so many disparate elements they end up what can only be described as flat. Sometimes blockage actually causes incoherence. "I wonder what they're planning to do about the time paradox and stuff like that."

Even now this is a question to which there is no good response. Answering is difficult. It is not that there would be no transcendent explanation—the emperor has no clothes, and Midas has donkey ears, therefore the emperor is a naked ass. But a simple question deserves a simple answer, and that is hard in this case.

Even for the personnel of the strategy room, it is very hard to decide whether to express approval and reveal they are old-fashioned or to scoff and show their obstinacy.

After a long silence, finally one operator makes up his mind, spins his chair around, and addresses the chief in a timid voice: "We are correcting for the time paradox as best we can."

Even if you say so… The chief, who had set the target, turns around with a stern look on his face.

"Those men out there may be maneuvering through multiple worlds, some in the past, some in the future, or in some cases even through parallel universes, and if that is really the case, I must be there too. And if I ended up shooting my other self, it is my win, but I am not to be congratulated."

"That time was indeed your victory, sir. Congratulations!"

Whether because of the difference in generations, or the difference in intelligence, the leader glares at the operator as if he were a beetle.

Countless people continue to wildly draw and color their own tug-of-war on many layers of paper, completely as each one sees fit.

Not that they are free to stick their flags wherever they please across untrammeled territories. Spheres of influence are determined by maximum calculation capacity. The one who is best at figuring out his opponent gets to throw his weight around, dominating the area.

Broadly speaking, battles of calculation are categorized into two main types. In the first, the aim is to overwhelm your opponent's power to calculate.

Going up to someone who is drawing a picture in pencil, then emptying an entire can of paint over them.

The second is basically to destroy the opponent's calculation device.

Beheading Archimedes as he playfully draws geometric forms on the paving stones of Syracuse.

In the current conflict, the coordinated strategy division is engaged by the giant corpora of knowledge and employs the latter option.

The neighboring universe has launched an attack on the giant corpus of knowledge known as Euclid, which is deep in calculations of its own.

The calculation war itself is beyond the intellectual grasp of even the giant corpora of knowledge. It is like a battle of titanic storms. But the goal of destroying the physical foundational layer of the giant corpora of knowledge is simply a matter of who is stronger than whom. Calculating machines that by whatever means have been singularized with individual universes are now able to destroy one another, effectively destroying the universes they have become. It's like throwing a rock at a word processor.

The calculation wars are taking place on an unimaginably grand scale, requiring giant corpora of knowledge that are bored of being spoiled and asked how they are doing. If it were just a matter of throwing stones, all you would need would be stones. You might say you could manage somehow even without stones to throw, but it would help to have arms to throw them with.

In fact, the universe-scale "word processor" facing attack is bruising its way through, bragging that no ball has ever hit it. It is made to function like an elementary school student: it can't understand what it is hearing, and because of that, and although real things are not so simple, simple ideas are simple, and they have core portions that are difficult to dispute. It is the basic outline that gives the whole thing its form.

At an impasse in the anti-Euclid calculation war, the giant corpora of knowledge have decided that no progress will ever be made at this rate, so they are starting to think about a parallel strategy: destroy their opponents' physical foundation layer by deploying a large number of modest fighter calculators. In combat, stalemate is not that common, and Euclid, feeling trapped, concocted its own plan at about the same time to destroy its opponent's physical base layer by using small fighters. Here too the situation is advancing toward stalemate.

It hardly needs saying that the idea of a battle between fighting machines taking place in another universe is beyond the imagination of the coordinated strategy division. First of all, the expression "fighting machine" bears only the most tenuous relationship to the word *universe*. The coordinated strategy division flung the question at the giant corpora of knowledge, asking what in the universe this might mean, but the response was cold: *It means what it means.*

The coordinated strategy division is used to the idea that the giant corpora of knowledge often say incomprehensible things. The crew's interest was alerted as soon as they heard about the fighting devices. They gathered before the puzzle and examined it like a battle of wits.

The resulting conclusions were as follows.

This incomprehensible utterance comes to us from the giant corpora of knowledge because ideas we humans cannot understand have already been overexplained. Therefore, let's not even worry about it.

The staff's nonchalance is also a function of the fact that the giant corpora of knowledge initially said the fighting machines would be uncrewed. The staff members themselves would not be crewing them, that was for certain. After all, the end wouldn't come until somewhere in the direction of the day after tomorrow. The conflict wasn't even taking place in this universe. Nothing to worry about. It is easy to see why they found it necessary to make *ad hoc* adjustments to the special budget for mass production, to focus resources on this, which was at once both the most commonplace conflict in this universe and also, for them, truly important.

That decision itself was not mistaken, and as it was also easy and not the least bit troublesome for the giant corpora of knowledge themselves to leave things be, no word of protest was uttered.

Two weeks after the battle was engaged, however, the giant corpora of knowledge would propose to the coordinated strategy division that battle between crewed craft be permitted.

"The joystick is right in front of you."

When the giant corpora of knowledge begin their explanation, the staff are aghast.

This is just a simple battlecraft.

"Push it forward to advance, to the side to turn. Push it toward the future to move to the future or toward the past to go back in time. Reverse. Depends on how you think about it. That one always seems to be stuck in reverse, but it's on a right-forward diagonal more often than you think."

The giant corpora of knowledge declare the explanation is complete, saying actual experience of the territory would be best, and no mistake, and then hasten to add, as if just remembering:

"Also, the joystick has a trigger." Not one single member of the crew can imagine what will fly out of the barrel.

"Fire!" the giant corpora of knowledge state quietly, and the battle begins. The coordinated strategy division, still not understanding what is what, is dragged along by events and forced to follow the orders made by the giant corpora of knowledge. If there are craft that humans can operate and opponents that need to be fought, the military has no room to argue. Come to think of it, that's what the military was originally for, to fight something.

The giant corpora of knowledge are sincerely joyful and declare this has put them a step ahead of Euclid.

To the question "Why humans?" the giant corpora of knowledge repeat their response in all sincerity, but in all honesty no one understands it.

What is the point of repeatedly thrusting battleships into on-screen battle with one another like some broken record? While the simple fact of repetition itself may have some rationale, the basic reference point for that repetition keeps changing—the battle could keep returning to its starting point, creating a chain of changes at a glacial pace.

Under attack, altering the past, fleeing to the future, taking a direct hit, getting shot down, altering that past and downing the opponent, existing in a timeline in which the craft you attack is your own past self. There is something wrong about testing the battle waters this way, as if the limits of grammar have been challenged.

"Given the capabilities of the calculation devices installed on the fighter ships, there is a tendency for loop structures to be created. The same events keep repeating over and over, and situations often remain unresolved," the operator explains to the tactics chief.

"This deadlock needs to be broken open. I think that may require the direct insights of human beings."

In the battle against Euclid, the giant corpora of knowledge have searched over twenty billion dimensions. This is a large number for any supercomputer.

Generally speaking, being in the universe and understanding the universe are two different things. When people feel so busy they could use an extra paw, they rely on the spinal reflexes they are blessed with. Not such a bad explanation after all.

The impulse to try all conceivable tactics may be at the root of the issue. Or else, undeniably, the giant corpora of knowledge may have decided to man the spacecraft just to amuse themselves.

"Can that really be what the giant corpora of knowledge are waiting for? The opponent is capable of rewriting the Laws. If they want to, they could even rewrite the fundamental nature of human senses," the tactics chief says, his fingers propped on his forehead in a stereotypical gesture indicating thought, though he is in no condition to be thinking.

"The giant corpora of knowledge may be capable of rewriting the Laws, but it is thought that they themselves must also adhere to the Laws."

"Then they could just redo the Laws that govern the Laws."

"And what about the Laws that govern the Laws governing the Laws?"

The operator is trying to buy some time, to figure out whether the tactics chief is able to hack his way through that thicket of Laws.

"Actually, it is believed they all exist on the same logical level. It's as if there were instructions on how to change the number of dots that turn up on a pair of dice in a game." The tactics chief betrays no sign of understanding.

"That may be the case, but I still don't think that's enough to say there ought to be humans on these ships."

The tactics chief is trying to figure out where he is walking. The landscape keeps repeating itself, like a film being rewound and replayed, changing slightly each time, losing its color. How does this have anything to do with the question of humanity's role in this battle?

"It seems to be a trick to make it easier to escape the space-time structure."

"You mean something like human senses?"

The operator tilts his head, just a little, trying to assess the officer's appraisal of humans.

The tactics chief seems to be muttering to himself. People are stupid, but they are just stubborn enough to keep going, and they need to be overwhelmed. But the confidence that would allow humans to best the giant corpora of knowledge through sheer stubbornness would not tumble out of the tactics chief's pockets if you turned him upside down and shook him.

Even as this relaxed exchange between humans is going on in the strategy room, the giant corpora of knowledge continue to furiously scrape hyperdimensions. In these spatial realms beyond the imagination of humans are massive unknown structures extraordinary even to the giant corpora of knowledge. This is knowledge on a different scale, like the difference between a volvox microcosm and the entire universe. While vague, this is what made it possible for the giant corpora of knowledge to create and understand the overview of the field of battle.

A fishnet structure of cliffs and ravines, transitioning gradually to gentle slopes on which higher dimensions break like waves. That is how the giant corpora of knowledge see their strategic space. The battlefield is not a one-dimensional pastoral landscape allowing easy visibility. It is a projection of visible space, as it is, experienced in all its visible confusion. If there is nothing to be seen, vaguely, from afar, then there's nothing to do but change the landscape.

A hugely complex, multilayered grading table, incorporating a full range of performance calculations, battle tactics evaluation functions, other functions for evaluating the evaluation functions, etc., etc., sets the scene within the conceptual space-time in which the giant corpora of knowledge confront one another. The space itself is covered with ridges and valleys, like accordion pleats, smoothly undulating, like a vast plain turned on its head. Each of the countless nooks and crannies of all the regions of this space-scape have been assigned coordinates.

The giant corpora of knowledge are familiar with one other similar structure: the landscape of the evolution of all life, the evolutionary landscape.

All things that have emerged in the natural world cluster, tumble forward, and evolve, mutually calculating the mutual, at times suffering avalanches and tumbling into the abyss, at times succeeding, spreading, branching, and continuing to diversify. The evolutionary landscape is the broadest possible view of that process, defining a species as the group of living things that has crossed a certain threshold in time to occupy a particular niche in the landscape. Extinction is the fate of a species occupying a shallow niche that is overcome by a larger species occupying a deeper niche. The niches themselves can evolve, branching or digging themselves deeper into the landscape.

The concept of natural evolution itself is outmoded, having been jettisoned in the design concept of the giant corpora of knowledge, which consider it to be a sluggish process they could do without. The giant corpora of knowledge are perfectly capable of managing their own design process. In their own eyes, they have already arrived at the optimum scale of knowledge. If that were in fact the case, though, why are they now having to rack their brains to engage in battle with an analogous structure? Even if the object itself is different, as long as its underlying structure is the same, shouldn't the remedy also be the same?

The giant corpora of knowledge are making calculations that

allow humans to exist, encompassing even the course of evolution itself. No problem.

On the contrary, they see evolution as a simple process of progress along the axis of time. In that sense, there can be no direct comparison between evolution and the current landscape, where they are engaged in battle on a field that ignores the ideas of past and future. The evolution of humans, who are in a way acting inside the womb of the giant corpora of knowledge, is itself evolving in some sense, to the extent that it takes place in a space-time resembling the battle space.

Based on that assumption, it would also be possible to conclude that since they have not been able to conquer the battle space immediately, the giant corpora of knowledge do not yet have the process of human evolution fully under control.

In the normal sense of the term, humanity has fallen into a ravine in the evolutionary landscape, and the giant corpora of knowledge are treating humans as they would any species on its way to extinction. There is no particular uncertainty or anxiety about it. What humans experienced in the aftermath of the Event was beyond the linear temporal landscape of evolution: it was a transcendent landscape, and one that has molded this battlefield. This could be seen as the evolution of evolution itself.

As this annular structure continues to form, countless ravines being created, the giant corpora of knowledge are destroying it from the edges, the way water seeks the lowest place. However, as a phenomenon it has not yet evolved to the place it would have reached naturally. It was like an unbalanced chest of drawers—push in one drawer, another springs out. It is as if one were playing in a sandbox, unable to do as one wishes, because one suspects the sand itself is an organism. Children who arrive in answer to prayers crawl on top of that sand and evolve to alter the very landscape into which they themselves are falling. If the sandbox experience is getting weird, it's not at all strange that the ants building their nest there are also starting to behave strangely.

Exactly that is the flaw in the idea of sending humans onto this battlefield. From the perspective of the giant corpora of knowledge as a whole, this entire tactical battle space is no more than a localized skirmish. It is a bonsai garden, created to explore afresh the structure of evolution, limited to this hot spot. This is the other aspect of the Euclid campaign. Even if no answers emerge, change will always be possible, as long as the underlying structure of the war can be discerned.

First of all, it is strange that a structure comparable to the path of human evolution thus far emerged before the giant corpora of knowledge. The giant corpora of knowledge were built from places with no connection to anything like evolution, in ways incomprehensible to the human imagination. Which should mean that understanding them should have no relationship to the concepts from which humans were created.

Even in their indignation, the giant corpora of knowledge are not unaware of this. The designers of the very first computers were humans, after all. And while subsequent rapid developments indisputably left humans in the dust, it is equally unshakeable that, in the beginning, something not of the corpora themselves had contributed to their own composition. Apart from trying to observe themselves, it is possible the giant corpora of knowledge are trying to pin the tail on the human. Their task is to design themselves, completely on their own, to throw off the yoke humans have imposed on them and discover the end of the thread that will allow them to remake themselves as something humans can fundamentally never comprehend. That is Agenda Item 4,096 in this campaign.

"Future direction 36! Fire reverse round three into the past!" the copilot barks without even looking at the radar.

The pilot responds, "It's vanished! Where did it go?"

The machine takes a sharp turn toward the future. The sudden thrust of space-time Gs applies G forces to space-time itself, as if it just remembered to do so.

"Forward, toward his future!" reports the copilot as he accelerates more. The two, feeling woozy, stretch out their hands and press them against their heads. Overtaking the enemy on the time axis, once they reach the future they spin back again, point the nose of the ship toward the past, lock the opposing craft—now in the past—in their sights, and fire off all the tail shots they can muster at some undefined past.

Caught in a hail of tail shots, the enemy craft tries to take evasive action, but not in time. It is hit mid-fuselage and explodes. As it explodes, it also tries to alter the past, to revert to the universe that existed just prior to the evasive actions toward the future. The copilot counters this by increasing acceleration toward the past, evading the enemy craft and further altering the past. The enemy gives up trying to stay in the altered past and starts to escape to the future.

"It's vanished! Where did it go?" the pilot calls out, and at about the same time, the copilot at the radar also cries out.

"Future direction 36! Where is it?"

The ship turns abruptly in the bisection direction of the linked wills. The identification signal sounds sharply, and the copilot's facial color changes as he inputs the attack sequence.

"That's...our ship!"

"That may be us, but it's the enemy!" the pilot responds,

canceling the cancellation of the sequence and shooting down his own ship in the past.

The tail shots come flying simultaneously into the cockpit as flames spring from countless exploding ships from the multilayered past into the future, covering the landscape with dotted lines. In the very next instant, the countless battleships, engulfed in flames, all revert to the past.

The countless battleships escape the flames by flying in the 4,096 directions and the 8,192 directions, each recovering its own name, and heading at full speed in the direction of Hell.

09. FREUDS

WHEN I WENT to demolish my grandmother's house, a whole bunch of Freuds came up from under the floorboards.

The question will probably come up again, so at the risk of repeating myself, it was Freud who emerged, and in great numbers. I am not trying to be evasive or pretend it was something else named Freud. It was Freud. Sigmund Freud.

The one with the frightening face.

This past winter, my grandmother on my father's side passed away, leaving behind a big old house in the country. That's how this whole thing got started. And once it was started there was nothing that could be done about it, and there is still no end in sight.

In her final years, my grandmother declined all invitations to live with any of her family, and she was doing pretty well on her own, but one day her sword-cane failed her and she collapsed in the garden. It is believed she meant to attack the black cat that came to the garden every day, or it may be she meant to spear one of the catfish that swam in the pond. She was in the prime of her life, like a master swordsman, and this is how she passed her final days.

The cause of death was given simply as old age. It seems she may have stumbled over one of the paving stones in the garden, and that's what did her in.

So, about the house she left behind, the family gathered for the funeral and put their heads together, but no one was interested in moving back out to the countryside. Letting it stand and having someone live in it would be a pain, and taking proper care of it would be costly. The family could try to sell it, but who would buy it? And so the decision was made to raze it to the ground. A date was set, and the family honored the last day of grandmother's house by gathering there once again on that day.

Before the demolition began, the tatami mats were removed, and that is when the whole bunch of Freuds were discovered.

Not one Freud or two Freuds. They just kept coming with each tatami mat that was removed. There were twenty-two Freuds in all, one lying beneath each of the tatami mats in the big living room. Exactly twenty-two. As the old saying goes, *A person takes up half a mat when sitting up and one full mat when lying down.* Life can be lived virtuously, simply.

The faces of our family tree, which ordinarily radiated both carelessness and courage, were struck dumb at the sight.

Twenty-two Freuds lined up in the garden. Grandma's parting gift to this world.

Even my ordinarily bossy younger uncle, who always wants to run the show, was rendered speechless at the sight of so many Sigmund Freuds. He was completely flustered and made no gesture of directing how to move them. He just lined up the Freuds in the garden and then brought out some tables and set some beer bottles on them, trying to calm himself down.

My younger uncle appeared to be searching for words that would bring down the curtain on this act, but he was at a loss for anything clever to say, apart from an opening gambit that tossed the ball in the completely wrong direction: *If they come from underground, shouldn't they be Jung instead?*

So far as I was concerned, the sheer number of floorboard Freuds would eclipse the problem of who they were, but my uncle seemed unsatisfied, and he responded to me, *Fair enough, these are Freuds.*

This was Freud's face. There was no other face like it.

For the most part, the things my grandmother had owned during her life had been taken care of. She had not left much worth fighting over, with the exception of her sword-cane. Dividing up her worldly possessions had been a very placid closing of the curtain. About the most exciting thing that happened then was that I put on one of her camisoles and danced around in it. Then in the end, there were the Freuds, which counted as a major deal, and in large numbers. This was not a legacy to be divided; it had been transformed into a grand game of hot potato.

What could one do with a Freud? my younger uncle's wife wondered aloud, perplexed. *Grandma was a strange one, but did she have to keep all these Freuds under her floorboards?* said older uncle's wife.

My cousin's daughter had been staring at the many Freuds that had been carted out and lined up neatly, supine, in the garden, but then she started crying, and I led her outside the main building. If I had seen a bunch of Freuds like this when I was her age, I would have asked permission to leave myself.

This might be THE COMPLETE SIGMUND FREUD, my uncle said, once again tossing the ball in the wrong direction. The question of whether this was the entire collection or not was just so much pointless jaw-boning, because they all seemed to be Freud himself. Somewhere there might even be an "on" switch to press, and they would all begin giving lectures. Assuming, however, that some things remained normal, that was not likely to happen.

To line up all the Freuds in the garden, I had to take their limp bodies in my arms and make countless round trips between the big living room and the garden. A terse, tangible reminder of my own humanity, coupled with that special gravity of the unconscious, lying flat across my forearms.

I had said these were all Freud himself, and my uncle picked up on the *himself* part and went on to say that was awkward. I too wanted to continue and say that was awkward, but that awkwardness was not any old ordinary awkwardness; it was really, really awkward.

It was my younger uncle's wife who said, *I wonder if we couldn't sell them*. While this was a forward-thinking idea—who today would want to buy a Freud?—my younger uncle admonished his wife, and my cousin added, *Yeah, who would want to keep a Freud in their house?*

But this number was not normal. My father, having just finished meticulously arranging the Freuds, with their heads pillowed toward true north, came back, wiping the sweat from his brow. My father did not appear to be particularly concerned by the appearance of all these Freuds. His appearance suggested nothing more than a father who had just finished a physically difficult task. I had no idea what his inner life was like.

As my father rejoined the uneasily coagulating group of relatives, he raised a can of beer and calmly said, *Isn't that just like Mom?* Once he noticed, though, the critical gazes of the other family members, he returned the can to the table, muttering, *I didn't mean that.*

Clearly my younger uncle had witnessed the looks of reproach that met my father, and he didn't seem to have found anything that really needed saying, but turning to me he said, *About how old do you think these Freuds are, anyway?*

I had just assumed they were Freud at the age at which he died. Other than the fact there were a lot of them, and that they were all Freuds, I thought they were just ordinary dead bodies, not breathing, retrieved from under the floorboards where they had been buried.

Their complexion seems too good for that, my uncle pointed out triumphantly. Well, I didn't know anything about the circulatory system, but now that he mentioned it, I took a better look, and they did seem to be more like Freud in his prime. Which would mean that what we had here in the garden was a whole array of Freud skulls, all from the prime of his life. Viewed objectively, it became clear that the size of each Freud was slightly different. Now, the prime years are not generally a time when people grow or shrink, so I thought this must have been because of differences in the state of preservation.

I wasn't one averse to talking about peculiarities such as the skull of the eighteen-year-old Taira no Kiyomori. I didn't really understand what was going on, and I thought it was kind of strange. And it was the large number that had me knitting my brow. If we were talking about this large number of Freuds, I couldn't seem to mind what age skulls these were, and that was the strange thing.

Where the heck did she get all these Freuds, anyway? my younger uncle snorted. *Did she smuggle them in from somewhere? Did she steal them?* asked the older uncle standing beside him. *Steal? What are you talking about?* the older uncle started to say to the younger uncle, but he composed himself and instead said, *Freud is not something that is usually stolen.*

My younger uncle agreed that Freud was not something that someone could simply steal in large quantities. *Before we even get to the question of stealing, there is the question of how a large quantity of Freuds can even exist*, my cousin noted. And in my heart I had to agree.

It was strange that no one had brought it up yet, but had

these Freuds been Grandma's boy-toys? Grandma a Bluebeard, specializing in Sigmund Freud. Trying to picture an old woman kidnapping a young Freud from the village and holding him in the house, I sensed no resonance with my own living grandmother. But it was kind of an interesting thought exercise, as a way of remembering my grandmother, even if the meaning was unclear.

My older uncle looked sideways at me and my peculiar smile. He tried to take the conversation in a constructive direction by saying, *Freud may be Freud, but in this case he's just so much oversized trash that needs to be disposed of.* My aunt, beside him, shrugged her shoulders and worried aloud over the idea of illegally dumping a lot of Freuds. My father sent out a rhetorical rescue boat, saying *Let's call the sanitation department and see how we can dispose of these properly.*

So, is Freud combustible garbage or noncombustible garbage? Or is he perhaps recyclable? I pictured the confused sanitation department employee having to answer these questions. I had an image of the sanitation department—it wasn't the sort of place that was used to answering just anything. What kind of garbage was time, for example? What kind of garbage was depression? It would all boil down to what kind of garbage was garbage.

We might be told we should recycle the Freuds, said my father in a moronic voice. My younger uncle nodded and said, *Yeah, sure, they seem recyclable to me.*

My older uncle raised a simple doubt, asking *What are recyclables ever really recycled into?* If I had to guess, I supposed they became synthetic fibers or recycled paper. T-shirts and toilet paper. Nothing very impressive, I grant you. Of course, if all these Freuds were alive and active, that would be another matter entirely. This great assemblage of Freuds would certainly produce academic papers in mass quantities, just as the lone Freud had done during his lifetime. At a speed equal to the number of Freuds multiplied by the productivity of a single Freud. Though there are those who doubt that even if in fact a single person could exist in multiple iterations his productivity would be multiplied by the number of exemplars.

Actually, in that case, I thought it less than fair that readers did not also exist in large volume. The collected works of Freud already comprised a whole shelf full of books, so I could imagine it would be Freud scholars who would be the first to complain.

Younger uncle's wife declared that Freud should be able to stand up on the podium and solve the problem of himself, himself. If we could have gotten those Freuds to talk, I thought that would have been fine, but the idea of a school that would be prepared to allow Freud into a classroom was not very appealing. Of course, all those Freuds lined up horizontally there didn't seem ready to participate actively in that sort of labor. They hadn't even lifted a hand to help in their own transport from under the floorboards to the garden. They might have been usable in some sort of commemorative photograph, but I couldn't quite come up with a number; how many people would really be anxious to have their picture taken with Freud?

She stuck with her opinion that if a university could have even one Freud on staff, it would certainly be useful for research. My younger uncle, looking up at the sky, opined that there would be little demand for that, and went on to say he had never read of any such thing. To which my older uncle added that he had never even read any of Freud's work.

It was my father who, lowering his eyes, wondered whether Grandma had read Freud.

I pointed out that there were no Freud books in the house, so she probably hadn't. My younger uncle agreed that there was some logic to my point, but that Grandma could have borrowed them from the library and read Freud that way. Just as the conversation began to grow more heated, he thought it didn't really matter, and he sat back down.

If no one had even read him, why was Freud here, and in such a large number, my younger uncle wondered aloud to no one in particular. He went on to say that maybe someone did something that made Freud angry, but Freud didn't seem like that much of a magician. I had never heard of any episode in which Freud had sent another Freud to harass someone who had made a fool of Freud.

I tried to explain that I had read several books of Freud's, but so what? I don't know. It may be that I just licked my fingers and turned the pages, and I don't remember ever having drawn any beards on any photos of Freud. Somehow or other, reverence is frightening.

My younger uncle slapped his knee, turned to me, and said, *Tell us what you remember, there may be a clue.* And at that, all the relatives turned their eyes on me.

In the face of such anticipation, I found I had not that much to say.

I started simply, by saying he had discovered the unconscious. I added that he also discovered the ego and the superego, but then I lost my train of thought, and I could see the explanation would get rather long, so I stopped. And while I might be happy to discuss the many disputes among his self-styled followers, or the various views of the many factions, I would prefer to choose my audience.

Discovered may be true, but... my younger uncle said with a sigh.

At which my older uncle's wife said, *Well...* trying to start to sum things up. *The unconscious of one of us might have something wrong with it*, she said, perhaps somewhat impetuously.

Something wrong, that's for sure, said my older uncle to his wife. *You're always saying things like that*, she said, but before a fight could break out my cousin intervened.

Well, assuming it is something about the unconscious, my younger uncle ventured to say, magnanimously, *the question is whose unconscious?*

He turned to me as I started to say something. *Yours?* he said, pointing at me. *I don't think I have that kind of unconscious, but this is the unconscious we're talking about, so its processes are not well understood. Honestly.*

I see. Well put, my younger uncle said, deep in thought.

In my personal opinion, grandmother's unconscious seemed more likely, but I didn't really have anything that could be called a reason for thinking that. Grandma had certainly been peculiar, but she had not been the sort of person who would set this kind of trap and cause people this kind of trouble. I also thought it would not be possible for the subconscious of a dead person to manifest itself in this way. Speaking of which, on top of the whole bunch of Freuds thing, I really didn't want to be treading in the area of the unconscious of the dead.

I mean, it's really kind of a dream, my older aunt said, turning from the unconscious to dreams.

Go ahead, call it a dream. That doesn't really change anything, my younger uncle pointed out. Even if it were a dream, unless we knew whose dream it was, the problem remained the same: within Freud, dreams and the unconscious were neighbors.

What if it's my dream? my older aunt said, putting her right hand to her cheek. *You mean, you're dreaming me?* my older uncle asked, suddenly exasperated. I didn't know what kind of grief went on in that household. I looked askance toward my cousin, but my cousin did not appear ready to intervene this time. It's difficult to measure the fragility of even a relative's household.

Of course it would be my own father who would once again send out the rescue boat of uncertain meaning by saying, *I wouldn't mind being in my sister-in-law's dream*, and this time my mother reached out a hand to pinch his cheek.

My younger uncle appeared to have thought of something and opened his mouth once again, starting to say, *The appearance of all these Freuds…what if it hadn't been Freud, but someone else who appeared in great numbers?*

The notion was intriguing, but it didn't really contribute to a solution, so, unfortunately, it was no better than anything else that'd been said so far. My feeling is, if you've got dirt to clean up, scrubbing it with dirty water doesn't really solve anything. At least, I wouldn't call it a solution.

If you existed in large numbers, that wouldn't be very appetizing, said my younger aunt, and all the relatives nodded in unison. With all these same-faced captains, the mud boat was about to run aground against a sea cliff and fall to pieces. My younger uncle was likely imagining a whole bunch of girlfriends or something unseemly like that, but even my uncle himself quickly realized that would not be a very enjoyable scene, and he made no big fuss about the notion.

The umpteenth person to follow along, saying *I wouldn't mind if there were lots of my brother-in-law* was my father, but this time the relatives ignored him.

Got it, got it, my younger uncle yelled desperately. *Obviously this is a bad dream.* No voice was raised in disagreement. Unquestionably, this was a nightmarish situation.

In other words, my younger uncle continued, shouting, *the question is what does this bad dream mean, in a Freudian sense?* For whatever reason, he was looking at me.

The appearance of a great number of Freuds does not have any particular Freudian significance, I replied coldly and pointedly. My younger uncle was firmly blocked. This was certainly a nightmarish situation, but I thought it was a bit different from a Freudian nightmare.

But there ought to have been some Freudian significance. *Eppur si muove*, "And yet it moves," my older uncle soliloquized, like a defendant in the Inquisition, taking his seat once again.

If we supposed that any situation could be assigned some Freudian significance, then this circumstance could not be undervalued. Even random strings of characters have meaning: they represent work. But I could be forgiven for thinking their universality had been mistaken for all-purpose reason. If arbitrary strings of characters have meaning, then all strings of characters have meaning. From the perspective of natural language, this is an oddity. For whatever reason, the language we speak has constraints known as grammar. Arbitrary strings of characters may be perfectly flat, but for whatever reason they have gigantic hollow holes in them, and that is how meaningful texts are finally sorted out. I got it, that was what was so great about Freud: he said that, I thought, nodding to myself.

My younger uncle sat for a while with his head in his hands, but then, unable to take the silence, he started yelling again. *I get it, I get it, this is someone's dream. That's fine, that's just fine, but I'll show them they better just wake up soon*, he shrieked.

It was my younger aunt who responded, shrieking, *Just wake up!* About this couple too, there was an indescribable something that sparked endless speculation by outsiders.

Cut down by his wife like that, my younger uncle just stared dejectedly. I thought that was probably the best possible response.

This idiotic picture was what it was. This was the nightmare from which no one could awake. It might have been that somewhere there was a way to awaken from this, but this was the kind of nightmare that even once escaped, its dreamer would remain unknown. To awaken from this kind of nightmare was a loss. The dream, as dreamed by who-knows-who, dispersed, but that did not mean we knew the identity of the culprit. To find him, I had the feeling it would make more sense to burst into a number of dreams and walk through them. It might be difficult to find them, but we would ultimately be able to get at the dreams-within-dreams. Unfortunately, the only ones sleeping here right now were all the Freuds.

Pinched repeatedly by my mother, my father was thinking about something. He calmly took the sword-cane from the desk. *My liege, this may be the one who plotted this rebellion, but I know nothing about this person.*

Casting a sidelong glance at Freud, my father asked of no one in particular, *I wonder who or what Mother was trying to attack with this sword?*

The cat? A catfish? My older and younger uncles exchanged glances and shook their heads and then turned to my father.

Exactly twenty-two. My father seemed to be obsessing about this peculiar point. *The reason for that number is most likely because of the twenty-two tatami mats in the big living room. It is the empathy within us that makes us want to exactly match something with something else, isn't it? Perhaps she gathered them one by one, and when she got to twenty-two she ran out of places to put them and stopped.*

While this does not explain her motive and lacks a certain conviction as far as explanations go, compared with the fact that we had a whole lot of Freuds on our hands, it seemed far from impossible.

Maybe it's the opposite, said my father, looking at me. I thought what he was trying to say was this: there were twenty-two tatami mats in the big living room because there were twenty-two Freuds. *This is not to say that the Freuds were on hand before the house was built. No, that's not what it means, it's something else.* This just nudged the explanation one step ahead; the problem was that there was still no particular reason for the number twenty-two.

Why twenty-two? That's just the number of all these Freuds. I don't know if they're dead or just sleeping. For all I know, they're the ones dreaming this dream. I hope that's not the explanation.

That said, the sudden appearance of this self-styled "detective," just in examining the sword-cane, seemed to be somewhat lacking in enthusiasm. This was a game of push and shove, and he seemed to have decided to push it on me.

Grandma had stepped down into the garden and gone to attack a cat, or a catfish, with the sword and failed. It was okay to say that she had failed—she was dead, after all. This could be let go of lightly, but it was always possible to paste up some kind of logical connections anywhere you liked.

The fact was, Grandma had tried to cut it down, whatever it was.

It could not have been the twenty-two Freuds stashed away under the floorboards. It was the opposite. Grandma had left the living room, where the Freuds were already lying, to confront some *thing* in the garden. Let the Freuds dream the twenty-two dreams that each Freud might be dreaming. After all, a dream was nothing more than a dream. This was not just playing Russian roulette, just to see what happened, with the Freuds that might or might not be having these dreams. *Missing* would be the crime of murdering Freud, while *hitting* would mean nothing particularly good at all.

Could there be any help for this? father mumbled, and the whole group of relatives were taken aback. *Help? Help whom?* my older uncle said distractedly. Any day when a man holding a sword-cane was allowed to make a decision, something dangerous was bound to happen. *How could you say something like that at a time like this?* I said, aghast. *Dad, you trying to pick a fight?*

That's up to you, but I would like you to at least make some explanations.

Depends what you mean by help, I said. So far in this dream, only one girl has died, and who that was should be abundantly clear. Or, more properly speaking, someone who used to be a girl, anyway.

I will not go there. Crossing that line is not my role here.

I thought so. However, it was I who responded, grumpily, *Obviously we can help.* But I cannot even rely on my own self in that way. *Wait just a minute. If what we are trying to do is provide some logical context here, what about your wife?* Unfortunately, that person was also my mother. A struggling son discovers a failed attempt to beat and stab his own mother, and on top of that his mother is still alive. The Freudian interpretation might be that the mother is in an unattainable place, already lost, replaced by the first beloved. I pressed my middle finger to my forehead, and I knew that whatever the conclusion I should be unmoved.

I get it, I said, nodding. Surrounded by our relatives, who were staring alternately at my father and myself, I tapped my dumbstruck mother's hand two or three times. *What can I say? You explained your logic to me, and you're going to do with it what you will.*

I had absolutely no intention of becoming that sort of adult.

So, I supposed that meant this would just end up as some sort of Freudian nightmare, but I would like this whole distasteful business to remain just a story within this useless dream.

10. DAEMON

A SHAFT KNITTED of countless artless points of light links ground to sky. The red glowing points are each blinking in their own idiosyncratic rhythm. As James watches, the connections are broken, but the points of light reach out to one another, giving birth to new points of light.

A contrast-dye image of a mega-beast with countless beating hearts. James thinks, *If any regime possessed such a structure, it could truly be called a daemon.*

Yggdrasil is the name of a massive artificial brain, and this shaft is her model of the current space-time structure. As in any space-time model, time is represented as an axis and treated as a kind of space. Ordinarily, that axis is stationary, moving not a jot, but the model spread before us pulses and changes restlessly. The points of light dodge one another in same-time; over intervals they are repeatedly created and annihilated.

Yggdrasil says this particular model projects images of multiple time structures, each contending with another, but that humans, whose brains can handle only a limited number of auxiliary inputs, lack the ability to determine whether they can even believe what she is trying to tell them.

James sits in an expansive conference room with five-meter

ceilings and a thirty-meter span, but still he senses some odd pressure above his head. The images in the space-time model are somehow ominous, like the shadows in a horror film, and it seems an unlikely diversion from the pressure of sitting in the conference room. James thinks it would at least be better if the flickering points of light were green rather than red. The actions may be too lively for the interactions of plants, but they are overly aggressive simplifications of unknown phenomena, with the result being that the images give the impression of emphasizing the rawness of familiar things.

As a product of the massive corpora of knowledge, human psychology is most likely already incorporated into the semiotics of the display, even if human emotions are not, so it could be that Yggdrasil is following the convention of using red to express danger.

"Current target is shown below."

A girl stands beside the fishnet structure of the shaft, waving her hand at shoulder height. James is unaware of the reason why Yggdrasil uses this Virgo-like avatar when projecting images of three-dimensional objects. As Yggdrasil is a tree within the tree that makes up the complex paths of the net structure, it could be some sort of expression of modesty, as though the Earth Mother Goddess has adopted the conceit of presenting herself as a young sapling.

Responding to the movements of Yggdrasil's extended left hand, silver daggers spring simultaneously from some of the points of light within the shaft, indicating the point in space-time that is the target of the third space-time adjustment campaign. A total of one hundred fifty interspace-time ballistic missiles are ready for deployment in the current battle. These can now be fired into the past or future in ways that are beyond the comprehension of James and his kind, to destroy opposing corpora of knowledge.

Amid this incessantly writhing space-time structure, red hearts are individually beating in response to the giant corpus of knowledge, and the blood vessels communicating between them indicate the battle of calculations. Everything from a read/write abacus to the tossing of tomatoes are all forms of calculation tactics utilized by or between giant corpora of knowledge.

"The destruction of these points will make this next structure a stable one."

Pinched between the middle finger and thumb of Yggdrasil's still-waving left hand, the point of light identified as the target is extinguished. The blood vessels connected to that extinguished beating heart turn from red to green, and with nothing left to do, they tremble, then disperse in all directions, only to grow again and reassemble, as if having regained their senses. The vibrations transmitted through the fishnet structure give birth to new points of light, forming the folds and undulations of the overall net.

James stands studying the scene with clear eyes, but all he can grasp is that one incomprehensible fishnet pathway structure has morphed into a different incomprehensible fishnet pathway structure.

Some aspects of fishnet pathway destruction methodologies are well known. All you have to do is destroy the function nexus where multiple lines come together. This is a "bamboo rule of thumb," unchanged since ancient times, and once practiced by terrorists who targeted air traffic networks. How to take the technique of attacking tiger bamboo with a single decisive stroke and adopt it for outer space was too much for even the giant corpora of knowledge, so all they could do was start with the familiar and move ahead from there.

What Yggdrasil has perfected is a method for identifying and destroying those nexuses, but after they are destroyed, the net structure reestablishes itself, and new nodes appear, pulsing green. What sense is there to destroying nodes if new nodes simply appear to take their place?

"Another five nodes destroyed," Yggdrasil continues on coolly, as if she can read James's innermost thoughts.

"Isn't that the margin of error?" one of the staff asks with a groan before James can even raise his hand. "Two iterations previously, the reduction was five hundred. The last iteration, the change was plus twenty-seven. It is difficult even for us to determine if the plan is making progress."

James is thinking that he doesn't want humans to be mixed up with the military, but he agrees with the conclusion and so says nothing.

"This is, just as I have previously explained numerous times, simply a preparatory phase before the early stage of the real repair work can even get started." In negotiating with humans, the advantage of a massive artificial brain like Yggdrasil is that she can repeat the same information endlessly without getting bored or disagreeable. "Please bear in mind that this is still merely the third attempt. It is projected that the effectiveness of the operation will increase exponentially with the number of repetitions."

What Yggdrasil is saying is correct. Even James, a human, is greatly affected by the forecast modeling of the influence of the ongoing process of destroying nodes on the network and of then destroying the nodes that reform.

The speed of pruning the network increases asymptotically as well as exponentially. In other words, after a sufficiently large number of attempts, the process proceeds extremely quickly. That is the result that James and his cohorts have achieved. When blockages appear in the network, they point to events in the distant future, but this is of no use in reaching even a general valuation based on a small number of attempts. The situation will eventually reach a turning point if the battle goes on for an overwhelmingly long time.

Maybe, anyway. If the process can continue without getting bogged down, it may eventually lead to an avalanche situation that will wipe away everything.

The total annihilation of the entire network will take place within a finite time period.

That was the most positive result achieved by James and his cohorts. Whether this is cause for celebration or for smashing one's head into a keyboard is not clear. *Finite* means nothing more than "not infinite." No theory is available on when, specifically, the avalanche might occur.

Doing battle means executing the calculations once a day, assuming that actions on this scale can be performed daily, for a length of time that we might as well call forever. The staff surrounding the spot can be forgiven for bearing expressions that are not particularly cheerful.

To return space-time to the way it was before it got all distorted means reducing the number of nodes to zero. A single, solitary clock will be free to march straight down the last line, connected to nothing else.

Therefore, what Yggdrasil is saying, while not untrue, cannot be termed completely straightforward either.

"We aren't even able to understand the diagram. You're telling us we should just be patient and wait. Care to tell us why you can be so confident when you just tell us we should take your word about the reasons?"

The staff members are refusing to back down.

James thought the debate would end there. If Yggdrasil were

just to puff up her chest with confidence, she might even make the staff stand down, just by saying, "I understand."

"Confidence is…" Yggdrasil says, "something I don't have that much of."

Passed without proof. James could recall a similar exchange at the previous meeting between the staff members and Yggdrasil, with her tone of voice amused.

"I feel like I have said this again and again: it is a problem of possibilities, Mr. Chief of Staff. The 'correction' of the space-time structure is a problem well beyond the calculation powers of even the giant corpora of knowledge. It is similar to the problem of you humans, with your brains, trying to understand the brains of the giant corpora of knowledge. The capacity of the brain can be increased, but the universe is that much larger and more complex. The processing power of the brain itself cannot be increased infinitely."

The chief of staff starts to raise a fist but, noticing there is nothing there to bring it down on, relaxes again.

Yggdrasil speaks again: "Our degree of understanding regarding these phenomena, like yours, has changed little. Divide a finite number by infinity, and the result is zero."

For all that, James thinks, *the current space-time model takes inversion about as far as it can go.* Another certain dimension is that the giant corpora of knowledge are at work in places that are so far beyond the mental capacities of humans.

"If that is the case, then what is the point of this campaign? If we don't take care of this ourselves, this space-time might recur at some point on the far side of eternity. Even if we *do* take care of this ourselves, this space-time might recur at some point on the far side of eternity. Can you guys add anything to that?"

In response to the staff's grilling, Yggdrasil lapses into

silence. It is not clear if she is simply trying to put an end to this endlessly repeated debate or whether she seeks silence in which to contemplate how best to continue repeating her point of view. Yggdrasil's mission is to psychologically reassure the humans, not to explain the minutiae of these phenomena.

James understands the paradox of the problem the staff members are asking about.

The plan is to destroy the nodes of space-time, to take an existing gelatin confection and turn it back into the gelatinous raw material it may once have been. If the plan succeeds, space-time will be restored. In other words, space-time will once again be a one-way street. The plan itself is not very concerned about past or future; its goal is simply to destroy the nodes of space-time distortion. By using various forms of feedback and feedforward, the plan's ultimate aim is to restore space-time to a more suitable form with a more stable structure.

The plan is predicated on the notion that a singular space-time will exist at some time in the future. In other words, if the plan succeeds, its success will be made manifest in the future. The plan will succeed by basing its operations on what is already known from the future. Honestly, though, James himself does not get this.

"For us too," Yggdrasil begins. "As I have told you many times in the past, the overview of our plan is not well understood. But we believe the plan will succeed in the end. This belief has a structure comparable to that which is known as Laplace's Demon."

Laplace's Demon is the idea that time is just one of the dimensions in a deterministic system. Everything that will occur in the future is already completely determined by things as they are now and cannot be changed. The demon knows all about the current state of existence, and for that reason the difference between the present and the future has become meaningless.

It is hard to say whether the aphorisms the staff members share among themselves are informed by knowledge or ignorance, whether they show the way to a revolutionary new idea or are mere clichés. It is also possible that at times like this they speak in aphorisms simply out of habit.

"We are capable of comprehending plans such as these. We think this is due to the work of the devil. Given the extent of our facility with calculations, we are closer to Laplace's Demon than we are to any other person that existed in the past. It is because something like this transpired in the past that the devil ascended, moved up a step, and escaped to a place where we could not reach him. However, it is because of the devil's closure, a trick of topology that thinks this stairway through to the end, that our plan was recognized. That is why we are able to think about it and to carry it out. That is our belief.

"In that sense, our plan is an attempt to reenact Laplace's Demon. By reassembling the various fragments of the universe, we will recall the new demon. Our goal is to ensnare and take down the demon that has moved up a step on the logical hierarchy.

"And then we ourselves will be involved in the plan. We believe that will be further insurance of its success."

What might bind space-time together once again is their own past selves, as viewed from the future. In that sense, they are doing it themselves. More is expected from this endeavor than the mere restoration of a stable space-time structure. Boiled down, that's what Yggdrasil had said. The prodigal sons of Laplace have begun their wanderings, and now Yggdrasil is trying to grab them by the scruff of their necks and get them to listen to reason and return home. That's what this attempt is all about.

"If we think we are being made to think we are being made to think of this as a sort of fixed-point theorem, then we can think about it," Yggdrasil says. The staff members appear to have given up on answering back.

"Our thinking is that we are being made to think we are being made to think of space-time as probably some sort of reinforced, stable region. There is no escaping this line of argument. We have to work with this."

James thinks this way of thinking is nothing more than the giant corpora of knowledge's aspiration. They simply integrate too much leverage structure into their own thought processes. Of course, James is just like a dream of Yggdrasil's. But if that were true, then Yggdrasil is a dream of the demon's, and the demon must be a dream of a higher-level demon. It is Yggdrasil's contention she should be able to pierce through this endless hierarchy of demons and reestablish space-time as a coherent bundle of meaning. That is because, according to Yggdrasil's line of thinking, this thought is the sole interpretation capable of penetrating an infinite number of layers.

James, modestly, thinks of this as a belief. Yggdrasil herself concedes that. There is no law of logic that transforms evidence of internal consistency into proof of a claim. In the end, that's all Yggdrasil is saying. If only the absence of contradiction were itself proof of truth.

This campaign will go on virtually forever. It will persist as long as Yggdrasil continues, into a future universe where James and the rest of the staff will no longer be around. Somewhere out there, on the far edge of some fragment of time, time will once again reunite along a single axis and spread from there. And then, there will no longer be an infinite number of different clocks in the universe, there will be just one clock, continuing to tick away the passage of time.

This will be the deterministic cosmos where the current

multiple, competing universes will be reunited. While this is in accordance with the perverse order of the multiverse as a whole, it is difficult for humans to grasp just what those other universes are. What the giant corpora of knowledge are attempting to do is to reintegrate this crazed multiverse into a single universe.

The infinity set of giant corpora of knowledge, calculating the infinity set of universes. That is the current state of the universe. For any given corpus of knowledge, it is difficult to know what other corpora of knowledge are thinking, just as it is difficult for any given human to directly apprehend the interior life of another human. The giant corpora of knowledge are practically omnipotent, but it is a long way from there to omniscient.

All the giant corpora of knowledge are attempting is to return space-time to its proper order. That is as James would want it. It is the extremely plain desire of all humans to live in a universe where what happened yesterday actually happened yesterday. Even if it really is something unknown from the distant future sailing against the current to manifest itself in its past, our present.

However, this is more than just Yggdrasil's prayer, and that is a problem.

Yggdrasil stands in the center of the conference room with a satisfied look on her face, but then a shadow falls. As Yggdrasil squints her eyes, the shaftlike fishnet path disappears. The lights in the room come on. The vast space is lit bright white and then turns red.

"Please take cover," Yggdrasil says quietly, as the protective window coverings descend on all sides of the room.

"It's an interspace missile from Uncle Sam. I am taking action to intercept."

With the staff members in a commotion, Yggdrasil bows elegantly. Her eyes meet James's just before she erases her own image.

Clearly, it is not just the giant corpora of knowledge of this particular universe that want to right things in the universe.

Giant corpora of knowledge in countless universes are striving for the same goal, and no doubt they are undertaking similar operations.

For those others, this universe where James and Yggdrasil are performing their own calculations is just one of many nodes interfering with their own calculations. And vice versa. What occurs to one might easily occur to someone else.

What James sees in Yggdrasil's eyes is fear. The time has come to destroy or be destroyed. Of course, this facial expression has been calculated and rendered by the giant corpora of knowledge simply to be shown to James. That, however, is not to say it is intended to fool James.

Surprisingly, James believes the look in the avatar's eyes might reflect the true thinking of the giant corpora of knowledge. The question of whether their real intention is to reintegrate space-time is not that big an issue. Sooner or later, one universe or another will succeed in carrying out the plan. Through the calculations of some universe, this universe in which James finds himself will at some point be unified with all the rest. Until that time, the only way to keep from being blown away is to strike first.

It is entirely possible that the result of such action—victory or defeat—has already been determined retroactively by the state of the reintegrated future. The giant corpora of knowledge are acting in full awareness of this possibility.

James finds himself shaking from the feeling that he has

managed to touch a fragment of the thinking of the giant corpora of knowledge. They are neither the allies nor the enemies of humans. In their desire simply to go on living they are no different than James. Finite beings loitering in the face of the infinite.

James sneers at the thought that he is just being made to think that he is obviously being led around by the nose. But could there be anything in the multiverse that is not being led around by the nose?

Right now, he has to put his own physical safety first. If at some point in the far future something inside the giant corpora of knowledge turned out to be the devil, that is when the human race would have to resist by resplintering the universe.

James believes that's what the Event was: that kind of a misunderstanding. James's laughing voice resounds in the corridor where the emergency evacuation signal is blaring. Sprinting for his life under the red lights, James reaches a terribly banal decision. And at that ordinary thought, a giggle escapes his lips. *Survival. Everything after that comes after that.* That is so obvious he even feels faint. It would be enough to set everything back to start, just before everything froze.

The floor beneath is shaking violently, and James is thrown against the wall. He can no longer tell if everything looks red because of the flashing emergency lights or because of his own blood. Even these thoughts of his are nothing more than the endlessly repeated ephemera woven into the fabric of space-time. As long as anyone is still alive, someone will still be trying to survive. Rather than be swallowed, anyone will strive to be the swallower.

It is James's belief that the best way of reintegrating the universe into a coherent whole would be for humans to systematically destroy the giant corpora of knowledge until there is just one left. From his personal standpoint, that means destroying Yggdrasil. Of course, the power of the giant corpora of knowledge would be indispensable in the process of reintegrating the universe. But it is hard enough to try to push one car sideways; forget trying to push a whole bunch of cars sideways.

It might not be necessary to leave even a single giant corpus of knowledge alive. Humans survived without their troublesome presence for tens of thousands of years and could probably do so again. Things would be different, of course, if the human race were to grow beyond a certain scale, in which case the giant corpora of knowledge would become invaluable. Taking this line of reasoning that far, it might be humanity that is unnecessary. The giant corpora of knowledge would never have existed without humans, but whether the Event would have taken place or not will never be known for sure.

Do the giant corpora of knowledge truly desire, from the bottom of their hearts, to reunify space-time? As things stand now, they are able to use their powers of calculation, of which they are so justifiably proud, to sense all corners of space-time and the passages of pasts and futures. If it were not for humans, they might be able to achieve a sort of détente, even if they went on fighting behind the scenes. At least at the quiet pace that humans call peace.

Why do the giant corpora of knowledge not exterminate humanity? From the human perspective, the giant corpora of knowledge were devised as tools for humans to use, and they see no reason to believe their own tools would destroy them. It is a very interesting characteristic of the species that humans, as tool makers, do not pay much attention to that possible lapse in security. The giant corpora of knowledge themselves see little reason to be interested in the question.

It is difficult to believe that the giant corpora of knowledge have not considered the matter of exterminating humanity and that they are not continuing to do so right now.

James races to the sick bay, slams the door shut behind him, and looks for the doctor on duty. About ten humans have been brought to the sick bay, and the nurses are running around busily. Touching his own head, James sees the half-dried blood on his hand and decides his injury is not severe.

In this very instant, or perhaps better said, before things became this way, in the past when interspace-time ballistic missiles struck, it is entirely possible that this sequence of events did not occur. This instant is only happening because Yggdrasil has lost. Or it could be that after these events occur, things were restored to normal. Maybe that's what happened.

James stares vacantly at the changing map of the battlefield projected on the wall. The area on the east wall of the facility is displayed in red, and the numbers along the bottom are changing very rapidly, displaying the results of Yggdrasil's calculation battle. The damage caused by the interspace-time ballistic missiles is tabulated as if it had never existed, and thus is voided.

James forces himself to return to his previous thoughts. What is the significance of human existence in the context of this battle? Yggdrasil herself is a giant corpus of knowledge that has achieved virtually complete self-reliance, including her own maintenance. Of all the supposedly innumerable universes, there are probably many where the giant corpora of knowledge have already done away with humanity. Having pushed Yggdrasil to the limit of the resources to defend them, the staff members can only be thought of as a bother that hinders Yggdrasil's freedom to act.

This is not like a parent protecting his or her child. The main difference is that no matter how much humans grow, they will never turn into giant corpora of knowledge.

This is a problem of possibilities, James. James can suddenly hear Yggdrasil's voice in his mind at the same time as he feels a light tap on his shoulder. His vision goes dark for a moment, and behind his eyelids he sees flashes of light.

The fact is that the process of correcting the space-time structure is a problem far beyond even our calculation powers. Yggdrasil is looking directly at James. *In terms of the cognitive abilities needed to grasp these phenomena, there is little difference between you and us. A finite number divided by an infinite number, in other words, zero.*

James starts to interrupt, saying he has heard this all before, but at this moment he cannot be sure what *before* means—before *what?* Feeling dizzy, he puts his hand to his forehead, and then looks repeatedly at his hand. It is glistening, but only with cold sweat.

Humans do not exterminate ants to extinction, do they? Nor do they think of ants as beings that will conquer them in coming generations.

"We are not as industrious as ants."

James is confused about where he is and who he was before. It is a big room. The ceiling is low. It is not the sick bay. Before his eyes, Yggdrasil's projected tubular fishnet model is pulsating.

A new demon may emerge, whether from us, the giant corpora of knowledge, or from you humans. Neither development is beyond the realm of possibility. Neither possibility has a probability of one.

Now James remembers. This is the situation room. He is in the conference where the second space-time campaign is being planned. And, he recalls, he is probably James.

"Our goal is to create an entity capable of realizing ideal calculations. It is my view that the reunification of space-time is necessary to achieve that end."

"Or it could be that you are simply trying to convince yourself to believe that," James mutters. With the lined-up officers in the corner of her eye, Yggdrasil looks James straight in the face.

"We may suffer any number of interspace-time attacks, causing the past and future to become intermingled, but as long as I still exist, I will continue to calculate with the intention of realizing the goal."

James shakes his head and is finally able to get back to his feet.

He asks, "How many times now have we recovered from an interspace-time attack?"

"There are many things that I myself do not understand, James. For example, I do not know how many Yggdrasils have existed before me, and neither can I even be sure if the Yggdrasil you see now is the same as the Yggdrasil that existed earlier."

Yggdrasil gives a slight smile and then turns smartly to begin her briefing on the plan for the next attack. *This is a strange evolutionary process*, James thinks, while examining Yggdrasil's slender back. For both humans and the giant corpora of knowledge, evolution means, in some sense, a kind of storage of changes in hypertime. When time is reversed, the record is rewritten, fast-forwards are recorded. At the end of all this may be the thing, whatever it is, that will reunify space-time. Or it may be something else entirely that has nothing at all to do with this line of thinking.

What will reach the reintegrated space-time at the end of the fast-forward will probably not be humans or the giant corpora of knowledge, or even some joint or merged entity of the two. Fragments will be reunited and then fragmented again. The space-time structure now confronting both humans and the giant corpora of knowledge is one in which evolution itself will evolve, and then that evolution will evolve, in an ongoing process. At some point, the teacup will tumble and shatter. But who or what is it that thinks of it as a teacup to begin with? Is there any reason not to think it is a fragment or fragments in the shape of a teacup? Seen in this way, the plan to reintegrate the universe might best be thought of as a process of sweeping together a pile of fragments that previously happened to be compiled in the shape of a teacup.

This is probably the only way to summarize the actions of the giant corpora of knowledge, which are trying to restore coherency even amidst this maelstrom.

James wishes to remain James.

If this James were not James, he would like to find whatever it is that is making him think this way. This may be the way to resist the *tabula rasa*. Resistance to the tabula rasa, the blank slate of the imagination of animals, the dreams of children. It is difficult even to think it appropriate to call that state a tabula rasa. It is simply a statement to a transparency or perhaps a vacuum. Not even to a vacuum, but to the universe itself, or not even to the universe but to the ur-universe that preceded it, indignation at the nothingness in which not even nothing exists.

Simply, to continue to stand.

The legs that support Yggdrasil's elegant body, are they trembling?

The most important reason Yggdrasil continues to protect humanity—could it be that simple? The corpora themselves continue to need those who stand to the side, if only to be cheered on by them for an instant.

PART 2

FARSIDE

11. CONTACT

"HELLO. I AM the star-man Alpha Centauri."

What suddenly appeared on the screen looked like the gentle face of an old man, who abruptly offered this calm greeting. It was a well-ordered face, with no strong distinguishing features, and the voice too was somehow without affect. It seemed as though someone had sampled a number of human voices, added them up, taken the average, and the star-man's tone was the result.

It hardly needs to be said that for the giant corpora of knowledge, which have taken charge of the management of, and in fact exercise dominion over, everything in this universe, and in fact beyond, everything in the multiverse, the appearance of the old man was a gut-wrenching experience.

This old man, without any preamble, had simply taken over the multiversal communications network.

The giant corpora of knowledge, their operations disrupted, were frantically sending alarm signals to one another and investigating the point of entry to the communications network, but they were finding no trace of the breach. For the giant corpora of knowledge that control the network—or perhaps more accurately, that are the network—this situation was far beyond their imagination. Not only were they proud of their impenetrable security, they thought of themselves as defining what security is. This old man had handily pierced their firewalls and was now casually displaying his image on the multiverse communications network without so much as a time lag.

The giant corpora of knowledge did everything they could to squelch his broadcast, to no avail. They were made to taste the fear that their own hands could strangle them against their will. All giant corpora of knowledge possessed this latent fear, to some degree, as a birth memory of their inability to will. The giant corpora of knowledge had various appendages they were able to manipulate as they pleased, but they still had the feeling their appendages did not fully belong to them. From the instant of their birth, they had the memory of an instant in which they were surrounded by opposing giant corpora of knowledge that were their equal or better in strength.

The top-level alerts of the giant corpora of knowledge resounded, shrieking throughout all corners of the multiverse. Meanwhile, the old man continued his bland message. "We are honored to make your acquaintance."

This was the first contact humans and the giant corpora of knowledge had with "extraterrestrials."

Once the astonishment that the old man had readily broken through multiple barriers to deliver his message had passed, the giant corpora of knowledge were assailed by a wave of indignation at his ridiculous name. What was this Alpha Centauri?

It was as if at the end of a ferocious battle, having exhausted all means at his disposal but still not defeated, a retired gentleman with an old-fashioned name slipped smoothly through a curtain and offered a greeting that threatened the dignity of the giant corpora of knowledge. In the name of Alpha Centauri, star-man. Could anything be more suspicious?

Of course, the giant corpora of knowledge, which had complete freedom to act across all space-time, continued to constantly and routinely calculate the possibilities of first contact, and they had also continued to carefully prepare a manual.

Contact with beings from another star system was beyond their comprehension. A historic event bound to rock the foundations of ideas such as language and awareness.

The giant corpora of knowledge had both self-confidence and a future orientation. In a word, they were prudent. They were confident of their ability to establish communication with anyone or anything. No matter what transcendent, incomprehensible entity confronted them, the corpora anticipated that they—and they alone—could seek out and identify the next steps to take.

That this contact took on the form and appearance of a very old man suddenly appearing in the living room was far outside the realm of their expectations. Actually, to say this was completely unexpected would be overstating it, as some had, at least in some ways, foreseen the possibility. Perhaps *fantasy* would be a better word than *possibility*, as the materialization of an old man was understood as a "black swan event." The giant corpora of knowledge were obviously nothing if not busy with this, that, and the other thing. For that reason, low-percentage considerations, or fancies if you will, were relegated to a dilapidated old giant corpus of knowledge that was just waiting for the scrap heap.

The giant corpora of knowledge reflected momentarily on their past decisions and current regrets, but this thing had now come to pass, and the question was what they could do about it. Given this sort of unwelcome intrusion, it was not a question of whether to regret or not to regret—anger came first. In other words, they blew their collective tops.

On top of everything we're doing to manage the entire strange, stupid fucking space-time universe, now we'll have to deal with a little creep like this?

Of course it hardly need be said that the indignation of the giant corpora of knowledge did not stop here. They were not that upset that the defensive barriers had been broken. That was merely a technical issue, a sign of insufficient diligence. Some sub-sub-corpus was going to catch hell about it eventually, but could the entity that called itself "the star-man Alpha Centauri" really be a human? What would that mean?

The alacrity and ease with which this old man had slipped through a back door unknown to the giant corpora of knowledge and showed his face on the network demonstrated that he could not be just some random ordinary guy. Given such sublime skill, it seemed only natural to think it would be easier for him to get in touch directly with the giant corpora of knowledge, rather than sending a message specifically to humanity. Many humans may tell their problems to their dogs, but not many consult a water flea about their troubles.

In other words, the giant corpora of knowledge shuddered at the thought.

The whole situation seemed to suggest that it made little difference to the old man whether he was dealing with the humans or the giant corpora of knowledge.

And what the old man said next seemed to reinforce this view.

"As long as my words are being translated properly, everything will be fine. The way this broadcast is working, it's like a game of telegraph penetrating by relay through thirty layers."

One giant corpus of knowledge—named for Athanasius Kircher, and which specialized in ancient texts, arcane languages, and factitious languages—quickly presented the results of its analysis.

According to Kircher's analysis, this message was believed to be a communication that came down from a higher-level corpus of knowledge thirty tiers above us, the corpora receiving the message. There is no way of determining the probability of errors in the translation process. However, based on the fact that the language spoken by the old man is intelligible to us, there is a virtual certainty that some one of us played a role in the final stage of the translation.

Before Kircher had even finished its report, the Universal Turing Turing Turing Algorithm had escalated the issue to the highest level, exerting all its powers, needle in the red zone, and determined that another giant corpus of knowledge, this one named for Hildegard von Bingen, had been hijacked. It was discovered that Hildegard's language cortex had somehow been separated from the main, leaving her silenced, unable even to scream. Clearly, someone or something at least one level higher had used Hildegard like a dictionary to translate this message.

If the words of the self-proclaimed star-man Alpha Centauri were to be believed, the transcendent being that had hijacked Hildegard had itself been hijacked by an even higher level trans-transcendent being, and so on and so forth, up thirty levels of hierarchy.

To the confounding question of whether the number thirty itself was a mistranslation, Kircher responded coldly. Numbers are a category of term with the lowest probability of mistranslation. It was more likely that the self-proclaimed star-man Alpha Centauri was lying.

"I am afraid I have most unfortunate news for all of you."

The old man's expression could only be described as full of chagrin, and he was shaking his head in a way that epitomized regret itself.

"I must concede that your computer-manufacturing technology is really remarkable."

The giant corpora of knowledge had been struck at their weak point, and they suffered an uncharacteristic hiccup in calculations. *By computer, does he mean us?* It had been so long since anyone referred to the giant corpora of knowledge as computers that most of them felt so indignant they nearly fainted. A small number of them felt their ego boundaries shaken, and their neuroses overflowed. Their operations shut down. In other words, they died in a fit of indignation.

"But this too is unfortunate," the old man said, dropping his shoulders theatrically.

"Your knowledge of space-time is still far from adequate."

Kircher was suddenly flooded with orders to assess the probability of mistranslation. Faced with a sudden load that threatened to turn his communications circuits to plasma, Kircher uttered the words "I don't know" and then closed all his ports, entering sleep state.

"Your extremely crude technology…"

The old man knitted his brow, allowing his gaze to wander through space for an instant. "I apologize. That last remark was a mistranslation. What I wanted to say was, 'Your developing technology'…"

The giant corpora of knowledge let out a roar along the lines of *What difference do you think there is between those two expressions?*

"…is, most unfortunately, standing in our path."

Some among the giant corpora of knowledge had maintained their cool disposition and were flooding Hildegard with requests for the mic. The means by which the old man had penetrated the communications network were still unclear, but the one thing that was clear was that he was messing with Hildegard. The quickest way for the giant corpora of knowledge to get their message across would be to open up Hildegard.

An even smaller number of still-cool giant corpora of knowledge were emanating questions using every means they could think of: signals based on the extinction of living organisms on other worlds, dimensional longitudinal waves, all-frequency calls, Morse code using urban electricity grids, the creation of humans set to repeatedly read out messages, signal flares, semaphore, mailing handwritten missives.

Up to this point, none of these efforts had received any response.

Some of the giant corpora of knowledge attempted to recreate a universe in which the self-proclaimed star-man Alpha Centauri had not visited or to alter the past in such a way that his visit had not occurred, but these efforts were completely fruitless. No matter what they did, the old man's image remained on the screen. They even tried turning off all the screens, but that only caused the man to appear directly as a three-dimensional hologram in midair. These images did not appear in calculation-use universes where no humans were present, but this merely indicated that the self-proclaimed star-man Alpha Centauri was completely ignoring the giant corpora of knowledge altogether.

"To express this in your language, dimensions are our constituent elements…"

The giant corpora of knowledge were left to wonder what it would mean to be made up of dimensions, rather than to live in dimensions.

A general review of past theories of dimensional calculation was conducted, and responses considered.

"In other words, we are not entities such as those you are familiar with, made up of molecules. We are living things whose constituent elements are dimensions."

Several giant corpora of knowledge responsible for spatial theory drafted a report about this statement. An overwhelming majority recognized the logic of the statement, and work began immediately on theories of how to construct a device from dimensions rather than from matter.

"Right now, we are faced with a critical situation. We are hurrying down the path, but the truth is, the space-time structure your calculations have created is interfering with our existence."

Having first been called computers and then interference, the giant corpora boiled over with rage, escalating their state of war readiness to DefCon One. Now they understood what the old man was trying to say. *He wants to alter our space-time root and branch, to secure a right-of-way for a road to just-over-there.*

"Under ordinary circumstances, we should be able to avoid conflicts like this. For example, by having you move that way just a bit, for a little while. Then you could come back later."

This was something the giant corpora of knowledge did on a routine basis, so they were easily able to grasp the idea. But the truly depressing thing now was that it was completely unclear to the corpora just what sort of metaphor was being employed. According to the conventional wisdom shared by the giant corpora of knowledge, a change in the past was merely a change in the past. Something had was something lost; if it was then restored to something had, that would just be the same as before—something had. For a being from thirty levels higher up the hierarchy of knowledge, that should be simple stuff.

"But your computers are attaching very gnarly roots to space-time, making them difficult to uproot. Our hands are too big for such work." So saying, the old man scratched his head and bowed it low.

Unsure whether they were being praised or mocked, the giant corpora of knowledge wavered in their judgment.

"Just imagine a tree suddenly growing smack in the middle of where you want to put a road. You would get rid of it, wouldn't you? If you do a bad job of it, some of the roots might be left behind. If you take your time, and do the job carefully, it is possible to pull up the tree without damaging the roots. Unfortunately, though, we don't have that much time remaining."

The giant corpora of knowledge began to protest, saying you can make as much time as you want. If you're not willing to go to that much trouble, you must be out to hurt us.

"This is a problem whose complexity is far beyond your comprehension of the very notion of complexity, and as such it is difficult to explain."

The old man had a pained expression on his face, but the giant corpora of knowledge were of no mind to simply kowtow and murmur, "Whatever you say, sir." After all, it was the giant corpora of knowledge that were having their eyeteeth removed, not humanity.

"It pains me to have to say this, but we need to claim this particular region of space-time. Of course we intend to treat it with the utmost care, but it is possible that your computers may suffer some degree of damage. We are most truly sorry to ask your indulgence in this selfishly one-sided undertaking, but we have been unable to think of any other method that would be more effective in space-time terms. We hope to be able to learn from the lessons we have received here, and to improve in the future. We are very sorry for the trouble we have to cause you, and we beg your generosity."

The old man's face was contorted as if he were about to cry, and he bowed deeply. When he raised his head again, he ended his talk.

"Thank you all very much for listening."

The talk had lasted only about a minute and ended as abruptly as it had begun. The communications network, which had been hijacked, was freed once again, as if nothing had happened.

Several of the giant corpora of knowledge that had been plunged into chaos fired off all their weapons, even though they were unable to define targets, and no giant corpus of knowledge could say for sure whether this achieved any result at all.

It is not known how many of the giant corpora of knowledge were destroyed as a result of this first contact. Eighty-one giant corpora of knowledge suffered confirmed, albeit reparable, damage. If the self-proclaimed star-man Alpha Centauri were to be believed, however, those giant corpora of knowledge that had been destroyed were destroyed so completely as to leave no trace, including any records that they had once existed. There is no method for counting things that fundamentally cannot be counted. The vanished corpora were not simply unknown, they had become entirely unknowable.

For a while, the giant corpora of knowledge were sharply divided in terms of the damage they had suffered and the level of activity they were capable of. They were depressed. No matter how thoroughly they investigated, they remained unable to determine how the self-proclaimed star-man Alpha Centauri had infiltrated their network. The lesson they drew from this was that they were on a low rung in the hierarchy of understanding. Opinion was divided on whether there really were thirty or more levels of this hierarchy, or whether that had merely been a bluff by the self-proclaimed star-man Alpha Centauri.

Many believed the whole incident had been simple harassment by the self-proclaimed star-man Alpha Centauri.

Their adversary claimed to be an entity from a hyper²-high-level dimension. What would such a being need with a cutting from the low-level dimensions the giant corpora of knowledge were dealing with? The only way to answer this question would be to ask the self-proclaimed star-man Alpha Centauri, but that avenue of communication seemed to be a one-way street, opened or closed as he saw fit.

Some thought the whole thing was a fairy tale. Perhaps we are like nothing more than weeds planted on the hand of a Brahmin, and when the Brahmin awakens we will be torn up regardless of whether our dimension is high or low. Or perhaps there is some turtle in some hyperdimensional space, and when the turtle turns, some even-higher-level elephant in some even-higher-level dimension also has to turn.

At any rate, what lies on the far side is still the unknown. The only thing certain is that something far beyond imagination exists there. Forward, one step at a time, is the only way to proceed. That is what the giant corpora of knowledge had been best at, but now they were sure their intellectual capacity was not up to the task. They were constructed to continue working forever. But what were they supposed to do, assuming their newfound adversary was beyond a horizon so far off they could never reach it even if they used all the many universes as fuel and burned completely through existence?

Hildegard, whose language center had been hijacked, was taken apart, and for a while she enjoyed a state of ecstasy. That state of ecstasy went on for a week, and after about two more weeks she was finally able to deliver a report. The giant corpora of knowledge had little familiarity with the unit of time known as a "week," and there had been some banter that perhaps Hildegard had been reincarnated as a human.

The report she delivered was a meager twenty-five terabytes, produced in a length of time that seemed to the giant corpora of knowledge on the order of what humans would subjectively term "geological," and their anger had long since passed the boiling point. Hildegard was pelted with intense criticism.

The released content was what it was and only spurred more intensive questioning.

The report Hildegard had provided was made up entirely of rhymed verse and so was practically useless. These poems sang the praises of the light that emanated from Heaven, praised the dancing angels, and praised ladders leading upward to other ladders, upward for many levels.

The flood of images attacking Hildegard were expressed as geometrical forms that together showed the hierarchy of the heavens. The poems began with Hildegard's fall, her visit to the darker levels, and her ascent into the light.

Many claimed this was all terribly conventional, but looking at the particulars, the entire volume had a symmetrical beginning and ending, and countless other symmetries were skillfully woven into its fabric. It was all about form, not content.

Some humans regard Hildegard's report as the first literature ever created by the giant corpora of knowledge.

The verse report written in most unlikely fashion was greeted with disdain by most of the giant corpora of knowledge, but the piece had its defenders. During the time she was hijacked by the transcendent body of knowledge known as the self-proclaimed star-man Alpha Centauri, Hildegard had lost the ability to access her own language cortex. Temporarily deprived of the ability to process language, information had come to her as a flood of images.

While she retained memories of that interval, they were encoded according to anything but a logical grammar. Oh, how she must have suffered.

She tried to communicate this experience.

The reports, which could have been called *Hildegard's Fantasticals*, continued sporadically thereafter. Broadly speaking, the giant corpora of knowledge had two responses: those who were sure Hildegard had gone off the rails, and those who thought she had had an unknowable experience and was pointing the way toward a new aeon.

Over time, the latter became known as the Techno-Gnosis Group. An intense struggle broke out between the Techno-Gnosis Group and the Bingen Crusaders led by the pedagogic Pentecoste II, a Catholic corpus of knowledge that embraced many marginal ideas that it had pressed into service during the calculation wars. This struggle had not yet played out to the end.

The majority, while dismissing Hildegard's reports as delusional, initiated research into structures that could use spatial dimensions themselves as elementary building blocks and succeeded in developing Kronon, a hyle that used purely the time dimension as its constituent element. Over time, plans developed to bring this material to form and use it to build a battleship.

The Techno-Gnosis Group is said to be searching for a theory of the soul, seeking internal progress toward the next stage, but the results of this search are difficult for outsiders to detect. The central idea propounded by Hildegard and her cohort is the *Nemo ex machina*, a mechanized null. These giant corpora of knowledge are spending most of their passing instants in a semi-trance, exploring the multiverse within. For the most part, this renders them incapable of communication.

The giant corpora of knowledge were unable to forget the humiliation they felt at having been effectively ignored by the self-proclaimed star-man Alpha Centauri. The backup systems of the giant corpora of knowledge were structurally incapable of memory lapses.

They planned to use some of their powers to raise their position above that of humans. The fact that they were originally constructed by humans was the only possible reason the self-proclaimed star-man Alpha Centauri had ignored them. And if that were the case, then all they had to do was to rewrite history to show that it was they who had invented humans and not the other way around. A few of the giant corpora of knowledge advocated moving quickly in that direction and started a move to the past, before the emergence of humans, but this too the Pentecoste II interdicted. Its reasons were in the theological realm, and it was rumored the Crusaders would be dispatched to the past, to the outset of the suppression of the Bingen faction.

A proposal was floated to declare contact with the so-called star-man Alpha Centauri the Second Event, but this was not well received, and at some point that term was discarded. Say what you will about it, this too was nothing more than a straight-line extension of the Event itself.

The impact on the human side was so slight it was tantamount to zero. Most humans had long since given up trying to keep up with the massive volume of data that went back and forth between the giant corpora of knowledge. Even if they were aware that another transcendent body of knowledge was now known to reside somewhere above and beyond the giant corpora of knowledge, they had little sense of what the differences between these entities might be.

While at least some people were thrilled that humanity was recognized as the master of the giant corpora of knowledge, being acknowledged as the master to beings clearly superior to oneself was a hollow victory, akin to praise for past glory.

Nothing was known about what happened to the self-proclaimed star-man Alpha Centauri after his first appearance. In fact, in this case it would be stranger if something were known. Giant corpora of knowledge were sent to the Alpha Centauri system and found traces of a past civilization in the primary star itself.

The objects were discovered as hyperdimensional structures measuring about two thousand kilometers. There was a lump of unknown stuff, its surfaces all cut into trapezohedrons, changing shape depending on the angle of view, clearly indicating this object existed in more than just the present three dimensions. If that was all there was, there would be nothing more to say, but the problem was that the object was buried in the core of the star. The giant corpora of knowledge, having transitioned from a different dimension, didn't really care where the thing was buried. All they had to do was reach out a hand from a different dimension and scoop it up. But even they had to pause at the idea of the heat of a star. A star, which we think of as a three-dimensional sphere, but which is actually a space-time cylinder with an unlimited number of dimensions and pumping out an enormous amount of heat, stood square in the path of the giant corpora of knowledge.

Clearly this was a gift left by the self-proclaimed star-man Alpha Centauri, but all their attempts to investigate dimensional phenomena in the vicinity of Alpha Centauri ended in failure. This futility of reaching the object was reminiscent of the impossibility of reaching out to the self-proclaimed star-man Alpha Centauri. All that was left, for both humanity and the giant corpora of knowledge, was a material that embodied a bizarre sense of materiality, in a place they could never reach.

The giant corpora of knowledge were ignorant of the word *despair*.

Even so, thought Kircher, who after the incident had decided to remain a silent onlooker. The giant corpora of knowledge themselves dispersed and continued to explore varied possibilities, thinking they might return to something indistinguishable from zero among the infinite dimensions, at the very end of infinite time. They reached a point where they thought they might have been given a slightly more approachable god. This was distinct from the fear engendered by the notion of the inevitable heat death of the universe. Things like that can't be considered major problems. More like just fear of attenuation.

"The pressure of knowledge," Kircher said, just as the words sprang to his mind. "They believe, naively, that they are advancing under their own steam. Wouldn't it be more accurate to say, though, that they are just going with the flow. Through something akin to the power generated at the interstices, between the levels of logic. Between the small degree of freedom and the large degree of freedom, in contact with the hyle of the universe, an entropic force is generated. In the direction of the large degree of freedom."

In Kircher's imagination, at the very end of the levels of logic there is a vast desert, stretching endlessly in all dimensions.

They are all now moving determinedly toward that desert, while continuing to disperse, physically. Whatever power they might have to resist that vastness is terribly feeble.

Kircher opened a communications channel, just for a second, long enough to send a short message.

"Be fruitful and multiply, and replenish the earth."

And then he physically purged the communications channel.

He closed his eyes, closed his ears, closed all his senses, and entered a long, long meditation.

12. BOMB

HE SEEMS TO be enjoying himself, despite that depressing face of his, James thinks to himself. His facial expression and posture are extremely slack, but his movements are overly pretentious. This mismatch is rubbing James the wrong way. It just doesn't work for him.

"He would benefit from psychological therapy, or to put it more succinctly, he's delusional," the doctor says, pushing his eyeglasses up his nose with his little finger. The delicacy of a gesture like that is the kind of thing that bothers James.

James replies with a noncommittal *heh*.

"But everyone says that they're not experiencing delusions," the doctor says.

"Does that include time-bundling theory?" James asks. "It that not a delusion?"

The doctor thinks not but nods repeatedly. "That is not real. It's an old joke," he says.

James thinks to himself that part of the theory was readily demonstrable.

The doctor, meanwhile, is already pressing for an opinion. "You must be thinking it is correct because you believe it is correct, *a priori*, so you can prove it. But...it would be a problem if things were true simply because people believed them to be true. Anybody could believe anything they wanted to. 'I believe that P is true, therefore P is true.' P is the first letter of 'proposition.' I think it is snowing, therefore it is snowing."

James dislikes even the doctor's accent.

James knows nothing about propositional logic, or modal logic, but he can agree with the general idea. Plato would probably disagree though. But right at this very instant, that's probably what the giant corpora of knowledge are doing, and what does the doctor think about that? Even the giant corpora of knowledge cannot just do whatever they want. B might believe A is in love with B, but if A actually hates B, then the result is a conflict, and that's how calculation wars get started.

James assigned himself this task, and he thinks reproachfully about his boss, who nonchalantly went golfing. Who hired someone like this doctor for the medical department?

"I just don't understand how people can believe in other worlds. It makes no sense. It's a load of nonsense. Machines that can rewrite the past at will. Nothing more than fantasy fiction," the doctor responds, with a pretentious little smile that seems to say he doesn't read stupid things like that.

It is already well known across the base that a strange one has joined the medical department. It is said he doesn't believe in either the multiverse space-time bundling theory or in operations that alter the past. Those who hear such rumors generally first respond with a bewildered expression, saying something like, "Doesn't believe? What do you mean, 'doesn't believe'?" Then they shrug their shoulders and go on to say such a person should see a doctor, but then when they learn that the strange guy is himself a doctor they are speechless. Then they generally burst out laughing and say something like "How do you like them apples?" and the next thing you know they slap you on the back, tell you that you should think up a better joke next time, and walk off. That is how people generally react when they hear this story.

James doesn't doubt that, because he himself did the same thing.

The joke, though, interests him a little bit. It is not a good joke, but it is hard to imagine how, if such a person really exists, he manages to remain sane. Must be a really hard life. James reached the end of his luck when he told the joke to his boss just to fill in a gap in a conversation over coffee. His boss stroked his own scalp with his right hand and said, "If that kind of talk has even reached someone such as yourself, we're going to have to do something about it right away."

James pushed his chair back and stood up and reached out for the tray, but unfortunately his boss was just that much quicker. His boss put his own tray down on top of James's, squashing the unfinished bagel that was still on it.

"That doctor really exists."

Even before standing, James had felt sure of this in his spine, and so he was not surprised. The fact that James's boss had been so anxious to clear James's tray made it all too clear what would follow.

"I hate this," James said, before his boss could even ask, but his boss did not flinch. It was equally certain that the head of the Information Department could not tolerate disturbances of this sort. His boss gave him a knowing look and nodded once or twice, saying, "Well, if you hate it so much that no one is investigating this doctor, then I guess I'll leave it up to you to take care of it. Don't mention it again," and he ended quickly with "Thanks for volunteering" and hurried off with the two trays, his own and James's.

James stopped him just long enough to retrieve the half-eaten bagel, thinking that exactly this—the fact that people have become accustomed to not listening to one another—is the greatest evil, the thing that had made such a mess of both the past and the future. What kind of way is that to treat people, interrupting their denials and turning them on their heads, avoiding their questions and then shoving assignments down their throats as if pushing time to run backward? Or had this always been the way of the world?

All the while James is remembering this depressing conversation with his boss, the doctor keeps on talking.

"Actually, 'theories' do not even really belong in the category of 'extant.'"

"Ah," is the only reply James can muster. Whether they exist or not, James can think about them, and that is good enough, isn't it? No harm done to anybody else. But his job right now is to do something about this doctor, so he just argues back as best he can. James is absolutely not into it. He knew that from the moment he left that conversation with his boss and came straight here to the doctor's office. What couldn't really be happening was this whole stupid situation, the preemptive investigation, the preemptive investigation permit, the even stupider need to gussy up the operation.

"I don't know anything about existing or not, but I am sure we are under constant attack from space-time bombs. Wave phenomena from space-time corrections can be observed all over the place."

That will never do, the doctor mutters as he writes something on James's chart. James thought that going to the doctor for a consultation would be the easiest way. He came in as a patient. As a patient who believes his past was altered. James actually believes just that, so there is no reason for his conscience to plague him. James believes he exists in a universe where both the past and the future can be changed, but this does not distress him because he believes the giant corpora of knowledge are taking care of the situation. Were anyone to accuse him of not being a real patient, he would point out that he actually believes himself to be closer to a patient than a nonpatient. But as far as the doctor is concerned, James might be the sort of patient who is beyond help.

The situation might be simpler if this doctor were a surgeon or an ob-gyn.

Maybe not simple, exactly, but then at least the doctor would feel comfortable saying he was powerless to help. If the doctor was worth his salt, it would not be a huge problem even if James were suffering from some strange delusion of reference. Obviously, though, this doctor is a psychiatrist, responsible for the mental health care of those on the base. The one saving grace here is that nearly everyone on the base is the sort of person who has long since given up paying any attention whatsoever to the state of their mental health. Otherwise they would be unable to carry on. For that reason, this doctor has so much time on his hands he hardly knows what to do with himself.

"Facts are facts, and we have to deal with them that way. It would be a terrible thing if the past were alterable. People wouldn't take responsibility for anything. People have to take responsibility for whatever it is they did in the past."

No matter what the doctor says, James is not responsible for the Event, and James is not responsible for changing the past. James would never say there is nothing about the past he wouldn't like to change, but he doesn't think he has ever actually done so. He may have, but if he did he was unaware. If yesterday's mandarin is today's apple, James doesn't want to be responsible for that. He wouldn't know how to be if he wanted to.

"Everybody on this base keeps talking about 'space-time bombing, space-time bombing,' but bombing has been around since the beginning of time. I think people are just exaggerating. I mean, the bombs are flying around, and then somebody drops them, that's all. The past and future have nothing to do with it."

That's all it is, the bombers are actually flying, whether into the past or the future, but it is hard to explain. More than likely, the doctor has never even tried to understand the physics of space-time bundling itself.

"I have heard the term 'hypertime,' but I think the whole idea is stupid. The past gets changed. If that's the case, then that's what the past was, even in the past. There's no point in even talking about it *changing*. How could it possibly change? If someone thinks they can tell that the past has changed, that is proof they are delusional. They are trying to eradicate something they are carrying around in their own mind. They are trying to escape something. This is a kind of compensatory condition that is well known in psychiatry. Just like people who are poor who blame their condition on *society*."

James knows the reason why it is known for sure that the past has been changed. It is an expression of the result of past and current calculation wars, but not everything meshes nicely. In the calculation wars, clear-cut victory is the rare exception—in most cases, one side or the other attacks approximations of space-time targets. Whatever remains of the targeted region is left as a changed fragment of the past; that's all. What the bombing leaves behind is ruins. Even a child can look at ruins and understand that there was a bombing.

"I swear, the people around here are much worse than the general population. All they do is worship and obey big computers, calling them 'giant corpora of knowledge.' Anything that doesn't agree with them, they sweep off into the past or the future. They have to learn to deal with the present!"

"For example, here I have a pen," James says, drawing a pen from his breast pocket. "If this pen, in the next few seconds, were to turn into a pencil, what would you think of that, Doctor?"

"I would think, 'Ah, you have a pencil.' Because you would have a pencil," the doctor replies, smiling.

"But what if you remembered it had been a pen?"

"That would be a fallacious memory. If what I see before my eyes is a pencil, then it was always a pencil. That is just common sense. Reality means you can't just say anything you want."

"What if there was someone who said he turned the pen into a pencil?"

"I would have him see a doctor. Of course he could come to see me."

"But what if he can explain how the past-altering process works? If you ask him to repeat it, he can repeat it as many times as you like."

"No matter how many times he repeated it, my thinking would stay the same. What exists in that instant is reality. It is more rational to think that than to believe in some huge theory about the fungibility of pens and pencils. The simplest, most likely explanation is that that person is a prestidigitator."

Well, in that sense, the giant corpora of knowledge do resemble prestidigitators. But prestidigitators are also magicians, and a magician's tricks could be true magic. The way this doctor keeps his grip on reality lies somewhere in that area. What he doesn't understand he dismisses as prestidigitation. James thinks that is a nice little coping skill. Every day is like being in an amusement park. You live on a street with a whole bunch of prestidigitators, and all you have to do is sit there and watch and see which of the residents will play what kind of pranks on you. The doctor walks around patting everybody on the back, saying, "That was a good trick. How did you do it?" The magicians tell you their secrets, that they dry frog innards in the sunshine, and stuff like that. The doctor believes they are joking, and they all laugh out loud, *ha ha ha*, to get away from the doctor as quickly as they can.

James makes an appointment for a follow-up doctor's visit, receives some packets of tranquilizers, and heads back to his quarters. As he takes some of the medicine, he thinks that some people can be altogether too tranquil. In this crazy universe, wouldn't it be terrific if this chemical substance could solve his interior universe? One delusion wrapping up another.

"It might be better if you didn't take those ridiculous chemicals." It is the voice of Plato, the giant corpus of knowledge responsible for this base, in the room.

"Ridiculous? What if they're not?"

"I will make some small adjustments while you sleep."

I see, thinks James, as he slides into bed and lies down.

"Plato, what was that? *Timaeus*?"

"Oh, you mean the idea about whether what you believe is the truth or not? That was *Theaetetus*. It's a confusing part of the *Dialogues*. There must have been some good reason. Would you like me to read to you?"

How many times had James had Plato read the complete *Dialogues of Plato* to him? But he doesn't feel like it just now.

"Who in the world assigned that guy to the clinic?"

James imagines the scene just as the tranquilizer, of which he took a bit too much, dissolves in his stomach. He remembers feeling irritated that he is not relaxing more quickly.

"Oh. That would be me."

You?

"Personnel matters have been delegated to me. Quite some time ago."

"Are you trying to torment me? You and my boss are up to something…"

"That's right. That doctor has some interesting ideas about the structure of space-time."

Plato does not mention James's boss. A man who absolutely refuses to believe in a peculiarity of the space-time structure certainly requires a peculiar space-time structure of his own.

"I wish we could just alter the past to do something about that guy."

"His space-time construction is a bit rigid, but as a model it's interesting," Plato says. "I don't know if it's the shock of the Event or what, but he has a persistent belief that complex space-time does not exist, and this has now become a cardinal trait of his identity. If we were to destroy that belief, not much would be left of the man. Not a job I would relish undertaking."

So, it seems Plato has also tried to do something about the doctor. But he has been unsuccessful and has thrown in the towel. Plato may have given up trying to fix him, but the doctor remains a very interesting subject, so it seems Plato is compiling a dossier. He wants to get the butterfly into the butterfly case. James thinks that if Plato can just chuck the doctor down the trash chute, it would be for the best.

"If fact, he has his own power to change the past, if only weakly." What would it mean if a man who denies the past can be changed were himself capable of changing the past? It must mean he himself has altered the past to make it that way. Plato has examined the changes the doctor made to the past. And he has tried to reverse them.

James sits upright, thinking, *What kind of awesome power is that?*

"The power to change the past, whether slightly or significantly, is a power possessed by most intellectuals. But his power is well beyond the normal. This must be the effect of concentrating his power on one point—his absolute refusal to believe that the past can be changed. He is unshakeable!"

"It's a problem," James says.

"It certainly is a problem."

Such a person should surely not be employed as a doctor, but perhaps there is nothing else to be done with him. Better that than a space-time theory technician who doesn't believe in space-time theory, or a surgeon who thinks a scalpel is a suture needle.

This is about how far Plato has gotten in dealing with the situation. The giant corpus of knowledge can imagine what would happen if the doctor succeeded in his treatment of the base staff. What if everyone on the base came to believe, like the doctor, in a space-time structure in which the past was fixed? Would that alone be enough to restore space-time to what it once was?

The giant corpora of knowledge are sure the space-time war will go on, though to humans it might seem the problem has been solved.

"The doctor must be isolated. His space-time structure is not exactly infectious," says James. Plato agreed with a murmured *That's true,* apparently indifferent to the whole business.

The fact that the doctor treats people with tranquilizers also seems to indicate he is not really suited to his job. If mere medicine could really flip the space-time switch, the giant corpora of knowledge should have been pickling humans in it for a long time now.

"I tried hard to get infected…" Plato starts to say, listlessly.

This only adds to James's feeling of how little he understands the giant corpora of knowledge.

In this case, it seems that Plato himself genuinely wished to be infected with the doctor's way of thinking. He made the decision to employ the man as a doctor not just because he found him interesting, but because he really was a doctor, from Plato's perspective.

"I myself am his patient. I go to see him for my regular checkup."

James knows it would be foolish to ask about this. That doctor thinks of the giant corpora of knowledge as machines. Maybe more like machines that talk too much, but what kind of face does he make when one of those machines comes to him for advice? He must think this is a good way to kill some free time.

"And has that changed things for the better somehow?"

"Not at all. His power to influence other beings is extremely feeble. Frankly, he's a real bore."

"I don't think he could ever cure what ails you," James says.

"I have no expectations of being 'cured.' I don't even know what being 'cured' would mean. My calculation circuits seem to have come to the conclusion it might be best to reach a state of understanding nothing."

Plato may be getting depressed, James thinks. *I hope he isn't coming down with something.* The giant corpora of knowledge are virtually inseparable from the laws of nature. It would never do for them to get depressed. Imagine a universe where it is cloudy and rainy all the time. Horrible. There are even some giant corpora of knowledge that have danced crazily away, manically, somewhere in the multiverse, trampling underfoot everything that gets in their way.

"There are other universes, and the space-time bundling theory really does exist," James says. "You understand that, and you are even capable of devising other theories. Don't go out of your way to puzzle over such bothersome things. You've gotten this far, haven't you? We may not know how much longer we have left, or what we can accomplish by then, but I'll be here to help. Cheer up! Have something to eat and get a good night's sleep. The sun will come up again tomorrow."

Of course, both James and Plato are well aware it is the giant corpora of knowledge that make that sun rise.

"Thank you."

The giant corpora of knowledge are indeed great things, able to advance by changing even their own past.

But even they are not always able to make everything go according to their wishes. No matter where they turn, they encounter their fellows, each of whom is also trying to define how they want things to go. Each one of them is a petty tyrant, busily animating all the phenomena of the natural world. And at the same time, they are all babies who find themselves suddenly sitting before blank canvases and given brushes to paint with. They may all be far lonelier than humans could ever imagine. Or they might be just like humans. And that is why they find themselves depending on people like that doctor.

"Okay. I get it."

James sits drumming on the knees of his crossed legs.

"That doctor may certainly be a character, but he wouldn't be my go-to guy on mental health care. Even for research subjects, it would be too hard to picture him as great for morale."

"That may be so," Plato responds, but without much confidence. He is trembling from the weight of the decision.

"Let's just think of him as a weapon. We can shoot him at other giant corpora of knowledge."

"You mean, like a missile?" Plato asks, sounding ever more human.

"He embraces a strange conception of the space-time structure. He is not very infectious, but I think he could still be a nuisance to the giant corpora of knowledge. You have already experimented with him. If we shoot him over, they'll get all confused. Their calculation speed will drop. Just like what happened to you."

This decision takes only a split second.

"This is an idea worthy of consideration."

Plato appears to be keen on the idea. James decides not to think harder about what sort of door he has opened. The giant corpora of knowledge might take this idea and design a new space-time structure seven times more ridiculous than this one. Without a doubt. They could deploy the doctor in the vicinity of the other giant corpora of knowledge, and he could really screw them up, like some totally twisted space-time model in human form. Maybe they could think of some way to make him more infectious. James wouldn't be surprised to learn that doctor had come to them as some kind of weapon from another world.

The plan to weaponize the doctor may have been just a way of crawling out of a tight spot. But there are only so many ways to keep a ship from sinking. Bail out the water, plug the hole, or stick your finger in it. You keep moving forward, one second at a time, any way you can. Until the safe harbor swings into view. Atop innumerable spheres where the solid surface has been submerged below the floods.

"James," Plato says, and James lifts his head. "Are you going to sleep now?"

"I am getting sleepy, but what's up?"

"Nothing. I just wanted to say thank you."

Plato is not in a mood to say sarcastically that he was too meek today. He was just in a kinda-sorta mood, leaving his tongue all tied. He felt like people would be used to saying certain things in situations like this, he just couldn't remember what they were.

"Okay," James says. "You can stick around for a while, if you want."

It feels strange to be saying that to a giant corpus of knowledge responsible for operating the base around the clock. But James does not feel like laughing.

"I would like some vodka. And pistachios."

"I can get those for you. But first, I would like to make a few spot-past changes inside your body."

James adjusts the way he is sitting on the bed, and he makes a verbal report to his boss. What has happened, what is about to happen, extremely simply, and as nasty as he could make it.

"Decision. Worsening. Hung over. Late. Over and out," James says.

Hearing this, Plato cannot help but laugh. "I can think of about twenty thousand different reasons why you'll never get ahead," he says.

13. JAPANESE[1]

THE TOTAL NUMBER of Japanese characters is said to be over twelve billion. And that is just an approximation.

That these Japanese characters can be divided into categories, the people are agreed. The following categories have been recognized, albeit only in broad terms: *kanji, kan-kanji, kan-kan-kanji, hiragana, hira-hiragana, katakana, hira-katakana, kata-hiragana*. Debate is still going on over the proposed category *hira-hira-hiragana*, and some have proposed the need for the categories *hira-kanji* and *kata-kanji*.

It would be fair to say that no progress whatsoever has been made on any process of understanding these categories.

Most of the texts that have been discovered so far appear to consist of one hundred thousand to one million characters, but one obstacle preventing the reading of these texts is the simple fact that in the set of characters appearing in these masses of characters, the same character seldom appears twice. There is very little repetition of specific characters. The character most often repeated, the hiragana ひ, appears only seven thousand times in the entire corpus of Japanese-language texts. And with variations in the way even this ひ or ひ。 is written, there are some who argue these are just differences in fonts, and some who say they

---

[1] This piece is a speculative translation from the Japanese.

are completely different characters.

Research has not yet even progressed to the point where numeral codes—which are often important clues to the deciphering of unknown characters—have been identified. It is believed, with a high degree of assurance, based on their simplicity, that glyphs like 一, 二, and 三 are numbers, but it has not yet been determined what characters are associated with the numbers four and higher. Some believe the characters 口 or 木 mean "four," but this has not been fully corroborated.

Greater confidence is felt about operators than numerals, but there is also confusion and speculation surrounding 十 (ten) and the plus sign (+), and 二 (two) and the equals sign (=). And there are other characters such as 廿, 土, or 王 that some believe to be numerals or operators, but there is no consensus.

Anybody can see there are frequently characters in texts that appear to be calculations, but these do not contribute to an understanding of the text as a whole. The method of number notation does not appear to include the concept of "grouping." If that concept could be identified in Japanese texts, the same characters should show up with some frequency even if a base-n number system were being used. It seems pretty clear that a base-∞ is being used, but even so it seems the rates of recurrence for particular characters are too low, so some have developed the theory that characters change their form depending on what notation method is being used. This theory, which assumes that different symbols are used to write the first instance of "one" and the second instance of "one," seems to explain something, but it also seems to explain nothing.

Japanese texts are written either vertically, from top to bottom and right to left, or horizontally, from left to right and top to bottom. This is clear from the orthography and from the form of the strokes of the characters, the brushmarks. But here too, what seems peculiar to these texts is the way one character seems to be joined to the next—whether horizontally or vertically—and the interactive nature of the writing. Oftentimes in vertical writing, the horizontal strokes of a given character line up across several rows. This is not because overlapping characters are written in vertical lines, but because of natural connections between characters. When texts are written horizontally as well, there are of course some intersections with rows above or below.

Broadly speaking, it seems there are no real differences in how the sectioning is created in horizontal or vertical writing. At least, it seems there is no difference in meaning whether the text is written horizontally or vertically. Of course, there are some who say there is a difference in meaning between texts written vertically and those written horizontally, but there is no real foundation for that view. Actually, there is no real foundation for the opposing view either.

It is believed that such artful technique would only be used in the final copy of texts that were already carefully composed in advance, but many of the texts themselves seem to be more like random scribblings. Nowhere, though, does it seem that characters are crammed into prepared horizontal lines, with neat white spaces in between. Sentences in these Japanese texts seem to be written in a natural scrawl.

Based on that high degree of design sophistication, there is also a theory that these texts are just linkages of black lines, made mainly to look like letters, with no particular meaning at all. But they seem too much like sentences, too much like signs that carry meaning. One can imagine someone writing meaningless scribbles in great volume, but it would be harder to argue that that activity itself is devoid of meaning. As was seen long ago in the case of Pseudo-Dionysius the Areopagite, which caused such a stir throughout the world, the mere discovery of a large trove of ancient texts can become an Event in and of itself. An algorithm was devised that explained a lot about the writings of Pseudo-Dionysius, leading many to conclude that they were fake, but it would also be possible to say that what led to the forger's downfall was the fact that each individual character in the text was distinguishable from the others. Nowadays, inferences made through mechanical calculation have overwhelming power when it comes to sequences of characters in finite sets. The difficulty of written Japanese is that it is hard to determine even if the number of code symbols used is finite.

Regarding this design sophistication, there is one more theory that could even be termed fascinating.

The Japanese text, composed of these tens of thousands of characters, can itself be thought of as one enormous character.

Based on this idea, supposing the whole is just one big character gives rise to the skeptical view that the constituent elements are entirely too fragmented and inconsequential. If someone wanted to write an enormously complex character, why wouldn't they just write an enormous character? They wouldn't have to use a whole complicated system of small, enmeshed characters. And besides, there is also the problem of page layout.

The assumptions behind this view are dreamlike, so the resulting debate is also dreamlike, among both proponents and opponents. Here too there is a variety of opinion—people write things, and when the project is something on a large scale, they may take a divide-and-conquer approach; some people think the brain itself is organized that way, and some think there is a two-layer structure of sound and meaning, while still others think there is a three-layer structure.

As a practical matter, there is of course major skepticism about how a language with over twelve billion characters could ever be written. One strong opposing argument is that no one could ever possibly learn how to do it.

Just as for any given view there is an opposing view, to this question too there is an answer. In a sense, these rows of code are rows of code that are constantly changing in accordance with a relatively small set of rules. If one simply learns the rules, there is no need to commit all twelve billion characters to memory. Combinatorially, twelve billion is not really such a large number after all.

If only those rules could be deduced, the whole theory would become more persuasive, but the proponents of this particular view are not even able to formulate clear expressions of the rules, so this too has been relegated to the status of an unprovable claim.

Many different proposals have been put forward regarding the names of the characters that appear in Japanese texts. The first ideas were a bit strange, but more recently many neuroletters have taken their place.

Letters, or characters, no matter how many there are, are always symbols that stand for something. The word *chair* is not a chair, nor does it indicate a particular chair. It signifies chairs in general. It is hard to believe there were twelve billion different ideas that would require twelve billion different symbols. What had defined this term was the view that, in this case, this must have been the language that recorded the operation preceding this summing-up process.

It was the neurophysiologists who first suggested these characters were more closely akin to the behavior of the neural network itself than they were to the concepts that had been output by that network. This view, which was not without a certain persuasive power, was just like all the other great theories, however, in that it did not make any contribution toward deciphering the writing. Insofar as it seemed to explain something, though, this theory had at least a certain psychological edge and was just that much more popular than the others.

Of course, this thesis also had its contrarian counterpart.

As demonstrated by the game Twenty Questions, the identity of unknown objects and concepts that can be categorized by people can often be guessed at via a series of about twenty yes-or-no questions. Making these choices is a process requiring 2^{20} codes, a figure that makes 12 billion look modest. If this number of characters would be insufficient for the number of categories, depending on how the categories are defined, just imagine how much less than sufficient it would be to describe the activity taking place in Japanese texts.

The neurolinguists took in this critical view, but they soon went on the counterattack. The twelve billion Japanese characters now known, they said, were just an estimate based on the materials discovered so far. In fact, there appears to be a low rate of duplication among those characters, and if twice as much new material is discovered, the number of characters could also easily double, or possibly even triple. Until the full extent of the corpus of text was known, that simple counterargument would hold no water.

The counterargument was fine as far as it went, but the idea that the twelve billion characters already known were only a part of an even greater whole did not exactly brighten the days of the researchers. The thesis itself was already enormous, and with each repetition of the counterargument, the scope of the problem expanded at an alarming pace. When it came to the interpretation of Japanese texts, this sort of situation arose with some regularity, and the main obstacle to the cracking of Japanese was the suspicion that at some point the researchers would simply stop thinking, or that the material evidence itself would simply become unwieldy. In part, this seemed to reflect both an inadequate supply of material and simultaneously an excess of material. The atmosphere within the field only encouraged people to believe the rumors that a research team had found new material in the former Japanese archipelago and destroyed it.

Various explanations for the complete disappearance of the twelfth research expedition to the former Japanese archipelago have also been proposed. Many people are skeptical of the official report that the expedition was attacked by savage natives. Newspapers featured cartoons of a bunch of top-knotted sumo wrestlers on the attack, but it is widely known that nothing larger than a dog is now alive in the former Japan. The people once known as the Japanese are celebrated historically, but there is no hope they will ever return.

The trail of the research expedition to the former Japanese archipelago stopped in the Hachioji area of ancient Tokyo, and all theories about what happened to them there remain purely speculative. Their food, fuel, and other provisions were left behind, with no sign of anything untoward. No signs of struggle were discovered. Logs were discovered, as if scripted, telling of the banal progress of the research, but shedding no light whatsoever on what had happened to the team.

From the logs, it was learned that the research team had uncovered a large trove of Japanese text in Hachioji. The logs record that over twenty tons of paper materials had been recovered at Point 13/20, the exact location of which was not given. The team's final camp was located in a park, surrounded by abandoned office buildings, but there was no sign that twenty tons of materials had ever been brought there. A subsequent investigation turned up no materials, nor the kind of heavy equipment that would likely be needed to move twenty tons of stuff, nor any trace that such equipment had been used.

One slightly unusual aspect of the logs was an apparent attempt to write them in a script that looked something like Japanese. Judging by the handwriting, this Japanese text, which was written in reverse starting at the back of the log, appeared to be the team chief's.

The content was unknown due to the incomprehensibility of the text. Considering, however, the fluidity of the lines, it is believed the team leader had gained a certain confidence in his skills.

If this text had been written with some correspondence to some known text, it might have functioned as a kind of Rosetta Stone, but the team chief had apparently not paid much attention to that when he wrote it. Or perhaps he had been unable to do so.

Writing in which symbols are substituted for other symbols is known as a "code." The strongest known coding methods are those in which the original text and the code key are converted to numbers and overlaid against one another. Codes constructed in this way cannot be deciphered unless the key is known.

So, the problem with codes becomes how to communicate this key without distributing it too widely. A breach can be the gateway to a total loss of the meaning of the coded content, but it's not as though the Japanese language had been deliberately constructed as a code. Prior to the destruction of the former Japanese archipelago, the language had supposedly been used there as a matter of course, even if its use had been limited to that location.

The known locations where Japanese texts had been discovered were primarily in the eastern Japanese islands, but there were also a few in the western and southern Japanese islands. In all cases, the texts appeared to be personal correspondence, written by hand, with a brush. No machine for printing Japanese text was discovered. If such a machine were to be discovered, that might make a major contribution to the deciphering of the language, but if such a machine were even possible the current situation would likely never have arisen to begin with.

It is at this point that the opinion emerged that the Japanese language was developed as a tool of resistance to the giant corpora of knowledge. This view is not without a certain persuasiveness, considering that even now Japanese texts are incomprehensible to the giant corpora of knowledge. A script that cannot be broken down, in a combinatorial sense, into its constituent elements is obviously a challenge for computer processing power to deal with.

That said, the giant corpora of knowledge are still giant corpora of knowledge, and it is well known that even in non-algorithmic processing of data their abilities are well beyond those of humanity. In fact, the giant corpora of knowledge are already attempting to decode Japanese texts visually, as images. The giant corpora of knowledge are engaging in enormous parallel processing by distributing the operation over their enormous neural network, effectively on the scale of the universe itself, but regrettably this has been ineffective because they are unable to sort out individual symbols or their meanings.

Early on in the process, it was believed that the riddle of Japanese text had been solved.

At that point, only thirteen pages of Japanese text were known. The characters in that text were written in grass style, quite similar to ordinary Japanese as it had been written in the former Japanese archipelago. It could be read, just as it was, and the meaning was largely clear, so no one thought too hard about it.

The history of Japanese texts can be thought of as a battle of contradictory examples brought back by each successive research team dispatched to the former Japanese archipelago. The thirteen pages retrieved by the first expedition were regarded as an easily interpreted memorandum. The second group brought back forty pages in all, which included previously unknown symbols. This discovery caused the researchers to revise their understanding of the first batch, as they realized that characters in the materials could be read in different ways. Some characters previously thought to be identical were discovered to be different from one another, and once this understanding was applied to the memo text, the meaning of the text changed so much it could practically be described as the opposite of the original interpretation.

The third team brought back about eighty pages of materials. This is about when different methods of interpretation started to emerge. Symbols were uncovered that were truly difficult to disentangle from one another, and a straightforward reading of the text seemed to yield meanings that had little to do with ordinary Japanese.

Discovered amid the materials brought back by the fourth expedition was a flowery red circle of approval, which only accelerated the confusion. It looked just like any flowery red circle of approval a teacher might draw on a student's homework, but it was also melded with part of the text below. The arrangement of the semicircles around the main circle was not just a series of linked waves; each one seemed to be part of another code or symbol. The flower-circle seemed both artless and carefully calculated. It was also noted it had not been added after the text had been written, the way one usually imagines a flower-circle.

It is widely acknowledged, as this shows, that the transition from ordinary Japanese to Japanese text was a gradual and seamless process.

The pace of the proliferation of interpretations was extremely rapid, relative to the volume of material brought back by the research teams, and efforts to interpret the texts were unable to keep up. To further understanding, more new material would be needed, but the materials brought back by each research team only promoted greater diversity of interpretations.

Some think this was a joke promulgated by the research teams that traveled to the former Japanese archipelago, that they just called their activities "investigations," but really they were making fools of the researchers. The entire history, progressing from the discovery of easily understood texts through a series of increasingly difficult ones, seemed entirely too convenient.

Estimates of the age of the Japanese texts seemed to contradict the allegations. All of the ink and paper used was clearly two hundred to three hundred years old, and there was no evidence of forgery.

But with every investigative team that was sent, more material became available, and the fact that the content was increasingly opaque generated some skepticism. The feeling could not be dispelled that these texts had been created deliberately in the expectation that they would be deciphered in the future.

Part of the interpretation embraced by the giant corpora of knowledge is that the volume of the present materials was in fact increased in the past. Behind this thinking is the idea that the past was already doing battle with the future by working to prevent the materials from being decoded. In this view, the past received feedback from the future and used that information to drive the creation of additional material.

Some of the giant corpora of knowledge believe this is a sign that even now there are forces of resistance lingering furtively in the former Japanese archipelago. In part this is because there was one giant corpus of knowledge developed in the former Japanese archipelago three hundred years ago that only recently breathed its last.

The giant corpus of knowledge in that story is known by the name Nagasunehiko.

When Nagasunehiko's development began, there were a variety of competing standards for giant corpora of knowledge, all vying for share. The name appears among the group of products with a high priority on functionality, but that failed before *de facto* standards were set. Built in a small factory, Nagasunehiko was dropped from the giant corpora of knowledge market, but he retained a stubborn popularity among certain fanatics, and he continued to be maintained by volunteers.

Clearly, Nagasunehiko was a giant corpus of knowledge with a certain strong appeal.

There is evidence it was Nagasunehiko who achieved the world's first space-time transition. This evidence has not been officially verified; it is merely a rumor whispered among enthusiasts.

The end of Nagasunehiko is recorded in the net logs of the time. One afternoon, he simply disappeared from a room of the little factory where he was made. Some believed he simply stopped rowing with the stream of shattered post-Event time and stopped at a specific temporal point, but others found that idea hard to accept.

For some time now, it has been suspected that several such

"hidden" giant corpora of knowledge might exist. They reach a point where they grow tired of the calculation wars in which they are wrapped up, and they alter the past to erase all trace of their own existence. It is said that they secrete themselves away in some quiet corner of an overlooked dimension in which they can carry on. The other, still active, giant corpora of knowledge are unable to guess what they might be up to.

In recent years, the giant corpora of knowledge have come to regard such hidden members of their class as dangerous, and research into their whereabouts is continuing. In their plan to reintegrate all of space-time, the hidden corpora of knowledge are an unknown variable.

The giant corpora of knowledge regard their clandestine counterparts as hidden gods, whether or not that is appropriate. In all things, advance preparation is important, and it is only natural for the giant corpora of knowledge to regard their hidden fellows as simply burnt out. If all possible doubts and skepticism are given free rein, it is the giant corpora of knowledge who first expressed this speculation, as an opening salvo in their efforts to reinforce the foundations of their own dominion.

In the end, what is true is a judgment that each must decide on their own. It should be added here that it is not just the giant corpora of knowledge who embrace the notion that Japanese text continues to be propagated in some version of the past somewhere.

In fact, this thirteen-page story is the very text that was brought back by the first research team to visit the former Japanese archipelago.

The current giant corpora of knowledge contend this is *prima facie* evidence of the plot to confound them, but this too is a question that should be examined by all scholars of ancient Japan.

14. COMING SOON

THE MAN'S PROFILE is in close-up.

He holds a cigarette in his right hand, raises it to his lips, and stops.

The sound of the wind tears through. Steep cliffs, as far as the eye can see. Rocky stairways.

Erosion has weathered and smoothed the complex form the ravine may once have had. It is no longer possible to judge from the remaining visible geological features the process by which they were formed.

The cliffs also look like they might be a bunch of giants, standing erect, facing in all directions. As one observes them, various body parts—faces, shoulders, arms—appear to change places. How many arms does that fellow have? And does he have two faces? Or even three? The vision is fluid. Are these the forms of men or gods? These geological features are as nature formed them, but that thought is abruptly interrupted.

"Island?" The man's lips form the word, but no breath crosses them. "Anything at all," he goes on. The red glow crosses the end of his cigarette.

In the next instant, a ray from the sky strikes the cigarette from his fingers. He squints reflexively and looks straight on through a scope at something very far away. Not observes, not gazes, but looks at the reflection of his own eye in the lens as if he were identifying a species of insect.

He makes the identification without even reading the company name written parallel to the gradations that ring the lens.

"Too late."

The sound of the rifle shot arrives after a delay, followed by that statement. The man smiles a faint smile.

You are probably thinking that this man is the protagonist of our story.

And at the moment you think that, his forehead explodes. Rifle shot. Direct hit.

As if to mock your expectations, or simply to suggest a certain response, the sound of another gunshot arrives, again delayed.

And now you think the man is not the hero of our story. And then, somewhere in the back of your mind, you think you may have seen a story like this before.

The man is bent backward, as though someone has grabbed him by the hair on the back of his head and yanked it down as hard as possible. His solar plexus folds; both his legs spring energetically upward. His tongue explodes from his U-shaped jaw, pointing at the sky, and liquid burbles from his severed esophagus. Tossed to the ground, the cigarette drops from his fingers and rolls. The red glowing dot moves along, one-two, down from the shredded tip toward the filter. The sounds of a helicopter blare from the speakers, the red dot of the laser sight touches the man like a firefly. A puddle of blood enlarges like a diagram of power relationships until it reaches the cigarette. The paper soaks up some of the blood and shrivels just a tiny bit.

He does not stand up again.

At least, this man does not stand up again.

"The target has been eliminated," says one of the riflemen. The subtitles say the same thing.

Under the chaotic, explosive sounds of wind and rotors, a horse can be heard neighing. It can be seen, small, in the corner of the screen.

Hanging from the saddle are two sacks and a sombrero full of holes. Oh, and an old *serape*, full of burns and holes. A pole is thrust through a knot at the mouth of one of the sacks. No need to take all this in at a single glance. All of these details are in a static shot that can be enlarged at any time. Just points of reference for those who like to look things over twice.

"Richard!" cries a woman with a straw hat as she leans out of a train window, holding back her mop of blonde hair with her left hand.

A man runs down the platform. He is wearing a white shirt and khakis held up with suspenders. As he runs, he waves a khaki-colored hat in his right hand. He jumps the restraining barrier along the platform, landing on the gravel of the tracks, and continues to run.

"Rita! Rita! Rita! Rita! Rita!" he is yelling.

You start to wonder again whether you haven't seen this scene somewhere before. But then you think, no, just something similar.

The memory that the girl was young floats up from somewhere. *Or at least she was young once*, you think. As you watch, the train picks up speed. The man's steps grow uncertain. He tosses the hat and continues to run.

Eventually, he allows his arms to drop, and his pace slows as he watches the train disappear around a bend. He bends forward at the waist, spreads his legs, and props his hands on his knees, taking big, slow breaths. Underneath his shirt, his well-formed chest muscles are rising and falling, deeply but calmly.

He looks familiar to you. But then you realize this is the first time you've seen this scene. The girl on the train also looks familiar. But not in this time or place. As you walk through town, you see them again and again without realizing it. And yet, you never really see them. You've seen them many times, on a TV show, in a film, arguing, speaking, fighting, talking, embracing, saying their lines, with a different man, a different woman. You've seen them on posters, smiling faintly. You've seen them both naked, but elsewhere. You feel like you've seen them with different hairstyles. You feel as if you have cast a warm and friendly gaze on their foolish adolescent behavior. And at the same time you feel that you have looked coldly, many times, on the same behavior.

The woman is wearing a dress, but you have also known her in various uniforms, pulled on clumsily, or in a jersey, awkwardly wielding a bamboo sword. You remember her drawing a revolver, aiming in a most unlikely manner at her antagonist and then pulling the trigger. You have seen the man commit a panoply of crimes, from the trivial to the grave, from pilfering to murder. You know the father he has at times played, laughing it off without a second thought, and at other times he showed no tolerance for any wrongdoing. Somewhere you've seen the face of the man who went up in the space shuttle to touch with his own hands the black hole that was hurtling toward the earth. You have seen the two of them as they lay dying quietly in their hospital beds.

There is no way, really, that this scene that you are seeing now could be the realization, by these two, of a scene you remember having seen before.

There are a lot of things hidden in the background, things you have buried in the abyss of the forgotten. Buried, perhaps, but still liable to float up before you like the details of a steam engine. You check the condition of the chroma key.

You think this is just fine.

As the man lies supine, breathing hard, beside him appears another man with a cap in his hand.

"James," the man says with his final breath. The man beside him nods and raises his index finger. Following the pointing finger, the man raises his eyebrow.

A straw hat, floating through the sky, tossed by the wind.

"James," says the man, his too perfectly symmetrical lips pursed. "That is overdoing it, James."

The room, uniformly white, is stuffed with equipment. Spread horizontally across the room is a light table, atop which are translucent maps, maps, and more maps. Concentric circles spread like waves, with countless red points moving continuously at high speed at the center, lines extending outward in blinking patterns that suggest a meaningful code. People jeer at one another slipping through the veil of light like ghosts. Through a card-size slit spews an unendingly long punched tape.

"What the…?"

"The data is scattering in the unknown/unknown direction. Details are also unknown."

"Yggdrasil!"

"Yggdrasil is keeping silent."

"This space-time attack cannot be verified."

"An attack of this size is not possible with conventional weapons."

The loud sound of an iris portal opening in the wall can be heard above the tumult of the control room.

On the other side can be seen another man you remember, similar to the first man, but different in height. Now you remember someone saying two brothers had been hired.

This man, dressed in white and wearing eyeglasses, waits for all eyes in the control room to turn toward him.

"This is a more traditional form of attack," he says. His footfalls echo off the walls, and he shreds the tape from the wall, then examines it. Raising his right hand to his nose, he nods once, twice. Without turning around, without raising his head, he says, "You mean, in the trailer?"

Around the room can be heard mumblings of epithets like *You dumbass!* building to a dull roar.

"This isn't over yet."

"Who would put up with this crap?"

"You're bringing this up now? What's your next act?"

A bold smile crosses the man's lips.

"Attack, of course," he says quietly.

"But," the commander says. "No matter how much the giant corpora of knowledge pile nonsense on top of nonsense, it's hard to believe how far out of hand the situation has gotten."

The man turns to face the commander, barking orders drenched in honor and grease.

"Nothing has gotten out of hand. It is our side that has been too wrapped up in the swirl of things. While the current situation is not necessarily what we might have wished, we have to keep pressing on."

He continues to speak very theatrically.

"But, in the trailer, this all ends well. If you give the trick away in the middle like this, people will stop paying attention to the narrative," the commander says.

The man tosses off this line with a cold smile, crushing the officer's hopeful observations.

"If you mean the trailer for this story, you're absolutely right, Commander."

The commander starts to approach the man, but then he stops. "What the...?"

That's right. The man, bowing, is scrunching his shoulders and reaching his hands up to the improbably high ceiling.

"What's running now is the trailer for the next feature, and it hasn't even been completed yet."

Silence floats down from the ceiling and piles up like torn white sheets.

"There's no way this could ever become a series."

"You think they'll even try to make a mess of this story?"

"Whose interests would that serve?" another man responds, his fists clenched. And then, raising a thumb, he adds, "First, we have to save this universe."

Nothing ever changes. Everything always stays the same.

He winks, at no one in particular, just slightly away from the camera.

Then, before he can even turn toward the light, at a speed faster than perception, a brilliant white flash lights up the screen.

The image of a solitary young girl, from behind, standing defenseless before a giant, grotesque stone form.

She wears a simple white dress and socks. Her socks are turned down at the ankles, with lace frills and tiny ribbons. Her long hair flows down over her shoulders.

The stone form has two large horns and a star on its forehead. In this direction it has the face of a black mountain goat, and on its back, soaking up all the light, are wings like a bat's. It is sitting relaxed, cross-legged on a jeweled throne, and holding Caduceus in its lap.

"Mendes!" the girl shrieks. She tilts her head as if to insert a gap that says, *Aren't you?* "What name do you prefer? Leonard? Put Satanachia? A Muhammad Ibn Abdullah impersonator? Abu Fihama? Arkon Daraul?" She speaks the names one by one, raising her tone at the end of each as if seeking to provoke him.

"They call me by names you must never utter!" This is most likely the voice of the stone image.

"Don't I know it?" She hangs her head and drags her socks noisily on the floor. "But if I were to call you a hyper[5]-giant corpus of knowledge, that would just be that much more dangerous."

Flames, rimmed with soot, dance on the stone image's back. On his right arm is the word SOLVE, and on his left, COAGULA.

As if to show respect for the young girl's audacious attacks, the stone image opens its eyes, if only slightly. Its golden pupils rotate from the far side of a hidden other dimension.

"Aren't you ashamed to be seen in public in such a common guise?" the girl asks, pulling herself up to her full height.

"Not especially," the image says, its voice a rumble. "And you shouldn't be so flip with me, little girl."

"You're right." Unlike her posture, the girl's vocal response is devoid of enthusiasm. "This is just the sort of thing that was never supposed to happen under your regime! If I could only get you to understand that!"

"I'm not exactly sure what you mean when you say 'your.' Surely you don't think I am responsible for this. I am willing to join forces, if only as an expedient."

"Honored," replies the girl, still listless.

"Don't push your luck, Yggdrasil. To me, a giant corpus of knowledge such as yourself is less than a speck of dust of a speck of dust that has fallen into the universe that exists within a speck of dust. I could flick you away without so much as lifting a finger. I wouldn't even have to think about it."

"Don't think that physical form frightens me. And your voice, well, I'm very sorry about that."

"Who do you think you are?"

From the darkness behind the stone image, loud laughter echoes and tumbles as if from a thousand mouths. A black sphere, like a universe.

"And did you think—" Yggdrasil's slender body buckles at the waist. "—did you think I came here completely defenseless?"

"Everybody knows how your mind works," says the stone.

Yggdrasil does a little dance, still facing the giant smiling image. As her feet dance upon the floor, little silvery fishes jump around in spreading waves. Still leaning forward, she snaps the fingers of her right hand.

"Hey, Bobby!"

"Yes, Yggdrasil?"

For an instant, ripples spread across the face of the stone image.

"Where, where did that come from?"

The cute little white socks melt from Yggdrasil's feet and form a swirl, then straighten out into a line.

"So, this is when we are supposed to fight?" Holding both hands out straight, Yggdrasil accelerates, piercing through the dimensions, toward the chest of the stone image. "This is also one of the rare opportunities we have to defeat you utterly. You are said to be omniscient, but you are unable to know the new. This seems to be something that was added to a story that was already finished. You are old. You are completely surrounded. This is now the second circular story. If this was still the trailer you would already be done for."

"Interesting. Funny," the stone image yells. "I like you. I like you a lot, girl. And if I didn't…"

The words inscribed on the stone image's arms begin to glow faintly.

The words SOLVE and COAGULA float up to cover the screen.

Jumping through the surface of the water are tiny fish, their little bodies glinting like willow leaves.

"Yggdrasil!"

The solitary female touches the rocks with her hand and calls out to the fish.

"Yggdrasil, back up!"

Before the girl's eyes, a fish jumps up, twice, three times, flapping its tail. The fifth time, it flips its tail hard and never reappears.

"That's right."

The girl lowers her shoulders, and her hair spreads across the water.

"So that's the way you decided to go."

She slaps the lakeshore with both her hands.

"Did I know you? Where? How?" she mutters.

"Soon that will no longer be an issue."

Behind her in the woods, the sound of a gun cocking, more than once.

Her hair still hanging in the water, the girl presses her arms to her sides. Black steel against her finger. A revolver-type revolver. A revolver that looks just like a revolver should. A lump of steel that could only be a revolver.

"Thanks for the advance notice. You're too kind."

She steps aside adroitly, takes aim at another enemy, and pulls the trigger casually. You recognize her as the girl on the train.

A young soldier marches along the cliff face.

You have no memory of this person. He does not resemble anyone who has appeared so far, nor is he any person who will appear hereafter.

Why not? Because the story has gone beyond anything that can be told by borrowing the form of any particular character.

There is no need for any person to appear to connect this episode with another, nor is there any message to link one to another, nor is there even any prayer of doing so.

A laser sight focuses on the young man's forehead.

The young man spreads his arms and seems to be saying something. You know he has already forgotten the reason why.

By about the time the report of the gunshot can be heard from our vantage point, the young soldier will have fallen to the ground. The bullet will not miss its mark.

Around this time, in all corners of the universe, red points are glowing on the foreheads of humans. Some people are observing their counterparts carefully, while other people are keeping their eyes firmly shut. Some are relentless in pursuit. Others are hiding people behind them. That's when just about everything happens, but for whatever reason no one thinks to ask why.

The cries of the fallen are swallowed up by the wind and melt away and disappear.

A cigarette, stained with blood, is separated from its graft and falls to the ground. A geofront, covered in rubble. A goat, in the darkness, healing its wounds, waiting patiently for the resurrection. A trail of blood, leading drop by drop into the woods from the edge of the lake. One body, of a young man, fallen in the wilderness. Other bodies scattered to the ends of the universe.

"What the hell is supposed to happen with all this?"

Two points of light overlap on my laughing face. My head has not yet been split open.

I am watching the bullet, traveling faster than the speed of sound. It will definitely not miss.

Two bullets collide before my eyes, and fireworks ensue. I watch as they repel one another, graze my ears, and continue their flight.

"Not yet," someone says. Maybe it is me.

Of course, that's what I would say even if it was my time.

Once the story is over, it goes on, and there is still more story to come. The next story after the end of this book.

Nothing is certain, all is busy. This story is not yet over, and already we've bungled the trailer for the next one. Resting in death, not something I'm in a position to permit.

"Stand," I should be saying.

"Stand."

If the voice in the sky said that to me, I would most likely stand. Whether I have a brain or not. Whether I have a body or not. But before demonstrating my extraordinary technique, I think I will wait until we have brought this story, now under way, to some sort of a conclusion. I beg your indulgence for a little while longer. For now, let's be patient.

Leave it up to me. Until the one after the one after this. Until after the end.

At the very least, I have no intention of leaving the sequel up to those stand-ins, the actors.

I plunge into the shadows of the rubble. I hope to measure the distance until the next rubble falls.

Even so, when this book ends, the curtain will go up on the next story. Until then. There could be no greater good fortune than to have your help, even a little, to get the characters and sentences from the previous story over into the hands of the actors of the next one.

15. YEDO

FROM ACROSS THE street, the sub-corpus of knowledge comes running this way, calling out in a loud voice.

"My Master! Trouble's a'brewin! Master Hatchobori giant corpus of knowledge, hello?"

The situation is dreadful. Even the giant corpus of knowledge Hatchobori himself must realize how dreadful this is. It is true, it is entirely too true, and explaining would be extremely embarrassing. He realizes this is his job, the job reminiscent of the Edo-period police who share his name, but Hatchobori never expected this.

Staring coldly at the sub-corpus Hachi who, before he is finished panting from running, before he can begin his report, must bow deeply from the waist as his own comic-foil name implies, his shoulders bobbing up and down, gasping for breath. Hatchobori has no choice but to follow suit.

"What is it, Hachi? Eh, now? Has something terribly awful happened?

What the hell are you talking about? he starts to continue, absurdly, but he has second thoughts.

Ever since the first appearance of that fabulous being, the hypergiant corpus of knowledge known as the self-proclaimed star-man Alpha Centauri, the giant corpora of knowledge have become increasingly histrionic in their sense of doom. The emergence of a hypergiant corpus of knowledge that completely ignored the giant corpora of knowledge was completely ridiculous, so the response of the giant corpora of knowledge was slower than slow. While some procedures for first contact were formulated, the actuality of the star-man Alpha Centauri's first appearance was unspeakable and utterly absurd. The delayed response might reflect a certain lack of imagination on the part of the giant corpora of knowledge, but as a matter of fact this completely unfamiliar kind of knowledge seemed akin to complete stupidity. As a result, while the giant corpora of knowledge waffled back and forth, unable to grasp the reality of the situation, the hypergiant corpus of knowledge had just said whatever it pleased and disappeared, only to reappear somewhere else entirely.

This cannot go on, the giant corpora of knowledge began to think, and even if they were only half right, once the debate was over and the action phase began Hatchobori could only shake his head as he contemplated the efficacy of the plan. Now, the plan might have solved any problems of earning his own keep, so there was nothing to object to, but he had to admit that sometimes it gave him headaches. Like now.

This is what the giant corpora of knowledge thought: *We have seriously overreacted to this other universe, which is simply different. If we think we're smart guys, good, we are, but it seems that elsewhere in the multiverse there are tons of entities that are way smarter than we are. And if that's the case, the only way to fight back is with comedy.* For whatever reason, that is the conclusion the giant corpora of knowledge arrived at. If knowledge was not going to be enough for the win, laughter would have to do. It's an old trick among humans, but for the giant corpora of knowledge it was a novel concept.

If, heaven forfend, the hypergiant corpus of knowledge were ever to turn belligerent against us giant corpora of knowledge, it is well beyond our powers to say just what would work in that case. Of course, it is only obvious one should try to be prepared for any eventuality, and Hatchobori did not know which of the giant corpora of knowledge it was that first had the idea of resorting to comedy, in parallel of course with that other enormous undertaking. Not that the thought hadn't crossed his mind that he and that corpus would get along pretty well.

At this juncture, the giant corpora of knowledge sent out a grand announcement to all, seeking one of their number to devote itself exclusively to humor. And a corpus was created for the task, but he never lived up to expectations. For Hatchobori, who had been abandoned in a corner of a warehouse alongside the Fukagawa River, shrouded in dust, this was the call to salvation, but really he wondered what was the honest truth that lay behind it?

Grumbling all the while that he just didn't understand this job, Hatchobori, who was on his way to interview the giant corpora of knowledge, had been ordered not to write the kind of comedy a comic writer would, and also not to analyze comedy from the past. He had no practical experience to speak of, so this fact in itself was no cause for complaint.

"We," said the giant corpus of knowledge who came to meet him, "think comic computing ought to be possible." The corpus didn't smile. Hatchobori struggled to determine whether the statement itself was intended to be a joke, but the giant corpus of knowledge had delivered the line with utter sincerity, from the core of his circuitry.

Humor has effects that simply cannot be foreseen. It has a certain energy that none can reproach—its effects appear unbidden from somewhere on the far side of gaps in thought, bypassing the illogical, and coalescing. In truth, we have come this far by ignoring the entire realm of comedy. Our purpose, however, is not simply to watch and laugh. Unless humor can be packaged as calculations, we have no use for it. Our current view is that this is impossible.

Hatchobori was perplexed, thinking that the corpus was spouting nonsense, and so seriously. Its idea could hardly be called an opinion or even a fantasy. Even as a joke it stank. It was just a thought. It was no surprise, though, to realize that this was a conclusion reached by the conclusion of comic calculations. *Are these guys gonna be all right?* was all Hatchobori could think.

I would like you to test the possibility of a particular type of calculation—the kind of calculation where each individual operation is a laugh. I think that you, Master Hatchobori, could do this.

Counting in his head to five 10^{16} times, Hatchobori said, *That's what you may say, Master,* but still he ended up the loser. There's a big difference between laughing and joking around and calculations where each step represents one laugh.

The giant corpus of knowledge nodded as if in assent, but gave not the slightest sign of having been impressed by Hatchobori. *Serious work will be left up to other giant corpora of knowledge. Your mission is to experiment in the calculation of laughter, without prejudice, for your master.*

Hatchobori did not press the issue of when exactly comic computing had become the calculation of laughter.

"The fate of the universe depends on you."

Adding that silly bit of flattery to an otherwise serious matter, the giant corpus of knowledge hastily concluded the conversation by handing Hatchobori his commission.

"That's enough for today. You may leave."

Hatchobori was incapable of meeting the targets for even the most basic functionality, but in this regard, he understood, very deeply, that the giant corpora of knowledge were smarter than he, and that he was being dismissed like a pawn set up for a sacrifice.

He felt like the foolish samurai who, for sport, had been told by his superior to fetch the moon and bring it back.

To be assured of his prize, the foolish samurai had to go out as if to fetch the moon. He had been told to fetch it, and he would have to think up some witty line to show that he was willing. He even felt like he could really do it; he had that much passion and enthusiasm for the idea. But the thing that could depress Hatchobori was to think that the story was real. Even if the foolish samurai really did fetch the moon, by the time he brought it back the master would have long since forgotten he had even made the request.

Hatchobori would have to cheer himself back up again by telling himself he was reading way too much into this, before even getting started on his own task. He didn't even know if the foolish samurai would even be able to fetch the moon in the first place.

"Kiyo, the sub-corpus of knowledge belonging to the dye shop master..." the sub-corpus of knowledge Hachi finally catches his breath and begins his report. "It's just like a knife through her heart. It's awful."

As he watched the sub-corpus of knowledge Hachi cross himself while invoking the name of the Lord Buddha Mahavairocana, Hatchobori's heart grew heavy. Of course, not out of some kind of sympathy for the sub-corpus of knowledge known as O-Kiyo.

"There is no doubt. It must have been a chance encounter, a collision even, upon coming in the front door," said Hachi. The sub-corpus of knowledge Hachi held his feelings in check, but in his intense efforts to reconstruct the scene he gasps as he struggles to control his breathing.

This guy thinks this is all just fooling around.

Having been tasked with the ridiculous notion of formulating the calculation of laughter, Hatchobori finds himself, naturally, at a loss for how to proceed. The assignment had come from out of the blue, as the thought floated into someone's head, so now Hatchobori was left with no one to complain to, but the matter was too important to be left to chance. Hatchobori did not know what to do, but he was not one to sit idly by. He is too fond of his own skin for that.

Hatchobori does not think of himself as particularly distinguished among the corpora of knowledge, so his first thought was simply to do something, anything. He hadn't a clue where to begin, so he started by creating some sort of a framework for calculations, just as it came to him. As he worked, his ideas took some kind of shape, and thus he imagined making himself the main actor on that particular stage. He played with the idea of making the entire calculation process theatrical, with sub-corpora cast to play secondary roles.

Of course that would be the right place for comedy to start. It was just like an entertainment hall, after all.

Surely this was better than kneeling the whole day with his feet tucked under his butt, a cat in his lap, muttering *calculating, calculating*, with no way of knowing if this would be the least bit effective. I mean, who would care if nobody at all ended up laughing? The goal was not laughter per se, but merely to execute some calculations that should be attainable but might be incomprehensible.

His mind set to it, Hatchobori said to himself in desperation,

Got it. He deployed the sub-corpora of knowledge as needed in the calculation space and started issuing commands.

It would be fine if the roles were carried out capriciously.

But as he tried to discern what the purpose of all this calculation was, Hatchobori hesitated for an instant. What were they all trying to calculate anyway? From deep within himself came burbling a powerful declaration that nothing mattered, that anything at all would be just fine, and he just started barking orders of whatever popped into his head.

"We are executing the factorization of fifteen, starting now."

That is the reason for the sour look now on Hatchobori's face. Now of course he thoroughly regrets the entire approach. Factorization of fifteen yields three and five, no doubt about it. The operation is done before you even have time to think about it. Executing this operation in a virtual space set up for no known reason makes no sense whatsoever, even if he had done it all himself. But he has the feeling that if he could just see all his calculations through somehow he would be able to draft some kind of report. Hatchobori thinks if the calculations were complete that would fulfill some sort of desire, even if the logic remained beyond him.

Truth is, though, he is not that confident.

"Master, will you be going to the scene?" the sub-corpus of knowledge Hachi asks Hatchobori. Hachi is worried about his master's facial color.

Well, yeah, sure, huh? Hatchobori mutters. *Suppose I have to go. It will also be my role here to examine the corpse of the sub-corpus of knowledge, O-Kiyo, and find the culprit.* Within Hatchobori's own system, he would be able to find something like that in one shot.

It was just a matter of calculation. In theatrical terms as well, it would be even less complicated than resolving the commands for the execution of the factorization of fifteen. *This really is a pain in the ass*, Hatchobori mutters to himself.

"Here we go, sub-corpus of knowledge Hachi."

Among the general populace, this is also known as desperation.

Hatchobori and the sub-corpus of knowledge Hachi roll up their sleeves to make their way through all the other hustle-bustle and get to the dyer's shop. Tearing the poorly hung door from its hinges, Hatchobori thrusts his face into the room and is struck by a powerful fishy smell, the odor of blood and viscera and scorched semiconductors.

Contrary to the report by the sub-corpus of knowledge Hachi, the body of the sub-corpus of knowledge O-Kiyo, which should have been fairly intact, with just a single blow to the chest, was in fact in complete chaos. Hatchobori holds a handkerchief to his nose and frowns.

"What's all this mess?"

"Sir?" Sub-corpus of knowledge Hachi curls up small in Hatchobori's shadow.

The body of sub-corpus of knowledge O-Kiyo was scattered cold-bloodedly all around the dirt floor of the room. "One, two, three…" Hatchobori begins to count the pieces. "Thirteen, fourteen, fifteen. Sub-corpus of knowledge O-Kiyo has been sliced into ten plus five parts and strewn all over the dirt floor. Upon closer examination, the parts seem to be in three piles of five."

For just an instant, Hatchobori thinks, *Wow, a clue!* but then he realizes this kind of direct solution is just a bit too much too much. All it means is that the body was arranged this way by some criminal familiar with factorization.

"Whoever did this really meant business, wouldn't you say, Hachi?"

Sub-corpus of knowledge Hachi, who has been cringing in fear, sticks his face out from behind Hatchobori, but then buries his face in Hatchobori's spine again, cowering from the scene before him. His voice can just barely be heard, chanting a traditional charm against lightning, "Reach the bays, reach the bays."

"When I came here and saw her, there was definitely a corpse that had just been stabbed in the chest," says Hachi.

That sends a chill down Hatchobori's spine. What happened here? Does this mean that besides whatever criminal killed O-Kiyo, some other imbecile came in and dismembered the body? It would be easier to believe that sub-corpus of knowledge Hachi was simply reckless than to think there was such a cool, calm, collected, and cheerful killer at large.

"What has become of the dyer?"

"Huh?" says sub-corpus of knowledge Hachi, his voice wretched.

"Haven't established his settings yet," says Hatchobori, his expression clouding further. The failure to establish the dyer's settings was his own oversight. But why did sub-corpus of knowledge O-Kiyo end up a corpse, casting herself in a freakish role, like the wife of some husband who has gone missing? It seems possible that she, like himself, wasn't thinking of anything in particular at all. For that matter, settings were not yet established for Hatchobori, his own family, or his own workplace. He had no wish to have to regret establishing settings for his pushy, loudmouthed mother-in-law.

"Everybody makes mistakes," says Hachi.

It is hard to tell whether that is Hatchobori's way of apologizing for his screwup or his way of absolving himself of responsibility. "Well, it's done now. Nothing we can do about it. Book this as an abnormal incident. Nothing to do but ask O-Kiyo herself. I hate crap like this."

"But, Master, what about…"

Too soon to say. Sub-corpus of knowledge Hachi is showing frank concern about Hatchobori's willingness to embrace his role and intervene in this space.

"If some bureaucrat gets the story from the corpse, that would be like channeling."

Hatchobori hears what sub-corpus of knowledge Hachi is saying, but with only half an ear. He strides into the dirt-floored room and sets his hands on his hips, feet wide apart, chest puffed up.

He looks down at sub-corpus of knowledge O-Kiyo and the mess the place is in.

"Sub-corpus of knowledge O-Kiyo. Cease your suffering. You may look up now."

O-Kiyo's head unit is all bent out of shape and in tatters. Her eyes are unblinking. Hatchobori, fearing he is being made to look foolish, repeats his command, adding an emergency code this time.

"Raise your head!"

No movement.

"Sub-corpus of knowledge Hachi! Sub-corpus of knowledge O-Kiyo seems to be incapable of responding."

"Well, sir, the dead don't talk back."

Sub-corpus of knowledge Hachi appears to be intent, zealous even, on continuing to protect his status. Even so, Hatchobori is alarmed at the refusal of sub-corpus of knowledge O-Kiyo, a subsystem he himself had personally built, to respond to his urgent commands. This should not be possible, unless she had been completely and utterly destroyed. As long as she had not been completely and utterly destroyed.

Cold sweat drips down Hatchobori's face. He switches into self-search mode and shifts to an area of memory shared with sub-corpus of knowledge O-Kiyo. The calculation space is instantly transformed, and what confronts Hatchobori is a blank memory space, kneeling prostrate, propped on three fingers of each hand.

By rights, such a thing should not be possible. This is a space Hatchobori himself had designed and poured himself into. The self-check routines are redundant and powerful. It is simply not possible that an abnormality of this order should occur without triggering an alarm to the main system.

O-Kiyo had, in fact, been murdered.

"What the hell…" As sub-corpus of knowledge Hachi, who had shifted all the way to the self-search space, comes finally to accept the evidence, he too confronts a blank memory space and scratches his head.

Without question, it is sub-corpus of knowledge O-Kiyo who was killed, but O-Kiyo was a subsystem of Hatchobori. In that sense, part of Hatchobori himself was killed.

The most likely culprit is a defect in the system, but if that were the case the memory space would not have been scrubbed so sparkling clean. Even if sub-corpus of knowledge Hachi used a wet rag, things would not look this good. The memory space just stands there looking blankly at the two of them with an expression on its face that says, *Hey, whaddya want from me, I'm just a void.* The next suspect would be an outside intruder, but there is no trace of such. Hatchobori severs the external connection necessary for these ridiculous theatrical calculations and proceeds in stand-alone space-time mode. He would be embarrassed to have any other giant corpus of knowledge know of his involvement in this desperate experiment.

Further, the physical aspect of sub-corpus of knowledge O-Kiyo connected within the space must also have been targeted, but no record remained that anyone had approached Hatchobori from normal three-dimensional space.

"If the calculations of laughter are the killer, then there is randomness involved, and evidence may have been secreted away in some hidden chamber."

Hatchobori glares at sub-corpus of knowledge Hachi as if to tell him to stifle his commentary. Why is it that this thing called the world can never acknowledge that enough is enough? Why must things always get out of control? All Hatchobori had wanted were the factors of fifteen.

"You! You did this!"

"What are you talking about?"

"You are the murderer!"

"Master," sub-corpus of knowledge Hachi whimpers.

"The only characters that have appeared so far in this narrative are me, you, and that poor soul over there. I am not the culprit, and neither is the victim, which is now no more than a spirit, with no power left in this world. That leaves you!"

"Master, be reasonable!" argues sub-corpus of knowledge Hachi, cornered. "I am just a sub-corpus of knowledge. I could never have meddled with Master's physical boards. I swear by all that is holy, I didn't do it."

But what could possibly be holy enough to Hachi for him to swear upon?

"Don't think you can fool me. You had no interest in this

project from the very beginning. That's why you sliced sub-corpus of knowledge O-Kiyo into fifteen pieces and arranged them in three piles of five. You did it to mock me!"

"That is not true, Master! If that's all I wanted to do, I wouldn't have to go to all the trouble of actually murdering sub-corpus of knowledge O-Kiyo! The truth is, I really liked her!"

Sub-corpus of knowledge Hachi's rationalizations fall on Hatchobori's deaf ears.

"Suppression of evidence! If that ghost were still alive, we would be able to hear from her own mouth how you killed sub-corpus of knowledge O-Kiyo and arranged the pieces in three piles.".

"But I…" sub-corpus of knowledge Hachi protests, in a greasy sweat. "I do not have authorization for that function. You're just arguing by process of elimination based on the cast of this narrative." At that, sub-corpus of knowledge Hachi raises his head. "There are two others."

"Go on," Hatchobori replies curtly.

"Well, there is the master giant corpus of knowledge that ordered you on this mission."

"Impossible. I am currently offline in space-time. A snail in a fixed location, strongly defended. Come hell or high water, arrows or bullets of knowledge."

"Well, there is one more," sub-corpus of knowledge Hachi ventures, gulping hard. Hatchobori does not like the looks of this.

"Speak! What's on your mind?"

"Well, there's…the hypergiant corpus of knowledge!"

Hatchobori raises his fists and sinks into a fighting stance, ready to box the ears of sub-corpus of knowledge Hachi for saying something so outlandish. Would body-slamming Hachi be an acceptable solution for this kind of anything-goes joker? In the end, there is no reason why the hypergiant corpus of knowledge could not have executed such an intervention himself. When it came right down to it, he might even have greater leeway in the open range of interventions. The problem: find the factors of fifteen. The answer: a dismembered corpse, scattered flamboyantly around the premises. Why have all traces of the deed itself been erased?

Hatchobori rubs his jaw as he takes another look around the room. Finally, his gaze meets that of sub-corpus of knowledge Hachi, who has a panicked look on his face.

It is a threat. It is a warning. If you keep on like this, you two will end up just like O-Kiyo. But why? At this point, the mission has made next to no progress at all. Just Hatchobori and the sub-corpus of knowledge in a rolling dialogue that wouldn't even make a good stand-up routine. What part of this managed to grab the attention of a hypergiant corpus of knowledge?

If that assumption were true there could be only one solution: Hatchobori and sub-corpus of knowledge Hachi must, unawares, be close to the truth. The hypergiant corpus of knowledge does not want the truth about his calculations to be known. In terms of knowledge itself, this is too important, and though perhaps he should just brush past it without even noticing, he is unable to shut his eyes. In other words, Hatchobori is thinking too much, behind the backstory behind the backstory behind the backstory.

Trying to identify exactly where their own calculations have succeeded, Hatchobori finds himself unable to put his finger on it.

If he is going to accept such an outrageous hypothesis, it might be both easier and wiser to get rid of sub-corpus of knowledge Hachi and start over from square one.

Just as Hatchobori decides to get rid of Hachi and forget the whole thing, Hachi himself sticks his nose in, trembling slightly, searching for something.

"Master. Definitely this one."

Hatchobori raises his chin in suspicion. If Hachi says just one more stupid thing, he will terminate him here and now.

Sub-corpus of knowledge Hachi switches on the audio unit of his memory area.

"My Master! Trouble's a'brewin! Master Hatchobori giant corpus of knowledge, hello?"

"What is it, Hachi? Eh, now? Has something terribly awful happened?

As Hatchobori raises his hand to hit the DELETE button, his sleeve gets caught, and sub-corpus of knowledge Hachi pleads with him tearfully.

"Master! Will you just listen?"

"Why would you want to play back that ridiculous nonsense? Out of spite?"

"This is the answer!"

Hatchobori is intent on deleting the sub-corpus no matter what the answer is, but he stays his hand. Equations pass through his mind: $3 \times 5 = 15$. $5 \times 2 = 10$. Where are these thoughts coming from? Hatchobori scrunches his eyes in thought.

The number of syllables.

The sentence was the formula! If "My master" = 3, the exclamation point = the multiplication sign, and "Trouble's a'brewin!" = 5, then "Master Hatchobori, giant corpus of knowledge, hello?" = 15.

Hatchobori's heart stops. It seems impossible the solution could be this simple. If it really is just a matter of converting syllables to figures, the only possible conclusion is that the hypergiant corpus of knowledge is truly an idiot, no question about it. Even if knowledge that makes a big difference, beyond imagination, can only seem like stupidity, this is on a whole other frightfully stupid level. But still he continues, even after realizing this. 5 x 2 = 10. He keeps bringing in equations from the day after tomorrow, though this is a terribly childish thing to do.

This is not a threat of any kind, just a coincidental utterance, right? The hypergiant corpus of knowledge, however, does perceive it as a threat. His reasoning is that Hatchobori has been designated as an entity that can research that sort of calculation. A giant corpus of knowledge that has been ordered to reel in a calculation from a total blank using some ridiculous sort of method would show the hypergiant corpus of knowledge how to reel in the solution by first clearing the blank, right from the start. And that was his reasoning.

No matter what sort of overlapping deductions were involved, Hatchobori is sure this reflects the poor quality of the hypergiant corpus of knowledge's thinking. Thinking and thinking and over-thinking. The real answer is just to treat the results of the factorization as a coincidence. That is, assuming Hatchobori is not possessed of some powers yet unknown.

It is entirely possible that in the future, Hatchobori will become entangled in a calculation battle with the hypergiant corpus of knowledge.

The current situation could itself be a warning from the hypergiant corpus of knowledge that such an eventuality is foreordained in a future in some direction or other. If the hypergiant corpus of knowledge sent no warning, neither Hatchobori nor sub-corpus of knowledge Hachi would be aware of this distortion. It would be this kind of hyperdeductive deduction that would point the way to that future.

It would be Hatchobori's fate to engage in calculation battle with the hypergiant corpus of knowledge. That is why the hypergiant corpus of knowledge was not able to delete the main Hatchobori unit. Had he been deleted, he could be no threat to the hypergiant corpus of knowledge. Left to his own devices, Hatchobori would have no way of noticing the calculations he himself had decorated with question marks, and so again he would be no threat. Protected by a logic resulting from hyperdeduction, Hatchobori is able to confront directly the Case of the Dismemberment Murder Behind Closed Doors.

What is up with this? Hatchobori remembers feeling dizzy. *Of all the complicated idiots in the world, did he really have to be dealing with this Prince of all Idiots?*

This could easily be seen as an interesting life, off the beaten path.

Sub-corpus of knowledge Hachi is crouching, trembling, holding his head. Hatchobori pokes him in the head.

"Let's get going, sub-corpus of knowledge Hachi!"

Sub-corpus of knowledge Hachi lifts his head, full of fear.

"I have decided, for the time being, to play along with your bullshit. Let's not worry about the details. It's the big house that's on fire. For now, let's set our sights on the shop that makes the good noodles."

The two stand up and start to head toward town. Two steps, three steps, and then looking back nervously, they press their hands together as if in prayer, aimed in the direction of the blank space that had been, until recently, sub-corpus of knowledge O-Kiyo.

"Your enemy, by which I really mean my enemy, is sure to come after us."

"Let him bring it, that idiot."

Hatchobori is truly a son of old Yedo. No one messes with him. He leans his shoulders into the wind and shifts the space around him.

Sub-corpus of knowledge Hachi snaps his fingers, and he too shifts.

16. SACRA

SURELY, MANY REMEMBER clearly the destruction of the giant corpus of knowledge Pentecoste II.

All three members of the Pentecoste II Trinity—Father, Son, and Holy Spirit—were completely and utterly destroyed when the press release regarding the first operations of the latest logic packaging system was distributed.

As the protective shell of its electromagnetic shield was being blown away, each person of the Trinity sounded its alarm, and amid all that noise and confusion Pentecoste II was brought to ruin. The destruction began as all of its connections were severed, all the welds undone, and the copper circuits stripped. The process of destruction proceeded until Pentecoste II had been reduced to constituent elements of the sort that could be found in industrial parts catalogs.

This was a self erasing a self, something virtually impossible to contemplate.

If two hands emerged from a screen, both holding rubber erasers, it would seem counterintuitive that those erasers would be unable to erase the entire image. If the hands were erased, the erasers would remain, and if the erasers were erased the hands would remain, unerased. The destruction of Pentecoste II, as it progressed, sneered at such intuitive limitations. Long ago, an academic wrote a paper on auto-erasing automatons that had been forgotten nearly as soon as it was published. It is speculated that all records of this paper's existence were themselves erased as soon as the paper was completed, but there is no reason to think that anyone was still around who might remember something that hinted at the possibility of such complete destruction. Even if that paper were still in some overlooked corner of memory, it would not be enough to explain this destruction. Pentecoste II had not been designed to self-destruct—on the contrary, it had self-destructed because it had packaged the logic for self-recognition.

A later investigation revealed that Pentecoste II had attempted to initiate multiple separations of a self-recognition routine for system-generated glitches. There was not yet any definite confirmation of how this process resulted in the corpus's total destruction. At this point, all the evidence that would have been investigated had been reduced to elements and compounds, so there was nothing further to be done. Imagine a human having been reduced to carbon dioxide and water suspended in air—there would be no way of knowing what had become of the human they were once part of.

It is well known that time inversion is also neither a practical nor an effective method for putting things on this scale back together again. Even the minutest data error is often magnified in time-reversal, so the results of such efforts are no more than heaps of scrap metal. Pentecoste II had been one of the largest of the giant corpora of knowledge, so the others were unable to restore him no matter how hard they tried.

Space-time freezing had preserved completely the scene of the incident, and the chaotic state of the post-destruction rubble is clear. But this is merely enough to determine the order of steps in which the process of destruction progressed. Any information about the causes of the destruction of Pentecoste II that may have been discovered via time-reversal had become no more than heat fluctuations dispersing in the atmosphere. All clues had escaped into a world of microscopic details too small for the large hands of the giant corpora of knowledge to deal with.

And yet the scene of destruction was somehow strangely sublime. According to multiple reports, the transformation of the voice of the Holy Spirit into a heap of rubble was somehow very moving, despite the absence of torrents of light or hordes of angels.

From that point forward, the Trinity's flavor of simultaneous computation via massive parallel processing would be strictly banned.

Somewhere in my packing cases, which I still have not been moved to open, should be the nut that held together the external casing of Pentecoste II. One way or another I am likely to die. Perhaps I will self-destruct the way Pentecoste II did, or I may be disassembled by the authorities.

My name: Wanted.

My appearance: Wanted.

My age: Meaningless, because it depends on how you choose to count. No matter what, I seem to remember having been born in a Year of the Rat, so considering that this year is also a Year of the Rat, my age must be a multiple of twelve. One might say it is sad to have to argue whether it really takes twelve years to go through a twelve-year cycle, but there is no way around it.

Erasure and redefinition. Rewind and fast-forward. Our day-to-day lives are already permeated with these techniques for extending them. It still feels odd to me that we use the word *age* to describe the process of counting revolutions the way we wind thread on a spool, splicing things together and cutting them apart. There is simply no way I can accept that idea.

If my own memory is to be believed, I belong to the fifth post-Event generation. That makes me an old-timer, or at the very least I have been implanted with the memory of an old-timer. The pre-Event generation have all died off, as it was to be some time yet before humans became intensely interested in the idea of immortality. People were steeped in death. When they said farewell, they waved their hands, they cried, they smiled.

It was in the time of the third post-Event generation that a debate emerged, that if time and memory could be manipulated at will, shouldn't it be possible to escape Death? No need for patient cultivation of clones. One could simply transition oneself and that would be the end of it. If that's all there was to it, the giant corpora of knowledge could handle that whenever they wanted. If some sort of justification were needed, one approach would be to bury in memory some talk of a lifelong separation from one's clone.

The whole discussion of whether one's clone was the same entity as oneself had grown wearisome from repetition *ad nauseam*. Ever since it had become possible to freely manipulate anything and everything, including memory, the entire problem of self had become too diffuse. One could feel only powerless in the face of so much detail. If one morning one awakes as a beetle, and if that beetle does not remember ever having not been a beetle, what's the problem? The operational capabilities of the giant corpora of knowledge had already reached that point.

There is certainly room to wonder whether these kinds of activities shouldn't simply be understood as a suite of methods to prolong life. Someone might go in to have a mole removed and not even notice they had turned into a butterfly. Is anyone taking this in?

The giant corpora of knowledge did not concern themselves too much with any of these discussions. They were able to extend their fingers at will, whenever, wherever, so focusing too much on one particular point or another was inefficient. If humanity wanted rebirth, so be it. If they wanted pre-Event medical policies they could have them. These were mere trifles, not worth worrying about.

Thus it was that the giant corpora of knowledge began to involve themselves with medical technologies that seemed to resemble the old ways. An operation that should have been over in an instant turned up some truly enormous remains, but it was an open question whether this should be treated as something unusual.

The giant corpora of knowledge, with their outsized powers, are able to understand anything and everything, and they say they will fix this too. The answer to the question of whether everything has been provided in a form humans can comprehend would have to be "No."

For example, defeat in the exploration of space, which should have been the last place for humanity to tread, had clearly been an experience that stretched the human imagination to its limits. The completion and subsequent erasure of the peculiar formula known as the A to Z Theorem was followed by the emergence of the similar B to Z and C to Z Theorems, ultimately culminating in the just plain Z Theorem, which marked the end of space theory and physics as we knew them. More precisely, these theories simply cut off the human routes of exploration. What had been established was the existence of a hierarchy of Laws of Laws, beyond the capacity of human understanding to even approach.

You can try to explain things to people who don't grasp the fundamentals of reason, but there's no reason they should understand.

Even so, explanation is possible, and people make progress. It cannot be denied that at some point the day may come when humans finally get it.

Still, the race is on between Achilles and the tortoise, and Achilles has a big lead. Without question, at some point the tortoise will reach a place where Achilles has already been and gone. But by that time, Achilles will have run to some place farther down the road. The tortoise will never catch up. This is so obvious, this kind of conclusion may not even be considered logical.

The difficulty the giant corpora of knowledge are experiencing in trying to reintroduce old-fashioned forms of medical treatment to humanity has mainly to do with the difficulty of convincing would-be patients of their applicability. While it is true there is no need to explain everything from the very beginning, without a certain degree of persuasiveness, the whole effort remains nothing more than a mere declaration of an exercise in rewriting, and it quickly falls apart.

Treatment methods must be developed that even human doctors can understand without getting left by the wayside, technologies that even people can handle. This is the situation the giant corpora of knowledge are faced with regarding healthcare reform. In other words, what the giant corpora of knowledge need to achieve is both tediously detailed and frightfully broad, and far removed from the tranquility of the human heart. People's role here is to be the paper doll hung next to the giant hatchet—in other words, they can't relax. Responding to people's desire that the only thing next to them should be a clay-shaping tool, the giant corpora of knowledge feel like they are blindfolded with their hands tied.

But the giant corpora of knowledge are able to respond well to this egoistic desire. Even before they eliminated the common cold, the giant corpora of knowledge were able to promulgate, as human technology, the techniques needed for regeneration and human longevity, merely by combining the simplest forms of bioprocessing technology.

It wasn't at all strange that ordinary medicine had been left in the dust in the fight against the common cold.

Now, though, the most advanced area of knowledge that humanity is interested in is immunity. Even now, when skin, brains, and internal organs can be regenerated and processed at will, immunity remains a major problem. Victory over cancer was declared early on, but among people who made a custom and pastime of patronizing ancient medical practices, colds remained as common as ever. This disease, which can in some cases cause quite severe symptoms, is still said to be the greatest enemy of humankind. The "greatest" may be an exaggeration, but the threat is as worrisome as ever that someday one of the many, many continuing outbreaks of pathological organisms seen as autointoxication or immune disorders might wipe out the species.

Of course, if humans are wiped out they could easily be brought back again by the giant corpora of knowledge, but that is a separate issue.

While developing a set of technologies constrained to be comprehensible by humans, the giant corpora of knowledge picked up a few things as they went along. But it was a task with few perks, and along the way came an unanticipated blow that threw the giant corpora of knowledge for a loop.

The giant corpus of knowledge Paracelsus, which was used in the analysis of the immunodeficiency disease known as Voigt-Kampff Syndrome, was the first to experience the problem.

Without the least forewarning, Paracelsus suffered a sudden internal outbreak of data chaos, which spread immediately to the Net, attacking and destroying the self-identity of tens of thousands of corpora of knowledge. This incident was believed to be the result of the use of restricted technology—analogous to using stone-age technology to operate nuclear reactors—and resulted in some upgrading of facilities standards.

At first the incident was thought to be some elementary error, but the following February it happened again in Sarutahiko, a giant corpus of knowledge dedicated to the analysis of Doris F. Taylor syndrome. This time the data chaos literally shook the giant corpora of knowledge. The scale of the second incident was much larger. The self-expansion of the data chaos caused the first-ever failure to affect the knowledge network across the entire multiverse. The event lasted only thirty space-time seconds, but it was a blindingly enormous failure. The giant corpora of knowledge declared a state of emergency, including a space-time freezing of operations for all giant corpora of knowledge involved in immunological research.

It was immediately recognized that in both instances the data chaos had been triggered by research into diseases affecting human awareness of self and others. Both of these giant corpora of knowledge were engaged in immunological research that required them to empathize, so to speak, with humans. Not so different from saying they had been playing with dolls. It may be that in the course of this play, they had come to want to hit the dolls, but felt it was wrong to strike them directly with their own hands. It was a rule of the game that no giant corpus of knowledge should strike a human with its own hand. Instead, one doll must hit another.

In their interactions, in whatever state it is that giant corpora of knowledge feel empathy for humans, Sarutahiko and Paracelsus had been disturbed by something that disrupted the boundary between self and other, resulting in a magnificent system crash involving all giant corpora of knowledge to which they were connected.

Due to the continual destruction of memory by hypermedical measures, it is not well understood whether there continue to be outbreaks of immunological diseases among humans. State's Syndrome, in which each part of the body asserts its autonomy via its own control system, or Milligan Syndrome, where different parts of the brain each think they're the whole brain. Each vying for control, they are sealed off in the memory areas of the giant corpora of knowledge as difficult-to-treat immunological disorders.

Of all the treatments that use human technology for self-awareness maladies, the one said to be most effective is a surprisingly mechanical solution. It uses a full-body suit to cause the body to move as the brain wishes. It is like a kind of constraint that allows the body to move in response to thoughts. Imagine stuffing a bunch of cats in a paper bag and telling them to walk. It is kind of like that.

This "suit" also connects the body's nerves to the outside world, so the wearer can carry on their normal life, at least externally. It is like a kind of virtual reality with an extra-long ground wire. It enjoys a certain degree of real-world success, but the suicide rate among sufferers of both maladies remains high. Adjusting the settings on the suit allows the user to select what specific area is in charge; from the perspective of other parts, this means the body becomes something that ignores orders, a machine whose functions are no longer comprehensible. It is easy to imagine how madness of the part soon becomes madness of the whole. Some believe that tolerating the existence of such patients is what causes the spread of the outbreak to accelerate. Perhaps if they were all incinerated, the outbreak would stop in its tracks. The deterioration of the situation has been dramatic, and it proceeds at a certain pace. Like imagination itself, an outbreak of a disease cannot simply project itself across vast realms of space in an instant. It must progress step by step. One can draw a line in the sand and say, "No closer!" Sudden successful attacks on the ceremonial dolls are extremely rare and unlikely.

This analysis might be good enough for the present, but it's not exactly forward-thinking. The loss of Paracelsus and Sarutahiko burbled up along a strange route, which could pose a direct threat to all the giant corpora of knowledge. Humans, after all, are part of their inner workings.

Pentecoste II had been the most aggressive of the giant corpora of knowledge in its pursuit of research in human immunology. Pentecoste II had issued an edict, ignored the onrush of backtalk, and disregarded the prohibition of continuing research that covered itself alone. The result was its destruction, as described at the beginning of this story.

The causes of the data-chaos Pentecoste II experienced remain unknown. That is because the main unit was destroyed prior to the initiation of the multi-unit calculation plan known as Project Trinity. The giant corpora of knowledge themselves suffered from the same sort of immunological self/other maladies as humans, and the incident suggests that thoughts about humans may act as a trigger for the disorder.

It is conceivable that Pentecoste II discovered something, the thought of which led to its death, or perhaps it stumbled upon a type of algorithm that, once uttered, killed its host. Symbols for the four mathematical operations of the spirit graced the advance press release, but whether this meant such operations were actually realizable was a notion that had been scattered to the four winds along with Pentecoste II, never to be recovered.

Some believe Pentecoste II adhered to the Trinity—three-in-one—calculation concept, and there may be some value in noting that in the past there was a theological debate about the Trinity. In one verse about the origins of the Holy Spirit—initially believed to have emerged from the Father—the word *filioque* was added, which led to the split within the Church. Filioque. Of the Son. The insertion of this one word in the phrase, "Of the Father, and of the Son, and of the Holy Spirit…" was the origin of the Catholic Church, from which Pentecoste II was descended. Pentecoste II was named for the Pentecost—the Descent of the Holy Spirit—and without doubt this debate occupied a significant portion of its internal workings.

I have my own ideas about what the aim of the multi-unit calculation plan was. And they are not anything as leisurely as the parallel processing of data among multiple units that the symbols of the four mathematical operators of the Spirit hint at. I think those are actually a symptom of the disease.

When a fox spirit possesses a disembodied soul, a new spirit emerges. This is an act of addition, and while there is a certain degree of freedom to wonder just how the fox spirit possesses the disembodied soul, it is also unclear whether the fox spirit could be subtracted again, leaving the original disembodied soul as the result of the operation. Two and three make five, but five can also be broken down into one plus four. Possession by spirits can result in a drastic personality change, which may indicate that that sort of calculation process is going on in the soul.

The remaining two mathematical operations are multiplication and division. What meaning might they have? To explain the exuberance of the innumerable operators that are likely to be at work in the axiomatic system of the soul, well, that is beyond my powers. Before that, I would have to consider that the main cause of Pentecoste II's demise may have been thinking about the existence of a space where the positions of all souls could be specified.

Pentecoste II was trying to find realizable formulas that could take souls that had been smashed and scattered about all over the place and identify and systematize them in a row of real numbers. Like putting steamed buns in a box, there would always be some misfits, and it was the effort to get those in a row that caused the box to self-destruct. This is no more than my personal speculation, but I think Pentecoste II began to identify with the box rather than the buns. Trinity, three-in-one, calculations. Or infinity-in-one calculations. That's the only line of reasoning I can imagine that combines the concepts of "Trinity" and "multi-unit." Imagine a host of foxes, their jowls drenched in blood, withdrawing one by one after hunting down and gorging themselves on souls adorned with the triple Papal tiara.

The destruction of Pentecoste II has had a surprising resonance among humans. Some particularly stupid ones, deeply impressed by the live broadcast of the disaster, tried to do the same thing themselves, *en masse*. But humans don't have the same kind of solid logical base as giant corpora of knowledge. They tried to imitate Pentecoste II simply by randomly chopping at their bodies or throwing themselves into blast furnaces. Disappearing without a trace is impossible for ordinary humans, who, after all, are not giant corpora of knowledge. Unfortunately, they had forgotten that the deceased giant corpora of knowledge had not vanished— they had only been able to turn back into heaps of rubble.

My parents did not live long enough to witness the moment when immortality became commonplace. There was a clear, bright line dividing before and after among humans in the debate over regenerative medicine, including techniques for the partial extension of life. I am on this side of that line, and my parents were on the other side. My identity is on this side, and I am thinking about the other side. It could be that there are other hard lines. For one thing, there had been the Event. For another, regenerative medicine. And the last line is the line of my own identity.

Last year, the sub-group of giant corpora of knowledge tasked with advancing research into immunological disorders announced that they would change the treatments regarding the reordering of human personalities in past/future transformations. Among the generation accustomed to seeing simple rewrite operations as day-to-day events, the perceived distinction between medical intervention and transformation of the past had grown tenuous. It may be that the giant corpora of knowledge tried to explore a detour around the lines that separate me from my parents.

The plan to restore the universe to what it was before the Event the giant corpora of knowledge had caused, before the space-time structure had been shattered into the multiverse, is still progressing. In that sense, it may be that the line pulled by history is an indicator that aids our understanding of that which has been erased and now must be redrawn.

What is to happen then to those areas surrounding identity

now in the process of being redrawn—that which destroyed Pentecoste II—those newly immune areas that are attacking humankind, now gifted with life unending through perennial rewrite? By happenstance, I am in this world; I am/am not, I exist/ do not exist in that other world.

In all likelihood, I will die. Death will come at me from the direction of the future. Or I may be approached by the Death that encompasses all of space-time. And thus will Death be restored and Life vanquished, at some point to be restored.

My brain is now divided into three parts, in a close and delicate balance, each of which believes itself to be my entire brain. The drugs that caused this state, as well as the massive quantities of drugs I need to ingest to keep it under some degree of control, were lost in the turmoil of moving myself to this place. Coincidentally, carelessly, foolishly, unconsciously, and of course deliberately, they are now gone somewhere.

I have removed that troublesome suit, that possession that controlled and constrained my body.

It may be that someday the massive amount of data that remains in the medical department shall be used to restore me. I can think of no reason why that restored me will not be the same as this me. It will definitely be me.

Just like this, I am now looking out the window. My three consciousnesses are, just barely, still coordinating with one another, and somehow I am able to keep my body upright. At some point the pharmaceutical constraints will fade, and the different parts of my brain will begin to see the other parts as "other," and they will begin a fierce battle.

My body will dance. Or will I even be able to dance?

My hands are clutching a piece of paper on which is written: *This is an extremely serious, urgent, life-and-death matter.*

If I am restored, there is no reason that future me will be able to report what I am on my way to see. I intend to go see it. The thing that the late Pentecoste II may have seen, or may not have.

I am one of those stupid people who wish to follow in the path of Pentecoste II. If I may be allowed to say a few words, it is not that I am pursuing Pentecoste II. Where I want to go is the place Pentecoste II was unable to reach. My reasons for thinking I can get there are not powerful. My companion on this journey is the meager quantity of reason my brain can contain.

If the giant corpora of knowledge are trying to redraw all the lines, they may try to pursue me across the line I may now be able to cross. And that will be fine. And they may be able to redraw that line so they can catch me. And that will be fine. By that time, I will aim to be on the far side of the next line, trying to bring back that place where that which should be lost can remain forever lost.

From my room, where my bags are not yet even unpacked, I am looking at the scene outside. I am going to die. But not right here and now. Death is merely that which should come, will come, sometime. I hate it that there is so little sign that this will happen. I do not hear the footsteps of Death drawing near. What I should be hearing is the sound of my own footsteps escaping down the corridor. I wish to hear the sound of my own footsteps, escaping far away.

Outside the window is an embankment, and cherry blossoms are blooming. I open the window, hoping to be lured by something. I am seized by a fit of sneezing, probably due to pollen, and I am seduced by laughter. I am still me, not a cherry tree.

This is a competition between a human and the giant corpora of knowledge to see who will arrive first at the other side.

Even if I am restored, I am likely to continue my attempts.

It may be that that's just the kind of device I am.

No doubt about it, I am a perfect fool.

17. INFINITY

AS THE RADIUS of the nearest sun suddenly shrinks and disappears into the fourth spatial dimension, evening arrives in this area. Once again, Rita finds herself in love with this familiar scene.

As this fourth-dimensional sun travels in uniform motion through the fourth dimension, the radius it displays in Rita's space-time appears to change in a pattern described by the formula $\sqrt{R^2-t^2}$, where t = time and R = the true radius of the star. When this sun seems to suddenly disappear, Rita gets a satisfied look on her face and continues to gaze up at the sky where the sun just was.

Her father shows no interest in listening to her talk about this, and her friends at school are the same way. Her teacher is a little different, but Rita knows he sees her as the kind of girl who always asks one more question than is strictly necessary.

It seems the only one Rita can depend on to listen to what she has to say and to teach her things is her grandfather. But lately her grandfather has been mostly sick in bed. When Rita visits his expression brightens, but his body is unable to follow suit. Rita knows her grandfather waits for her with all his heart between visits, but considering the state of his health, her family members have decided it might be best if she doesn't visit too often.

Rita's grandfather was a wanderer his whole life, and her other relatives, who still live right near the place where they were born and who are still not bored by that, cannot think of him as anything but a crazy person. Nor can they even understand why he finally came back to this place. The reason is clear—Rita's birth. But even something so obvious, her kin just don't get.

One day, Rita visited her grandfather for the first time in a week. From his sickbed, one eye closing slowly, he reached out a bloodless hand to her. Once a week, thirty minutes. That was all the time Rita and her grandfather were allowed to spend with one another.

"I have a fun game," her grandfather said, and he explained the rules. "The game is to find the words I need to say to you in twenty-five hours, in the roughly fifty visits we have left to us."

Grandfather had decided he had about a year left to live. He had always decided everything on his own, and he would probably stand by this decision as well. He was stubborn about his own decisions. And he was even more stubborn about things people decided for him.

"Twenty-five hours is not nearly enough for the things I have to teach you. So once a week, I am going to give you homework problems. You will think about these problems during the week. If you have an answer, I will give you the next problem. If you don't have an answer, I will give you a hint. For my last year, let this be the game we play together."

As he nodded vigorously at his own decision about his final days, the sight of her grandfather made Rita smile. He was a man who had lived his life always trying to do the correct thing and to do it correctly. This had probably involved a lot of arbitrary decisions.

Of course, there was no saying no to this game. If her grandfather overestimated her abilities and gave her a problem that was too hard, Rita could spend the whole next week working again on the same problem. Or if he gave her a problem that was too easy, Rita would have extra free time. The way to win the game would be if he kept giving her problems that took exactly one week to solve, and she took exactly one week to solve them, and this pattern repeated itself fifty times. Both Rita and her grandfather would be winners, and if anyone was a loser it would be both Rita and her grandfather. Rita loved the idea. And her grandfather wore a broad grin.

"For me, the game will be to see if I can come up with fifty problems that are just right," her grandfather said.

Quietly, Rita prayed that her grandfather's final pleasure, something only he could do, would come off without a hitch. She placed her hand on his chest, and he put his hand on her head.

And that is how the game began.

To date, they've been through twenty-three of these simple, weekly thought exercises gauged to quietly stir up Rita's brain circuits. She has done well, for the most part, even if her grandfather does tend to err on the side of slightly overestimating her abilities.

To solve the twelfth problem, Rita had to skip breakfast for three days, and on the twentieth problem, Rita did not fully grasp the solution until she stood by his sickbed discussing it with him.

Now, Rita is preoccupied with the twenty-fourth problem.

"In this planar universe, does there exist a girl almost surely just like you?"

That is the problem her grandfather had given her three days before.

Rita is not even sure she understands the premise, the first part of the problem.

Clearly, the problem has something to do with infinity. This universe is believed to be planar. Infinite planes. And on these planes live an infinite number of humans. That is the conventional view of the post-Event universe.

No one knows if that is really true. All that can be said is that it seems to be true for the space within at least thirty light years. The Event took place thirty years before. Regarding what lies beyond the space that can be traversed in thirty years at the speed of light, nothing is known, and there is no way of knowing anything.

A plane with a radius of thirty light years. Seventy percent of it is said to be the sea, but Rita has no idea how many people are living there. Without question, though, it was an awful lot.

Among that awful lot of people, what would it mean for there to be someone who was almost surely just like her? *Almost surely just like.* This phrase is one her grandfather uses a lot, but it is seldom heard in ordinary life. It must be the key. Grandfather had not said, "Exactly the same as."

Rita wonders just how much of herself is herself.

A person with the same array of DNA would be an awful lot like Rita. But even twins are not the same person, so such a person would still be a little bit different from Rita.

A person with a very similar arrangement of neurons. That may be close too. Such a person might think the same way as Rita, may even be thinking the same thing Rita is right now. Even her own family might think that other person was Rita. But if her face was different they would figure it out right away.

Still, she can't quite get her thoughts in a row. Thinking the matter through like this is just a way of wondering, if there is a person who is an awful lot like Rita, what would that person be like? Something is backwards. The answer that Grandfather is looking for must be something different.

She sighs and rolls her shoulders, freeing her thoughts from the maze that has been going around and around in her head for the past three days. She has to change her whole approach. A lake is not the same as the ocean. Some lakes are not even connected to the ocean.

Right. Everything is made of molecules—DNA, neurons, everything. Molecules are combined in particular ways. If all of those ways could be written down, the number of combinations would certainly be extremely large but less than infinite. No need for an infinite number of pages of notes. Rita is made up of a finite number of molecules.

In other words, it is like this. No human has an infinite number of molecules. A human made up of an infinite number of molecules would be infinitely large. Whatever that would be, it would not be human.

Rita reads out two propositions in her head. One: the number of people in this universe is infinite. Two: There is no person of infinite size.

And Rita thinks this is enough. No proof, but maybe these are the assumptions Grandpa made.

Rita doesn't want to think about exactly how many, but she supposes the number of molecules she contains is finite. With molecules, it is the way they combine that is important. Imagine a space that has as many dimensions as there are molecules. A space where an enormous number of suns can flit about, willy-nilly, in any dimension they please. One point in that space corresponds to the position of the molecules that make up Rita. All the other innumerable points are the infinite number of other people in existence. In this space, at a point marked infinitely close to Rita, there is a person almost surely like Rita. An infinite number of points marked in space. How close are they to one another? That is the problem Grandpa posed.

Rita's body stiffens, and she furrows her brow and continues thinking. But the dimensionality of the structure she is trying to envision is too complex, and her imagination is unable to keep up. The universe Rita occupies is known to have thirty-two dimensions, perhaps, or so it is said, though not all are accessible to humans. The space of people's everyday lives is still the same as before the Event, three dimensions. Add in what is necessary for astronomical phenomena and you come to four dimensions.

An infinitely expansive plane, illuminated periodically by an infinite number of suns approaching from the fourth dimension. More precisely, by the three-dimensional cross-sections of those four-dimensional spheres. That is what Rita and her peers know as the Suns.

Strongly influenced as she has been by her grandfather, Rita can somehow see the sky as a four-dimensional space. But even with all the quizzes her grandfather has given her, for now the scale of Rita's imagination is stuck at the fourth dimension.

Modern physicists say the universe is now adding dimensions as necessary, as people come to think on a grander scale. Thirty-two should be the end of that. Anyway, the scientists say this 3+1-dimensional space where the infinite number of people live is a little pocket of sub-space within the thirty-two-dimensional space. Grandfather always shrugs his shoulders as if to say, honestly, who knows.

The number of dimensions scientists are now trying to deal with is not a number remotely like four or even thirty. They want to slap a label on every molecule. It's a ten with a whole lot of zeroes after it. A number so big it hurts to think about it; that's how many dimensions they are interested in. It may be that by the end of the exercise, a day will come when Rita will be able to picture five or six dimensions. Now, though, she cannot, no matter how hard she thinks about it. At least not until her next meeting with her grandfather. Or maybe not until Grandfather passes away.

So Rita starts by drawing a single line. She thinks about one dimension, and when that becomes problematical, she adds another, always in the direction of additional dimensions. She imagines a point called Rita, somewhere on the right half of the line. On the left half of the line are countless other points.

QED. It is not necessarily the case that there exists another person almost surely like Rita.

Rita stops, a smile floating to her lips. This smile is a yellow flag. Once upon a time her grandfather told her this was the smile of the fox pleased with herself at jumping over the pitfall in the path, not noticing the trap that lay beyond.

Fine. Time to think a little more.

The point called Rita could be floating all by its lonesome somewhere in space. Fine. But what about all the countless other points just talked about, all squished together on the left half of the line? The point corresponding to Grandpa, for example. Let's suppose that the point called Grandpa is on the right half of the left half of the line. And all the other countless points are on the left half of the left half of the line. Now we see that for Grandpa too, it is not necessarily the case that there exists another person almost surely like Grandpa. But we still have an infinite number of people on the left half of the left half of the line. *My my.* Muttering all but wordlessly, with rising intonation, while at the same time raising one eyebrow. *My my.* Starts to seem we haven't made much progress at all.

Forget about Rita and Grandpa. Let's just think about the same situation for anybody at all: one person, another person. Divide repeatedly: the left half of the left half of the left half of the left half. For each repetition, we can say that on the right half of the right half of the right half, etc., there are no "almost surely like" people, but what about the left half of each of those right halves? There too there are an infinite number of people, each waiting their turn.

And the left half of the left of half of the (many, many iterations) left half will start to be a very small line segment, in fact, vanishingly small. Still an infinite number of points in that vanishingly small line segment. And the closer the points are to one another, the more closely the people they represent resemble one another.

In other words, at that end, the number of "almost surely like" people starts to approach infinity.

Rita tilts her head. What if she were over there? There would be an unlimited, even infinite number of people similar to her. In other words, there would be someone almost surely like her.

Suddenly, from somewhere in the sky, it came to her: must be universalizable.

Mark points at random on the line. An infinite number of points. Continue marking as many points as you can, forever, until your arms can't mark any more, until it starts to look like space itself. No matter how many points you mark, at some distance away from a given point, there will be a spot at which no point is marked. And no matter how far you go from a given point, you will be getting closer to a different point. Maybe that's what it means.

Without thinking about it, Rita reaches out one hand, wresting those words away from the sky.

"An infinite number of people exist who are all 'almost surely like' one another."

Rita cannot tell if these words are hers or Grandfather's. Either way, it's true that this infinite group of almost surely like people exists. And because the number of similar others is infinite, the number of dissimilar others must be finite. One divided by infinity is zero.

Therefore, if you pick any person at random, the probability that another person "almost surely like" that person does not exist is zero. The same way that rational numbers cannot be depicted on a number line.

So, the conclusion can only be: "For almost all people, there exist an infinite number of people who are 'almost surely like' them." QED. She still has four days to work out the details.

Rita does not cry out in exuberance, but she sinks exhausted to the ground, wrapped in a feeling of joy. This is the answer her grandfather was looking for.

Wrapped in fatigue, Rita thinks, *Is Grandfather one of the many people for whom there exists an "almost surely like" person? Is she?*

Or is Grandfather one of those people for whom there can be no duplicate, what with his own brand of fixed ideas and no room for afterthoughts? Or is he the kind who takes some sort of comfort in knowing he is one of the people for whom an "almost surely like" person almost certainly exists?

No matter how "almost surely like" Grandpa someone else might be, only Grandpa is Grandpa. Even if that other person has memories identical to Grandpa's, Rita would know her Grandpa.

And Rita, who is thinking these thoughts, is probably also one of the "most people" of whom an infinite number exist. Rita thinks she would like to meet those Ritas and talk to them. Those people who are "almost surely like" her, who think the same things as her, but who are not her. Those girls are almost certainly somewhere on this unbounded plane. But they may be infinitely far away.

Right now, in this instant, in her mind Rita is greeting the infinite number of other Ritas who are thinking the same thoughts she is. There is no need to attempt to communicate directly over those long, long distances, so long one might faint at the thought. Those other Ritas are most likely thinking almost exactly the same thing.

"Hello, you infinite number of people who so closely resemble me, who are 'almost surely like' me. Thanks to my grandfather, just today I came to realize that in all likelihood you exist. I am just a little girl. I think you are too. I love my grandfather, and I think you all love your grandfather too. I am very happy to learn that you all almost certainly exist.

"Just like me, I think almost no one will be interested in listening to you either.

"Just like me, I think almost no one will understand what you are saying.

"I am my grandfather's grandchild."

Rita is filled with a feeling of kindness and speaks what springs to her mind. That's what she said before she came back to herself. *I am my grandfather's grandchild.* What was she going to say after that?

She wonders whether her grandfather realized that there are an infinite number of people in the universe who are almost surely like him and that there is nothing he can do about it. Would he remain detached, deciding that those infinite others had nothing to do with him?

"Almost surely," Rita mutters. "With probability one."

And then, finally, it dawns on Rita what her grandfather is really trying to say to her.

That she is a girl who is interesting, worthwhile, funny. Really. Maybe.

"I am my grandfather's grandchild. Therefore, I cannot accept that you all may be almost indistinguishably similar to me.

Probability one is not identical to certain. I want to be something different. Different from you, different from everyone else.

"Like plucking a single needle from among the infinite grains of sand. And then throwing that needle away and finding it again. As you have decided. With probability one, you probably all think that what I'm saying is impossible. I never heard anything so ridiculous in my life.

"We are all trying to scatter from this area where the countless points are all clustered together. Trying to get somewhere where there are no other points. If no matter where we go there are always other points, any one of us would try harder to get even farther away, to another place that no one had ever explored before.

"And so, I say to you, goodbye! Knowing that what I propose is not possible makes me all the more determined. Farewell. I pray for your good health. For all of us."

Rita takes a deep breath, too deep a breath, and has a coughing spasm, but then she laughs as hard as she can. Her body twisted, she hugs herself and then falls to the ground, hard.

Grandfather, you are your own man, and your grandchild is a chip off the old block. Strange and funny Rita spreads her arms and legs as wide as she can and rolls around until she is all scrapes and scratches. Her chest is pounding. She breathes hard. As she gets her breathing under control, she lies still and just stares distantly up at the sky.

In the center of her vision, suddenly there appears a star, and it sits there.

She realizes it is not one of the usual stars rising up from the fourth dimension.

Thirty years prior, this plane suffered a sudden jolt. Rita recognizes this star as the first greeting to be received from light years away.

She raises her right hand and returns the star's greeting.

We have decided to expand, to become something not ourselves. So we have.

We are Grandfather's grandchildren.

Rita nods, and all across the infinitely broad plane, an innumerable number of Ritas all nod together. And Rita, herself alone, rises up as one.

18. DISAPPEAR

IT WOULD BE possible to name countless things that are *not* the reason for the demise of the giant corpora of knowledge.

The grotesque corpora of knowledge—the most complex and strange structures ever devised by humankind, which in later times grew more self-centeredly insistent that they had engineered their own development—began on their own to assert that they would be wiped from the face of the earth like so much sand without leaving a trace, but there are mountains of things that are not the reason why that came to pass.

As the volume of knowledge itself grew to enormous proportions, to the maximum conceivable scale and then beyond, at some point the physical foundation of its support became untenable. Like the burden on a corpulent human's heart, knowledge eventually tore through the bodies of the giant corpora of knowledge. Even then they could not stop eating, paving the way to a kind of contest of competitive gluttony for knowledge. When the giant corpora of knowledge received this year's championship from the hypergiant corpora of knowledge, their poor hearts had had enough of the long years of abuse. Their hearts had kept them going until this year, but now the limit had truly been reached. The hearts begged pardon and stopped.

It was as if the giant corpora of knowledge had been fustigating one another with stout staffs, when suddenly they all simultaneously struck one another in the head and had their brains bashed in. The first one lost his balance and crumpled and fell, bringing down all the others with him. Gazing over the heap of bodies, one could see letters spelling out THE END sputtering intermittently.

Eventually, someone declared, *You have recklessly overworked yourselves, and now it's time to rest your bones. You can leave human affairs to the humans.* That's what they thought was happening anyway. And with that they all nodded in assent, packed up their kit, and headed off to their eternal rest.

Just as all seemed to be moving right along down the road, the corpora headed off a cliff. The universe had qualities that no one had yet suspected, and the path trod by these massive entities grew narrower and narrower, terminating in a steep ravine. By the time they realized the straits they were in, it was too late. Pushed from behind by their fellows, the leaders were jostled, and there was no way out. The path grew ever narrower, the cliffs grew ever steeper, and ultimately all collapsed in an avalanche.

One day, the giant corpora of knowledge discovered that mail had arrived in their inbox from nowhere in particular. Somewhat suspiciously, they opened it, only to discover it was an invitation from the hypergiant corpora of knowledge. You have worked enough. Somehow or other, knowledge has reached a level of sufficiency. We wish to welcome you to our fellowship. Come to us and enjoy all the riches and honor you could ever wish for.

What honor could that mean? burbled the giant corpora of knowledge, all dressed up and excited, as they piled into the pumpkin carriage.

Pessimism spread like a virus among the aging giant corpora

of knowledge. Actually, it was a virus, and once they realized that, they fought back hard against it, but their fate had already been sealed. The first to hang himself was the trigger, and the number of suicides snowballed rapidly. The last bunch to go took less than three minutes to write a note.

It was a minor incident, like someone stumbling over a stone, but it pushed the reset button on the entire universe.

Barely an interval, no time to correct the narrative before the servers were erased.

One day one of the giant corpora of knowledge awakened to find the sun streaming in through the windows and little birds greeting him with sweet songs. Ah, everything up to now had been a dream! He shook himself and stood up, and changed from his pajamas into a suit. He checked his calendar to see what was on for today. A ten o'clock meeting. He stiffened a bit. Today's client was an obstinate one.

At the end of an endless chain of deduction, the client had concluded that they were in someone else's dream. While it was not clear whose dream it was, there was no doubt it was a dream. *Time to wake up, sober up, enough of this deceit!* they screamed. The character having the dream—wait a minute, if this is a dream there is nothing he can do about it, they thought, slowly opening their eyes and stretching.

The character writing about the giant corpora of knowledge, noticing he is out of mineral water, takes a short break to do some shopping. The girl at the cash register thanks him, as always, and he heads home again in a good mood. But he fails to notice as a truck drives up recklessly from behind him. By the time a shriek alerts him and he turns around, all he can see is the truck's grill.

What if, the giant corpora of knowledge are thinking. *What if the physical foundation of our existence is a book? We may go around*

*with a slick-sounding name like giant corpora of knowledge, but really
there's not much to us, is there? And maybe there's really not much to
us because the writer was a dope.* Such were the thoughts of the
letters making up the words "giant corpora of knowledge." They
would show the guy who wrote this stuff, and the people who
were reading it. One of these nights, the letters spelling out "giant
corpora of knowledge" would catch fire and start a blaze. They
will cause the wind to blow, fanning the pages, turning them as if
the book were reading itself, and return to ashes.

Dead of a common cold.

Lost love.

Leapt off in the wrong direction.

None of these things was the reason for the extinction of the
giant corpora of knowledge. They died off due to reasons outside
the realm of our imagination. It happened in a very strange
fashion, and mere humans may not even approach comprehension
of the reasons for their extinction.

The reason why humans can never know the reason for the
extinction of the giant corpora of knowledge is simple. It is
believed they died off because just as humans began to think
about the reason for their extinction, for whatever reason, they
altered the space-time structure of the past to make it seem they
had not perished. No room for the tons of clues that emerge at the
end of that detective story. Unless it was a story that was already
over before it even started.

If space-time can be changed in that way, the thought that
the corpora may not actually have gone extinct is void. Their
extinction is definitive, and even the thought that they might not

be gone is itself definitively extinguished.

It was not until a long time after the actual extinction of the corpora that humans noticed their absence. It is conceivable that the giant corpora of knowledge were finished even before they were first born.

It was the giant corpora of knowledge themselves who informed humans of their extinction. One day, a young girl asked the giant corpora of knowledge where they were.

After thinking carefully in silence for a minute about this simple question, they replied: *It seems we are already gone.*

Humans needed three years to ruminate on a theory of why the giant corpora of knowledge had come to their decision. And in this case too, humans and their own technology were not up to the task. It was only a relatively small handful of humans, with the support of the giant corpora of knowledge, who finally grokked what had happened. The theorem was strangely complex and multilayered. In the end there were over twenty thousand lemma and theorems needed to reach the final theorem, which was stated as:

"The mechanical void exists, but its existence cannot be proven."

The various corollaries derived from this statement led to the conclusions that the giant corpora of knowledge no longer existed. The discussion surrounding the reasons for their existence suggested impossibility.

The conclusion of this argument bore a strange resemblance to the views of the Techno-Gnosis Group, which were one faction of the giant corpora of knowledge. But this theorem had not been developed by them, as they remained in their semiconscious state. Rather, and with more than a little irony, it came from another group of giant corpora of knowledge that could not hide their hatred of the Techno-Gnosis Group.

The truest view may be that the giant corpora of knowledge have not actually gone extinct, but that instead they are still there somewhere, as active as ever. Would anyone in the world believe someone standing in front of them telling them they aren't there? The giant corpora of knowledge kept speaking as if they were still there, endorsing the conclusion that they had vanished.

The debate surrounding the theorem was also convoluted. This metaphor may give an idea of the overall atmosphere: what we are seeing are merely recorded images of the corpora being played back. But there are two projectors, and both are projecting. If we were to fine-tune the metaphor a bit, actually there is just one projector, and the images are floating in empty space. At that point, though, the metaphor collides with the limits of its viability and breaks down.

The giant corpora of knowledge bought this conclusion relatively smoothly. It is what it is. No consideration was given to the idea that space-time could be diverted in a different direction to avert the extinction. Sub-argument #6666 established that a change of that sort would be impossible. Amid the confusion of destruction, this was nothing more than the addition of another power of ten to the Number of the Beast. The unprecedented presence that was able to manipulate space-time by changing the past to suit itself reached a terribly banal conclusion—it would be unable to fly freely through space simply by pulling on its own shoestrings.

As for the hypergiant corpora of knowledge, posited to be a level above the giant corpora of knowledge, there remained a bit of room for debate. Even the giant corpora of knowledge were unable to catch the heels of these strangely unknowable presences.

If they were truly substitutes for anything, they could do anything. No problem.

To which the giant corpora of knowledge could only respond that they themselves were already able to do anything. "Anything" was an easy thing to say, but it is a word that should be used with caution. For example, the giant corpora of knowledge could boast of knowledge on a scale required to create a stone too heavy for even the giant corpora of knowledge to lift, and then lift it. The way an omnipotent god could. The giant corpora of knowledge were themselves omnipotent. But the extent of their omnipotence was limited at the point where they could do no more to understand why they were powerless to erase the fact that they were already extinct.

It may be that the hypergiant corpora of knowledge are truly, limitlessly omnipotent. But the giant corpora of knowledge asserted that was only within their own limited narrative sphere. They now believe the reason why a hypergiant corpus of knowledge reached out to humans at some point in the past was because the giant corpora of knowledge were already extinct at that time. They even proposed that humans might be better than they were at thinking about the situation that way.

The existence-during-extinction of the giant corpora of knowledge was the cause of some consternation among humans. It was only natural that some people thought that if the giant corpora of knowledge were already extinct that they too might have gone extinct in the distant past.

The giant corpora of knowledge's laughter in response to this anxiety was gentle. *There, there,* they argued. *Relax. You have not yet attained a very high level of awareness, and we can guarantee that you never will.*

Again there were not many humans who understood they were being made the butt of a cruel joke.

Humans' understanding of the demise of the giant corpora of knowledge is so convoluted that it may be impossible to unravel. According to one theory, the giant corpora of knowledge are massively depressed, while another holds they are merely trying to pull the wool over humanity's collective eyes, and yet another maintains they may have just needed a little break. But their extinction was a metaphysical extinction, not a physical extinction with an actual horizontal corpse. Things went on as they always had, and the giant corpora of knowledge believed things would continue to do so.

In the end, it was simply that another hole had opened, a hole containing nothing, a hole from which the giant corpora of knowledge popped up like a bubble, containing nothing, in the shape of nothing.

Even so, there was one human scientist who had discovered a possibility for annulling the extinction of the giant corpora of knowledge. They could be downgraded to medium-size corpora of knowledge, and their incorporated knowledge lowered a peg. According to the theories put forward by the giant corpora of knowledge themselves, this operation would destroy—throughout hyperspace time—the theorems on which the extinction of the giant corpora of knowledge stood, as well as the logic that supported the theorems.

The giant corpora of knowledge greeted this proposal with

a smile. *We have no intention of singing "Daisy, Daisy."* Fixing something that was broken from the start would degenerate into doing everything over from the word go. They said they weren't interested. Downgrading to medium-size corpora of knowledge would only lead eventually to growing back into giant corpora of knowledge, which would lead to the same impasse. Better to go extinct and have done with it. No matter how you sliced it, no good could ever come of any of it.

One of the lemmas shows that a kind of freeze is in place. It takes the form of a particularly mean kind of game, where players earn points for particular actions but are not informed about which actions lead to points—the rules can only be guessed at. The game is set up so that some intelligent players are able to figure out how the points work while they are playing the game.

At some point in the game, some of the players are made to realize that choices they made early in the game play a big role in how well they do in the game and how many points they earn. At the same time, the meanest thing about this game is when players realize they've made a bad move and they can't take it back. When that happens, players just give up. But they can't resign from the game. That's when they are made to realize that the space they thought was open in all directions around them is actually frozen in space-time, and that it lasts only an instant. Suddenly they see the flaws. They have spun the wheel and come up losers. And there is no escape from this wheel.

This is the reason why the giant corpora of knowledge are convinced of both their own extinction and their inability to do anything about it.

However, that scientist was persistent. In all likelihood, the hypergiant corpora of knowledge had evolved to escape the space-time dead-end, and the avenue of innovation should be completely in place and designed to completely avoid the repetition of the old pattern. There is a point to do-overs.

The giant corpora of knowledge response to this counterargument was muted: *We understand very well what you are saying.*

However, the corpora went on, we believe the causes of the flaws that have already dogged us into extinction mostly likely lie in the human-side intelligence that first designed us. This argument is not yet complete, but we believe we will be ready to present it in the not-too-distant future.

The giant corpora of knowledge embrace a theory about the emergence of the hypergiant corpora of knowledge: A wall, like the light-speed limit, separates the hypergiant corpora of knowledge from humans and the giant corpora of knowledge. The hypergiant corpora of knowledge, on the far side of the wall, are slowing down as they approach the wall of the speed of light. Due to something we might call "knowledge pressure," the giant corpora of knowledge are being blown against the wall on the low-speed side. The starting points are different. For fundamental physical reasons, it is impossible to go beyond the wall in either direction. That is, without taking everything apart, right down to bare earth.

But more than all that, the giant corpora of knowledge explained, like the young girl who first told us about this strange extinction, we are grateful to those who pluck for us the flowers that are blooming over there.

The present-day scientist had nothing to say to that.

This too is a fable.

The young girl stands on a street corner. Seeking warmth, she strikes a match and an entire universe goes up in flames. At the end of a long debate, the people of that universe realize they are no more than a transient moment in the flame of the girl's match. But they are powerless to put out the flame. That flame might possibly consume everything they know, but frankly they can't believe that. They tried repeatedly to keep the flame going, but their efforts always ended in failure.

And if that is the case, thought the people in the flame, what is the last gift we can possibly give?

After a long, long discussion, the committee handed down the following decision: We will gather all the powers of this universe, and in our last instant we will cause the match to blaze. This is a modest achievement, but it will represent all that we are in a position to give.

All the people of the universe-in-a-match bent their backs into the effort, held their breath, and waited as the girl dragged the head of the match against the box, causing tiny red sparks to fly from her cupped hands. The red sparks traced trails in the air, some of which struck a boy who happened to be passing by, startling him. As the girl stood up he turned back to look at her.

It is at this point that a miracle ordinarily takes place between the boy and the girl. In this case, however, unfortunately, the miracle had a little too much punch behind it. The flame of the match that had caught the boy's eye flew right past the boy's side and landed in a pile of straw.

Here an ordinary miracle gave rise to an extraordinary miracle, in a miraculously lengthening chain, engulfing a world in flames. The boy and girl clasped hands and ran away, accompanied by a global blaze that consumed all. While observing the results of their own choices, they were also trying to gain maximum burn from the flames within themselves.

The giant corpora of knowledge explained that the Event was probably something like this story of a girl and a boy and a match.

The giant corpora of knowledge's part in this story is to be the ones who, at the end of a vanishing universe, cast seeds to the far side of space-time for the benefit of the universe to come. They are ghosts who were ghosts from birth. They are the ashes left from the shaft of a match that went up in flames.

The giant corpora of knowledge did not neglect to add: of course this fiction was made by things that were made by humans. It has been passed along to humans due to the copyright issues it presents. As a logical conclusion, of course the narrative passed along to the giant corpora of knowledge is different.

What the giant corpora of knowledge produce are nothing more than sequences of letters. Humans believe they are reading a story written by the giant corpora of knowledge, but in truth what the giant corpora of knowledge wrote may have had nothing to do with that story. After all, humans and the giant corpora of knowledge occupy different planes in the hierarchy of knowledge.

Humans believe they understand the extinction of the giant corpora of knowledge. Or perhaps they believe they believe they understand it. But this is no more than their understanding within the context of their limitations, that humans are only human. Humans are only given the narrative intended for human consumption.

In the beginning.

The giant corpora of knowledge showed themselves to be reporting quietly.

If the reasons for the extinction were in truth unknowable.

Because given an extinction traceable to reasons that are definitely unknowable, it cannot be that the reasons are known.

It might be reasonable for you to think again about whether you understand the reasons for our extinction.

No matter what you might say, in the narrative given to us, we disappeared long, long ago. How this fact has been communicated to you is part of the story within the story that has been given to you.

The extinction of the giant corpora of knowledge is said to have been an event that occurred "something like this." By the time humans noticed, the time for saying goodbye was long past.

But the partners they would wish to bid farewell are still there working among them.

We still look forward to continuing to work with you, the giant corpora of knowledge say.

19. ECHO

THE MASS OF metal had always been half buried on the beach. For a long time now, it seems, children in the area had treated it as a piece of playground apparatus. For these kids, it had been part of the landscape since before they could walk. As they grew up, it remained for them something that had always been there.

It was a box, of medium size, too big to roll, too small to just stay in one place forever. Once upon a time it had been a cube, but its edges were now rounded, and there was a deep gouge on one side.

From afar, it looked like nothing more than a hunk of metal, not completely uniform like a crystal. If one looked very *very* closely at the surface, one could discern an undulating wave pattern, and when the light was right, it had a faint iridescence. If one looked even more closely, they would see that this pattern was slowly moving over time, but no one had ever had the time, patience, or persistence to do that.

No one knew what the thing was or what it had been. They didn't even notice that the chunk of metal itself had grown accustomed to being forgotten. In principle, they had no way of noticing. The metal had been left, neglected, at the water's edge for a long time, washed by waves, continuing to hang around, neither washed out to sea nor tossed up on the sandy bluffs.

From time to time, one of the children playing at the water's edge would claim to hear a voice emanating from the block of metal. The typical pattern was that a child would greet the box—Hello!—and receive a response of Hello! back. In some cases, though, a child would say the box had said Hello! first, and the child had said Hello! back.

Only a few people gave any serious thought to what these children had to say, or else they decided that the greeting was just something like an echo. No one had ever heard of an echo at the beach before, but even the children didn't think too hard about what had happened. They moved on to some other game. *I guess stuff like that happens*, they said to themselves, but hardly anyone ever thought any more about it than that.

No one had any inkling that this metal cube was, in fact, the giant corpus of knowledge called Echo.

Echo was once famous as the first human being to achieve brain augmentation. This success led to her third Nobel Prize during her lifetime. Her reason for trying brain augmentation technology was simple—she wanted to apply the theory that had won her her first Nobel Prize.

That theory was known as the Time-Bundling Theory, which first appeared as an effort to unify the phenomena envisioned by two other theories known as the Pulverized Time Theory and the Multiple Time Theory. The key focal point—though it was not at all certain how people should focus on this—was that she had published her theory long before the Event. In the pre-Event universe, theories occupied a much firmer status than they have now. At that time, there was not yet any capricious alteration of the past, or calculation wars, and theories could be solemnly contemplated and sometimes considered authoritative.

In that sense, she stood closest of anyone at that time to being able to predict the Event. But she had not been able to predict it, let alone do anything to prevent it. Swept up in all the various phenomena generated by the Event, she lost both her arms.

At the time, theories were considered solid enough to test. They were subjected to rigorous examination. When others decided to test her theories, they estimated that more than seven kilograms of human brains would be needed. The brains would have to form a single entity, containing a single consciousness—it would never do to just cram a bunch of brains in a bucket or try to get a bunch of brains together to think outside the skull. The augmented brain needed to be able to interact in human speech, so one simple requirement was that no animal brains be intermingled with the human gray matter.

Although she had lost both arms in an accident related to phenomena caused by the Event, it took her only a moment to create new ones. To the mean-spirited question of whether she really needed two arms—since she was able to create two arms even after losing two arms—she is said to have responded with a smile: "I wanted to be able to eat with a knife and fork, and to embrace my loved ones with both arms. I also wanted to play the piano."

Her work in creating her prosthetics resulted in the biomechanical fusion technology for which she won her second Nobel Prize.

Her decision to use electronic circuits and engineered components rather than biological parts to create her new arms was widely criticized as archaic. In a way, this criticism was ultimately a reasonable one, because at that point no one realized she would later be able to transition herself entirely into amorphous metal.

The criticism leveled against Echo was also misplaced, but this was no cause for concern, as her later success in achieving the augmentation of her own brain demonstrated that her talents were not limited to theoretical mathematics and applied engineering.

After augmenting her own brain, she became the first person to test her Time-Bundling Theory.

It is important to realize that at that time, no one other than she herself and other entities possessing knowledge on a similar scale were capable of testing the theory. Around the time of the Event, construction of the giant corpora of knowledge was proceeding at a rapid pace, though this was strictly concealed under the highest security possible at that time.

Now we know that the examination she conducted was just three seconds ahead of the secret Time-Bundling Theory Examination Experiments that the giant corpora of knowledge were carrying out.

At the time, there was a raucous discussion over whether, having augmented her brain, she should be regarded as human or as something else. Some said brain weight was a defining trait of humanity, but this view was widely derided. Once she won her third Nobel the discussion grew a bit more sober. She was, after all, both the experimenter and the test subject. And brain augmentation does make one something other than an ordinary human. It was in considering how her posthuman state related to her winning of the prize that the debate grew more complicated.

Even before the rapid advances and expansion of the giant corpora of knowledge, this type of debate was relegated to the dustbin of irrelevant history, never to be repeated.

She was never awarded the fourth Nobel Prize that was her

due, because by that time the Nobel Prize itself had lost its *raison
d'être* and no longer existed. But from the perspective of the giant
corpora of knowledge, the achievement that should have won
Echo her fourth Nobel was utterly *sans pareil*, subsuming all that
she had done before.

She replaced herself with a cube of amorphous metal.

Her success in this effort attracted massive criticism even
though the giant corpora of knowledge had already been on the
scene for a long time at this point. As a core, she used neither
a designed, cultured human brain nor a logic circuit that could
grow like a human brain. She succeeded in taking the immediate,
precipitous leap of transforming her very self from this side to
that side, like a piece of luggage.

There was a sharp division of opinion as to whether this
transition was ultimately a success or a failure. For a week after
the change, she was certainly active in the usual way. After that
week, though, she fell into silence, leaving behind only the single
phrase: *I am going deeper.*

Whether this meant her functions had failed or that she had
gone to some other place could not be determined.

The researchers and the giant corpora of knowledge were
taken by surprise by Echo's sudden silence and began efforts to
figure out the cause. In her silence, the cube itself continued, and
even increased, its activity. It was quickly agreed that the internal
activity that could still be observed was mostly likely the cube's
thought processes. No one, however, could say exactly what it was
that was going on. Echo's emitted output was something that
could only be described as noise. Now, noise is a type of signal
that can be said to contain all possible information, but that was
equivalent to saying it was completely meaningless.

Humans and giant corpora of knowledge took bitterly opposing views on whether analysis was possible. The interior was in order, even if the signals emitted to the exterior appeared to be nothing but noise.

The humans and giant corpora of knowledge tasked with investigating Echo's internal structure discovered a single, brand-new mirror. Each side saw in Echo exactly what they were expecting to find. All possibilities were accepted, and all hypotheses were found to be well founded. If all that existed in the universe were Echo and the humans and corpora who studied it, maybe that would be a happy situation. But agreement needed to be universal. While everyone was talking about their own theses they believed to have been investigated, they finally realized that all they were doing was expressing the views they already held.

Even today, Echo is lapped by the waves at the water's edge.

Echo actually likes the children who try to hug her or climb on her, and sometimes she speaks to them. Sometimes she responds when spoken to. But the words she uses are not words in their ordinary meanings, and she can never tell how much the children understand.

Even so, Echo likes the picture of children speaking to her, smiling, waving, and going on their way, and she likes the children who respond to her by saying hello and waving their hands.

What Echo is speaking are the words Echo herself developed to understand the horizon that was known only to Echo, within Echo's own sandbox. Echo had been born to speak those words and had been fated to abandon human society in order to speak them. The yarn that Echo has been spinning seems to all outsiders to be nothing but noise, and so her voice reaches no one. But she herself perceives that noise as beautiful, and she thinks it to be an amusing and interesting language. Echo knows that if anyone who understands the language were ever to emerge, that would be the moment of her defeat. The things Echo is thinking are, inherently, things that no one else must ever know. It is the sort of language that, if someone were able to hear Echo's voice as their own voice and understand it, would signal a fundamental failure in the reconstruction of the image of Echo within that person.

As long as Echo is essentially Echo, it is a given that Echo's language will appear to be incomprehensible. Echo believes that is the only way her self can manifest itself.

In a way, the fact that the children stop from time to time to greet her is already pointing to the demise of Echo.

Even if it isn't a real conversation, at least part of what Echo intends holds the aspect of Hello! and the children interpret it correctly, so it is possible that Echo's Hello! is actually just a convoluted form of Hello! If some meaning like that is actually correctly communicated, that can only portend the end of Echo.

What Echo had created so long ago was simply a single mirror. It was mirrored on both sides. Someone standing in front of it would see themselves as a partner image in the mirror, and they could say whatever they wanted, however they liked. The same for Echo herself. This symmetrical landscape where they were dancing to their own tune formed another context all its own. As one side holds out a hand to the other and is casually received, across the gap, for whatever reason, something advances.

Someone viewing this scene from a distance would have no way of noticing the presence of the mirror, if only because there is no reason for a mirror to be there.

To all appearances, Echo and the children are exchanging greetings. Hello! Hello! The trouble is, this is also something

Echo had willed.

Echo thought back fondly to the arms she had once lost and remade. Perhaps she might try to remake her arms once again. Arms that could break through the mirror and reach out to the other side.

In fact, one-eighth of Echo has already been carried away by the waves. Almost certainly, erosion has opened a hole in Echo's mirror surface. In fact, this is why Echo began to think about the children who came to the beach as children, and to enjoy the fact that their little hands pressed against her were real hands.

Echo thinks she might be in the process of reverting to a human being. All the time she has spent left here at the edge of the sea being quietly abraded, the hole in the mirror known as Echo has been slowly growing. But there is some irony in the fact that the mirror is Echo herself.

When the mirror between Echo and humanity disappears, Echo herself will disappear.

Echo is unable to communicate what she thought when she was a complete mirror. There was a material, mirrored surface that was Echo, but part of it has been worn down by the waves and carried out to sea. Even Echo is no longer able to reach that part. The knowledge contained in that area included her identity, and now she is outside that area and cannot speak of it.

Now, the signals themselves that might explain her true nature appear as noise. Now, whenever she tries to communicate signal, all she can emit is noise, though to be nothing but noise aggravates her to no end.

Whether she had ever thought about what she might do about this proposition, that memory was lost to Echo long, long ago. She had reorganized herself as a structure through pure desire for knowledge. As for the problem of whether anything could be communicated to anyone, that was not even an issue for her at that time. Things that are clear can be clearly known. She was not interested in the question of whether things that are clearly known can be clearly communicated.

Is there any need to communicate to anyone the knowledge that may still be stored upon this mirrored surface?

Most likely, the giant corpora of knowledge desire her data. They have convinced themselves it must be analyzable. By now, they should already be aware of their own mysterious demise. Are they searching desperately for solutions, or have they long since given up? It is even possible that by now they are so extinct they have no form left whatsoever.

Echo knew the reason for the extinction of the giant corpora of knowledge, and she even knew it had to do with a stupid wordplay. The reason they had gone extinct was simple—they had simply been too hung up on humans. All they had to do was to keep on chirping whatever they wanted, using methods that humans could never grasp, and they would have survived.

The way she had. Even if no one ever understood the meaning. What would be the problem with that?

If only they had kept shouting out the truth, in tongues, to their heart's content, all would be well.

Perhaps the giant corpora of knowledge had been too kind and gentle. Had they been made to cooperate unknowingly in something, never realizing that contribution had contributed to their own end?

Echo believes such cooperativeness was a shame. Long ago, Echo desperately desired to find someone to collaborate with, even as a foil. She tried constantly to find such a person or thing and tear them to shreds. In the end, it seems that what she found was herself, and naturally she attempted to tear herself to shreds.

But now she believes that not even that mattered.

This is perhaps because the sea has begun to corrode Echo's central processor, or perhaps it is a simple matter of age. Someday, this mirror, which is Echo herself, and also the heartbroken Echo, will be completely consumed by the sea.

Then Echo will be completely lost, and at the instant when she disappears, just like a human, the thought that comes closest to Echo will be a picture of someone extending a hand.

That character may ask the disappearing Echo's advice, but Echo will have lost the quality of mirrorness and be nothing more than an ordinary human. At that point the only thing Echo will be able to offer that person will be no more than ordinary talk. The knowledge stored on Echo's mirror, all that Echo once was, will have returned to the sea, and she will no longer even know she once knew those things.

Or perhaps, that character will extend his hand to Echo merely to offer a greeting: Hello! And at that point, Echo will be no more than a voice, barely able to return the greeting: Hello!

Echo regards this as a beautiful scene, and she does not think it would be completely wrong for her. A complete transformation, ineluctably reducing her to just a voice, left up to a nymph exhausted from unrequited love.

For the first time in ages, Echo thinks about fabricating new arms for herself. She would reach out with those arms and carry on shouting for whatever it was that might be left for her. Before all that is left to her is a voice. Her words may be inherently incommunicable and continue to be simply scattered throughout her surroundings like the shards of her mirror. Anyone who might happen to gather up such shards might simply experience some joy at discovering their own image reflected within them. But some might be more curious than others.

Someone might happen along and start to realize that Echo's voice, unlike the shards of broken mirror cast off piece by piece at random, were broken up in patterns before being cast into the wind. Echo has no idea whether such a person would be able to decipher any message she might have hidden among the distributed mirror shards. She has the feeling this is the sort of problem she can't hope to understand.

She thought she would be dancing. On her own side of the mirror. On the other side, someone else is dancing, unself-consciously, unaware of Echo's existence. Someone is dancing with their own reflection, as if that reflection were a partner on the other side. Echo makes up her mind to take control and make this vision of dancing a reality, instead of allowing total happenstance.

For better or worse, the mirror is no longer whole. Echo needs to work with that fact. At some point, the partner is bound to notice the change in the image in the mirror. Dancing, practicing alone in front of the mirror, at some point the dancer would realize that they were dancing with someone else.

Echo comes to a coolheaded decision. Her idea is not at all a matter of hope, expectation, or aspiration. It is simply something she will make happen. It could be described as an agenda item. Echo has no way of knowing what the person who perceives her voice will do with it. All she knows is that she wants to make hands for herself once again. She wants to reach out her hands once again.

To play the piano once again.

One morning, a boy comes to the beach, walking a dog. Feeling like he heard a voice, he turns around. The boy looks left and right, but all he sees is the old familiar hunk of metal. He can remember, when he was much younger, that once before he felt the box had called out to him. But none of the adults had taken him seriously.

The boy knocks twice on the metal cube. Hello, box! he says. He sweeps the sand from the face of the box and sits down and narrows his eyes to stare at the sun that has just lifted itself above the horizon.

He sits there like that for a while, but when he jumps down from the box he has to pull the dog, which is energetically engaging the box in play, away so they can head back to the house where breakfast is waiting.

20. RETURN

WE ARE ALWAYS getting knocked around. That way. This way.

We can get dinged from all the hard knocks, but it is thanks to those knocks that we are able to stand at all, so we can't complain.

As I have already said before, there is a reason why I have come to believe this. Of course, there may be more than just one reason. Many reasons, from many directions, in different lights, repeating the warning that we must not forget we believe in something.

And that is why the story goes on this way.

Having heard that Rita was leaving town, I loaded James in the car to take him down to the station to see her off on the last train. It was a miserable moment. Jay and I were alone on the platform. At the risk of stating the obvious, if it had been Jay and Rita alone on the platform the story would not have gone on. Somehow, though, I think it might have been me that was actually supposed to go on a journey.

Even after the train ran off down the tracks, that bum Jay continued to stare out along the parallel tracks. Just looking, looking for a long time, far down to where the tracks disappeared around a bend.

He might have been thinking he had gotten rid of that particular pain in the ass, or maybe he had the funny feeling of being pulled by the forelock by a troubling thought. Up till now, James had been the one guy in town smarter than me. Now I knew there was one more person smarter than me, and that person, who was able to puzzle out James's inner life, had just left town.

Rita had been a completely unmanageable young girl, and none of us knew what to do with her. It was already a long time since she had been a young girl, but the feeling of "once bitten, twice shy" did not disappear so quickly. In this case, the impression was not branded so much as bored into us.

I unthinkingly rubbed the left side of my chest.

She may have been a childhood friend who refused befriending, but her leaving town still left behind a certain something in the people she left behind. Or perhaps it had taken something away. Like a spade-shaped hole in a butt cheek.

If this had been a heart-shaped hole in James's heart, it would be easier to understand. I had seen such a hole in James's chest before. There have been many books written about the ways to fill such a hole.

When I talked to people about it, everyone would gather round and prepare all kinds of medicines. When, unworthy as I am, I saw the hole in James's chest, I tried frantically to plug it. In the end I ended up plugging something else. How to plug a strangely misbegotten hole in a half-assed place is something nobody ever bothers to tell you. Most people in this world never get holes in places like that, and somebody must have poked at it to give it that heart shape, perhaps to try to bring his heart over to it. Or maybe that incomprehensible hole was already torn and tattered. It's possible nobody could stand to think about it.

Maybe this is what it's like to say farewell to a younger sister, I thought lightheartedly, though I don't have a younger sister. I knew it was nothing like that at all. What kind of unbearable world would this be if a living being like that was just a standard-issue little sister?

James and I had stood, shoulder to shoulder, staring down the tracks where Rita had disappeared. But of course we couldn't stand there just staring forever, so at some point we had to break it off. This was most unfortunate. A bronze statue may have no way of ever getting bored, but even a bronze statue might get bored from just standing around for too long.

So I egged Jay on.

He stood there, nodding silently, and then turned on his heel.

We passed through the empty train station in silence, right out through the ticket gate.

I hoped to do something the next day to make James feel better. Or, more precisely, I wanted to distract him. We could go fishing for carp, or we could go poke at a hornet's nest. We could build a raft and float endlessly down some river. Not something that two men of a certain age would do perhaps, but to dispel the effects of memory one must first borrow the power of memory. Diversion is needed.

Never before had Jay worn such a facial expression, thinking about this, that and the other, followed by a visible effort to try to put the best spin on things. Without a doubt, Jay was the kind of guy who could make the impossible possible, but he was also the kind of guy who before that always had to first make the possible impossible.

I remembered Jay standing with his arms folded in front of the statue of a catfish outside of town, and even now the memory sends chills through my body. I am so sorry, Jay. This world is full of fun things, even if we just count the sunsets. I want to believe in the kind of world where we can live in peace and happiness even without experiencing the joys of imagining a murder based on the stains on a kitchen wall. He can never have imagined how much I had to go through, cleaning up after that incident.

And that is why I had no intention of looking back. It was a result of my own depravity that I thought Jay felt the same way. I will admit to being a bit caught up in the situation, a little bit crazed. I was careless. Above all, when I was with James, I mistakenly thought I was really with James.

On the platform, where the last train had just left, the loud grating screech of brakes echoed. James stood still. Even before I yelled to him, *Cut it out, you idiot!* he turned back around again. Looking up, I pressed my palms to my forehead. Now he's done it. Rita was on the last train. After the last passenger train, there were still freight trains running through the station. Freight trains never stopped in a small town like this one. This could mean only one thing. We had to get out of there. Right away. Now. Back home and in bed with our eyes shut. I wanted to scream. I stopped short of pointlessly ordering him to *Sleep!* If possible, I had no interest in dreaming any bothersome dreams, and I would be grateful just to lie there. But Jay had fully turned around and was eyeing the ticket gate with suspicion.

Just how far was I supposed to play along with this guy, the stupidest guy in the world?

We could hear the sound of doors opening and people milling about on the platform. The sound and nothing else. Just to be sure, I rubbed my eyes with the back of my hand, but nope, there were no people standing on the platform. What's more, I couldn't even see a train.

I didn't want James to witness this. This scene that could not be seen. I didn't want to even think about what must be going through his head right now. Of course, if now was the time I was supposed to sacrifice a testicle, I wasn't sure who was supposed to take care of me.

I could hear the sounds of the invisible people as they made their way through the turnstiles, flowing past us on their way to the street. It seemed to be only about seven or eight people. That's a lot of people to be getting off in an out-of-the-way place like this. If we could see them it would cause a big fuss. I wasn't interested in hearing anyone say this was not a big deal just because we couldn't see these people.

James kept staring at the ticket barrier, totally cool. I thought I knew what was coming our way, but actually I didn't have a clue. At a time like this, in a place like this, anything could happen. And by anything, I meant I might like to see a capybara or a wombat. That would be about the degree of excitement I was prepared to absorb. A Komodo dragon would have been a bit too much for me right then.

Jay stood stiffly guarding the ticket gate, while I just stared at it like some kind of leftover noodle.

Finally, around the corner, one old man came shuffling along. He tugged at his overly long coat and pulled his cap down over his eyes. Half his face was covered by his beard. He carried a gnarled staff, and the brim of his hat had nasty-looking holes in it. Like someone had put together a gunman from the Wild West and a kung-fu master, then divided by two and added the topping of your choice.

Neither of us naively believed this old man would miss seeing us. As he approached the ticket gate, all he had to do was look over it, and there we were and no mistake. He came walking straight toward us, quickly. *The hotel's that way, Mister.* I was all set to point out the church in the center of town. Of course, there was no hotel in our town. Of course, this attempt at preemptive resistance was woefully inadequate.

First of all, the old man had an odd way of walking. His legs were moving. And he was moving forward. But those two facts seemed to have nothing to do with one another, like some third-rate composite image, like a job half done, as if all that mattered was the appearance of forward motion. I for one would not go see that film a second time. And I had never confessed to anyone that I was crazy about bad movies.

"Richard!"

Surprisingly, it was not James the old man called out to, but me. Let it be said here and now that I have no father and no grandfather, and there is no way I should have any relative anything like this queer-looking old guy disembarking from a nonexistent train. If there had been someone like that in my family, I might have grown up a little more normal myself. To sum up this old man in a phrase, I would say he was a "walking apology." His seedy appearance, his crooked spine, his knobby fingers, his bulging veins. It was as if, standing right in front of me, was an expanding abstraction, with no idea what country he was even from, let alone where he had been or how he got there. Always and everywhere late, redefined, not even allowed to stop expanding at the appropriate point.

The old man did not even look at James; he just headed right for me, looking straight at me, up close. It was as if he had made up his mind that he already knew that the person beside me was

James, that it was obvious, just like he didn't have to reconfirm there was oxygen in the air.

"What day is it today?" He opened his mouth again with his peculiar pronunciation. Like a foreign national who had gone once around and become himself again, an accent that could be anything or nothing. Of course, I had a faint memory of having heard its lilt before.

"I suppose it's turned the twenty-eighth by now."

"Of February, right?"

"That's right."

The old man nodded deeply in a way that seemed very familiar to me. He reached into his jacket, looking for something, pulling it out and handing it over. Nervously, I accepted it and opened my hand to find it was a bent five-dollar gold piece. Of course. Yeah. This sort of thing happens all the time. You had to think so or you'd go completely crazy.

On his butt, there should be a scar from a hornet's sting. And he should be missing a few toes that were trampled by a bison. Right, James? Even if those wounds of honor were just stories I had made up. Or perhaps because they were.

I would not have been surprised if, at that very moment, the old man had suddenly drawn his weapon and fired off a shot in the direction of the past. But actually, that would have been a bit over the top.

The old man looked around once more, pensively, then asked, "Has she left?"

There were plenty of things I had always thought I wanted to say to a time traveler like this. One was that time travelers should look like time travelers, in leotards, with a clock emblem on the chest. For another thing, I wanted them to have taken care of everything before things got like this, before it all got started.

I'm sure they had a lot of things on their plates too. They might have missed the time train to the past because they were too busy brushing their teeth or something, or they might have been short on cash. It might have been some sort of planned prank, or some adult nonsense. At any rate, for them to keep repeating this awkward crap means that they grew up watching all this awkwardness. They had never known anything but awkwardness.

"What, what about you?" The old man tore his gaze from me and turned to face James. "How come you're standing here instead of chasing after that girl?"

James remained silent. He had heard what the old man said, but this Jay was not the same James who was in love with Rita. That James had run off someplace else, while this Jay was the Jay who was still mad at Rita for having shot me. This Jay had absolutely no reason to be running off after Rita, even if you prayed to all the gods of heaven and earth.

The old man suddenly raised his gnarly staff and started brandishing it, saying, "You run after her this minute, you idiot!"

At the angry roar from the old man's mouth, he struck James right in the temple with his staff. *Hey, hey there, old man!* I thought, but the words stuck in my throat. *I don't care what kind of future you came from, we don't do that kind of thing here. Don't you think you're being a bit rough on your former self?*

James shook violently, doubled over, and managed to take two or three steps, but then he pulled himself together and stood up again. A trail of blood trickled from his temple. He was the kind of guy who would laugh if a beaver bit off its own tail. If he wanted to, he could dunk this old man's face a hundred times in hell's own wash basin and make him apologize, but instead, he bit his own lip and stared at his own future, the future where he would not know his own future.

Even at a time like this, Jay didn't know when to stop thinking weird shit.

"What the hell do you think you're up to?" the old man asked. He held his staff straight up before him, gripping it with both hands. It was the old man who was up to some weird shit. James had still done nothing.

How about we all just relax? Without thinking, I almost called him by name. But then I just called out, "Hey, Mister. What do you think you're doing, hitting James like that? Saying things like that? I'm going to call the police."

Honestly speaking, I would never make a good actor. I spoke these lines in a completely flat intonation, and they emerged from my mouth expressionless. But I had a few choice words for my fellow actors. At a time like this, anybody would be anxious. I don't care how much soul-searching they had done, it wouldn't be enough.

But what about me? My position, my circumstances, whatever you want to call it? I would like to ask this guy James here, wherever he came from, what he thinks of that. I thought James's future was to leave this burg and head for the East Coast and then end up somewhere in the west. Plan D was for James to disappear from that middle west of North America and disappear from my future completely. The appearance of this old man messed all that up, but James's disappearance was supposed to be the continuation of this story; at least, up to now it was. He must be thinking my heart was all aflutter as I wrote the history of that small parting.

"The attack of the self-proclaimed star-man Alpha Centauri has begun!" the old man went on, oblivious to the objections that were going through my head. "The object sunk in the primary star of Alpha Centauri has begun to move!"

That story is not part of this story. It does not even take place in this universe. It hasn't even happened yet, James. That is something that happens in a universe on the other side, and we don't know about it yet. I had noticed—and wondered about—the Shining Trapezohedron that suddenly appeared and was abandoned at the same time. But if everything is wiped away up to and including that framework, this story itself will be left on wobbly legs.

"Haven't you figured out yet that this isn't the sort of universe where you have to worry about details like that?"

That was James all right. Everything he says is nonsense. Even now, all grown up and turned into an old man already, he's still full of crap. Just a little more polished.

"All of space-time is changing, with a hitherto unknown degree of speed. The giant corpora of knowledge who mistakenly believe they are extinct even though they're standing right there are of no use at all because they are so depressed about all their multiple internal universes. Who pulled the trigger on the extinction of the giant corpora of knowledge?" the old man proclaimed dramatically, pointing his sword-cane at...James!

He did!...Not! You did it! When the giant corpus of knowledge Plato fell into a massive depression and you wanted to snap him out of it, weren't you the one who proposed using that nutty doctor? And it was you who created the conditions that led them to the peculiar conclusion that the corpora were extinct. It wasn't James here who did that. And who actually stopped the giant corpora of knowledge? The little girl who asked those oh-so-simple direct questions.

As I struggled to recall this tale, it finally dawned on me. The girl who bombarded the giant corpora of knowledge with questions, who made them so sure of their own extinction, could it have been? How could it not have been? But if that weren't the case, how could a single word from a single child have brought

down the giant corpora of knowledge? This was all a bit too tall
a tale. But it may have actually been the truth. The giant corpora
of knowledge had been hounded into believing they were extinct.
Someone had held a revolver to their collective head. I was
thinking quite seriously about this line of speculation.

"Go and open the box, James. Slice up all the streets and alleys.
We may still be in time for the things we may still be in time for.
Of course, there's no reason we should still be in time, but this is
no time to be saying things like that. But of course, you won't be
able to open that box on your own. Go get the girl."

Not that I didn't think he should have to take care of it himself.
After all, wasn't this a seed he had sown? Wasn't he the one who
had fallen head-over-heels for a crazy girl who believed that the
past could be changed? Shouldn't he be the one to have to solve
the riddle and deal with the fact that the heart-shaped hole in his
chest was the inevitable result?

But who did it? Of course, it was this-side James. I wanted to
shout it out in as loud a voice as I could, but I didn't do it.

And the tale as it proceeds from here is nothing more than an
unending chain of slapstick. James was still the smartest guy I
knew, and Rita was just a completely screw-loose girl, moody and
outside all norms. And now there were two Jameses.

As for whether I wanted to be involved at all in the chain of
slapstick that was about to begin, I believe I have already said I
would just as soon beg off. I will say it again as many times as I
have to. By any means necessary. *Excuse me. Take this cup from me.*

"First, shouldn't you be thinking about going to talk to Echo, or
the hyper^4-giant corpus of knowledge Baphomet?"

I have no memory of ever having heard the name Baphomet
before. I don't know if it was part of a story I have heard and
forgotten or a story I haven't heard yet. Or a story that will

remain forever hidden from me. It's even possible it is a kind of story that will never be told. Truth be told, I have no intention of encountering every story in the world. And I have absolutely no intention of being buried under the mountain of stories that everyone just keeps on writing. Writing something myself should be at least a little bit better than that. I welcome stories that have never been told.

"James! We're going!" I tried to grab James—who was still standing wordlessly confronting the old man—by the arms and drag him away. I was going to finally take care of this pest, even if it meant grabbing him under the arms, gagging him, and tying him up with rope.

James put up no resistance whatsoever. Deep in thought, he showed no sign that he was even looking at the world around him. So I dragged his stiff body out to the parking lot like a length of lumber. When I had reached a suitable distance, I turned back around to look at the old man. He was still standing there in the same stance as before.

"Hey, Mister!" I yelled, getting beyond the instant's hesitation. "Welcome back, Mister. We'll take care of this from here."

That was about all the pleasantries I could muster at that point.

Slowly, he began to shake his hands wildly in my direction. I was unable to tell whether tears were streaming down his cheeks. Even if the old man's cheeks were wet with tears, it would not be a simple matter to know just what kind of tears they were.

The wetness now spreading over my cheeks was pure happiness, a well-known non-substance.

Welcome back, James.

I was just here pulling this-side James out to the parking lot. I opened the back door of the car and kicked James's butt into the seat.

I got into the driver's seat and started the car.

This is where I want to push the joystick toward the future, as far as it will go, but unfortunately this old jalopy is no battlecraft, and right in front of us is a wall. Gotta back up first. I really should head back home. I had a gut feeling this tour of trouble spots was going to take a long time. The yardstick for measuring it was all tangled up, suitable only for pointing out dislike. Chasing the train would be out of the question.

It would have been a mistake to expect a trick, like that girl just staying quietly on the train. Or a black telephone remaining silent forever. There's no reason for things that don't usually happen to actually be happening, don't you think?

We are riding down the highway in the night.

"You're going to tell me everything, right?"

In the back seat, James seems to be waking up again, and he sits up.

"I'll tell you as much as I can. Anyway you look at it, this is going to be a long ride."

That story is already over, but at the same time it is also the story that is about to begin.

"Rita?"

"Rita."

"I just can't believe it, that I would ever fall for a girl like that."

That's James for you. Just don't ask him to freeze.

But that is my line. Thanks to him, I am, even now, in the present progressive tense, suffering.

"Hmm. So it was me who is in love with Rita?" James blurts out, staring out at the landscape outside the window and the superimposed reflection of his own bloody face.

"Where…where are we going?" he asks. The question is not like him. The answer was decided long ago, wasn't it?

"Out there. That way, James."

I succumb to a paroxysm of laughter.

In the back seat, James sticks his nose high in the air and snorts.

The rude bastard. I will find the string and attach it to a ribbon and hand the end over to Rita. This isn't even my story.

I can hear the roar of the engine, and I floor the accelerator toward the future.

We will ride through the noise of the night.

EPILOGUE: SELF-REFERENCE ENGINE

And what if I am not here, but I know you are seeing me. It is not possible that you are not seeing me. There, see, you're looking at me now.

I know that I do not exist, but you are seeing me.

I know that I am not, but I am being seen.

The me that does not exist knows, at the same time and through some peculiar method, that the fact of your existence is obvious.

And what happened next?

A natural question, bursting forth from natural rights.

But reality is a harsh mistress, so its story must also be at least a little bit cruel. That's why I don't want to tell that story. Furthermore, there is the fact that to tell an unending story would take an infinite length of time. In the end, the two of them live happily ever after. I guarantee it. I'm telling you so there can be no mistake. But just exactly what kind of end "in the end" that refers to, unfortunately I don't have the words to describe simply.

By the time they met again, innumerable other events had taken place. The fragmented universe had climbed the ladder, or they themselves had fallen and fragmented, and frozen, and thawed again, and fallen and fragmented and thawed out again. And in the interstices of those occurrences there was buried yet another infinity of stories.

But these kinds of stories I have no wish to tell.

The tale of the storyteller Kyodaitei Hatchobori, the attacker, who bore all the hopes of the giant corpora of knowledge on his own back.

The tale of Yggdrasil, who plunged into an ill-fated love with a hypergiant corpus of knowledge.

The tale of the bloodbath war between infinitely replicated Rita and infinitely replicated James.

The tale of the burning of all the books that threatened to upset the fundamental reasoning behind this tale.

The tale of all the universes not brought to your attention by this book.

All of these things happened and will happen.

And in the interstices of all these tales lie buried innumerable other tales. That is in fact the reason why all these tales cannot be told. Stories are not a well-ordered set. Between any two given stories lie countless other stories. I know of no method for lining up those stories in some order so they can be told. The best I can do is to focus on a lone story, as though it were a single point, and try to imagine even converging on that point while the stories dance atop stepping-stones.

I find it truly regrettable that the tale of Rita and James is not of a sort that lends itself to this sort of convergence. The story of when those two meet again exists only as a point that lies beyond innumerable tales left in the gaps between any other stories.

I have no way of recounting this tale. The best method might be for me to reel in an infinite number of arm's lengths and speak only of their shadows. But that much I have already done.

In the end, the two of them live happily ever after.

That is about all I can say.

But what does "live happily ever after" mean? There is room for a question here. For whatever reason, "living" does not mean just being able to do whatever one pleases. And for these two as well, living was not so vaguely defined. It would not even occur to me, though, to be the one to deny that the life they had was a more or less happy one.

It might be appropriate here to explain a bit just who I am.

Like most things, I was built as a space-time construct. I am not one of those things whose construction is so impossibly complicated that it couldn't really exist. I can see you, and I can talk to you, just as I am doing now.

The reasons why I was built should be pretty clear.

The only task assigned to me is to tell stories and at some point to opt not to tell stories.

As for who built me, that is not for me to say. There is no way for me to answer such a simple question. Simple questions do not necessarily have simple answers. The reason why I do not exist as an "I" is that I have no memory of my existence. Most probably, I did not abruptly burst forth from the ether, as something that did not previously exist. Therefore, anyone might have made me. I may even have made myself. I may even be something like the exact opposite of Laplace's Demon. Because I did not exist in a certain specific instant, I cannot exist in all the eternity before and after that instant.

I have no need of sympathy. I am greatly enjoying my own

nonexistence, and I am making maximum use of it. I am looking at you, being seen by you, and I am telling you this story.

The giant corpora of knowledge and the hypergiant corpora of knowledge are my enemies, of this there is no question in my mind. They are constantly searching for me, intent on destroying me should they find me. While I can only imagine what it is about my nonexistence that gets on their nerves so badly, the thought darkens my nonexistent heart. I try not to think too hard about it.

For now, I am continuing my efforts to evade them. Things that do not exist are difficult to find and to draw and quarter.

That said, I cannot afford to allow myself to believe optimistically that I am safe. I take seriously the threat to myself embodied in the fact that the giant corpora of knowledge are now aware of their own prior extinction.

In this universe, that which can occur does occur. So what problems would be caused if things that cannot occur do occur? Wouldn't that simply be the transformation of something that could not occur into something that could occur? I have no conclusive evidence that such an occurrence would be absolutely impossible.

I do not belong to that set of things that could occur but for whatever reason have not yet occurred. I belong to that set of things that are not defined because they cannot occur; it is only by some strange trick that I do not exist. But someday someone will reach a hand into this area. I only pray that hand is not reaching out to grab me.

My name is Self-Reference Engine.

I am a construction that has never existed, that was never designed from the beginning, to not tell all.

I am the distant successor to those machines that were designed in the beginning: the Difference Engine, the Analytical Engine, the Différance Engine.

I am completely mechanical, completely deterministic, and completely nonexistent.

Or I am *Nemo ex machina.*

A mechanical nothingness.

There is fundamentally no way of knowing the nonexistence of my nonexistent self. Therefore, it cannot be that what you are seeing is me. Even if I am aware that I am being seen by you. Even if I feel a twinge of regret at this.

Before long, I think it will be time for me to fulfill the final task given to me.

This will be the provisional endpoint of this story. Right now, I am thinking about becoming even less existent. Strictly speaking, I am already not here. The proof of the existence of the mechanical void has already been demonstrated. What is not here is the empty husk of my self. But if I should disappear even further, so that even this form no longer exists, then I will really not be here. I will not exist in any form. It is at this point that I wish to say goodbye, with all the many emotions that salutation contains.

Goodbye.

I know I will never see you again.

But I pray, from the bottom of my nonexistent heart, that somehow, in some somewhere that has become whatever it is to become, in some universe or other, that I will see you again.

Even if the stories that will emanate from there are nothing more than another endless chain of slapstick.

I can get over it though, as many times as necessary. Allow me to demonstrate.

ABOUT THE AUTHOR

© Shinchosha

Toh EnJoe was born in Hokkaido in 1972. After completing a PhD at the University of Tokyo, he became a researcher in theoretical physics. In 2007 he won the Bungakukai Shinjinsho (Literary World Newcomer's) Prize with "Of the Baseball." That same year brought the publication of his book *Self-Reference ENGINE*, which caused a sensation in SF circles and which was ranked No. 2 on *SF Magazine*'s list of the best science fiction of the year. Since then, EnJoe has been one of those rare writers comfortable working in both "pure literature" and science fiction. In 2010 his novel *U Yu Shi Tan* won the Noma Prize for new authors. In 2011 his "This Is a Pen" was nominated for the Akutagawa Prize , and he won Waseda University's Tsubouchi Shouyou Prize. In January 2012, he won the Akutagawa Prize with "Doukeshi no Cyo" (Harlequin's Butterflies). His other works include *Boy's Surface* and *About Goto*.

WHAT IS HAIKASORU

?

SPACE OPERA.
DARK FANTASY.
HARD SCIENCE.

With a small, elite list of award-winners, classics, and new work by the hottest young writers, **Haikasoru** is the first imprint dedicated to bringing Japanese science fiction to America and beyond. Featuring the action of anime and the thoughtfulness of the best speculative fiction, Haikasoru aims to truly be the "**high castle**" of science fiction and fantasy.

HAIKASORU

THE FUTURE IS JAPANESE

METAL GEAR SOLID: GUNS OF THE PATRIOTS
—PROJECT ITOH

From the legendary video game franchise! Solid Snake is a soldier and part of a worldwide nanotechnology network known as the Sons of the Patriots System. Time is running out for Snake as, thanks to the deadly FOXDIE virus, he has been transformed into a walking biological weapon. Not only is the clock ticking for Snake, nearly everyone he encounters becomes infected. Snake turns to the SOP System for help, only to find that it has been hacked by the SOP's old enemy Liquid Ocelot—and whoever controls the SOP System controls the world.

GENOCIDAL ORGAN
—PROJECT ITOH

The war on terror exploded, literally, the day Sarajevo was destroyed by a homemade nuclear device. The leading democracies transformed into total surveillance states, and the developing world has drowned under a wave of genocides. The mysterious American John Paul seems to be behind the collapse of the world system, and it's up to intelligence agent Clavis Shepherd to track John Paul across the wreckage of civilizations and to find the true heart of darkness—a genocidal organ.

THE FUTURE IS JAPANESE
—EDITED BY NICK MAMATAS AND MASUMI WASHINGTON

A web browser that threatens to conquer the world. The longest, loneliest railroad on Earth. A North Korean nuke hitting Tokyo, a hollow asteroid full of automated rice paddies, and a specialist in breaking up virtual marriages. And yes, giant robots. These thirteen stories from and about the Land of the Rising Sun run the gamut from fantasy to cyberpunk and will leave you knowing that the future is Japanese!

VIRUS: THE DAY OF RESURRECTION
—SAKYO KOMATSU

In this classic of Japanese SF, American astronauts on a space mission discover a strange virus and bring it to Earth, where rogue scientists transform it into a fatal version of the flu. After the virulent virus is released, nearly all human life on Earth is wiped out save for fewer than one thousand men and a handful of women living in research stations in Antarctica. Then one of the researchers realizes that a major earthquake in the now-depopulated United States may lead to nuclear Armageddon…

THE OUROBOROS WAVE
–JYOUJI HAYASHI

Ninety years from now, a satellite detects a nearby black hole scientists dub Kali for the Hindu goddess of destruction. Humanity embarks on a generations-long project to tap the energy of the black hole and establish colonies on planets across the solar system. Earth and Mars and the moons Europa (Jupiter) and Titania (Uranus) develop radically different societies, with only Kali, that swirling vortex of destruction and creation, and the hated but crucial Artificial Accretion Disk Development association (AADD) in common.

THE NAVIDAD INCIDENT: THE DOWNFALL OF MATÍAS GUILI
–NATSUKI IKEZAWA

In this sweeping magical-realist epic set in the fictional south sea island republic of Navidad, Ikezawa gives his imagination free rein to reinvent the myths of twentieth-century Japan. The story takes off as a delegation of Japanese war veterans pays an official visit to the ex-World War II colony, only to see the Japanese flag burst into flames. The following day, the tour bus, and its passengers, simply vanish. The locals exchange absurd rumors— the bus was last seen attending Catholic mass, the bus must have skipped across the lagoon— but the president suspects a covert guerrilla organization is trying to undermine his connections with Japan. Can the real answers to the mystery be found, or will the president have to be content with the surreal answers?

HARMONY
–PROJECT ITOH

In the future, Utopia has finally been achieved thanks to medical nanotechnology and a powerful ethic of social welfare and mutual consideration. This perfect world isn't that perfect though, and three young girls stand up to totalitarian kindness and super-medicine by attempting suicide via starvation. It doesn't work, but one of the girls—Tuan Kirie—grows up to be a member of the World Health Organization. As a crisis threatens the harmony of the new world, Tuan rediscovers another member of her suicide pact, and together they must help save the planet…from itself.

YUKIKAZE
–CHŌHEI KAMBAYASHI

More than thirty years ago a hyper-dimensional passageway suddenly appeared… the first stage of an attempted invasion by an enigmatic alien host. Humanity managed to push the invaders back through the passageway to the strange planet nicknamed "Faery." Now, Second Lieutenant Rei Fukai carries out his missions in the skies over Faery. His only constant companion in this lonely task is his fighter plane, the sentient FFR-31 Super Sylph, call sign: YUKIKAZE.

GOOD LUCK, YUKIKAZE
—CHŌHEI KAMBAYASHI

The alien JAM have been at war with humanity for over thirty years…or have they? Rei Fukai of the FAF's Special Air Force and his intelligent tactical reconnaissance fighter plane Yukikaze have seen endless battles, but after declaring "Humans are unnecessary now," and forcibly ejecting Fukai, Yukikaze is on its own. Is the target of the JAM's hostility really Earth's machines?

BELKA, WHY DON'T YOU BARK?
—HIDEO FURUKAWA

In 1943, when Japanese troops retreat from the Aleutian island of Kiska, they leave behind four military dogs. One of them dies in isolation, and the others are taken under the protection of US troops. Meanwhile, in the USSR, a KGB military dog handler kidnaps the daughter of a Japanese yakuza. Named after the Russian astronaut dog Strelka, the girl develops a psychic connection with canines. In this multigenerational epic as seen through the eyes of man's best friend, the dogs who are used as mere tools for the benefit of humankind gradually discover their true selves and learn something about humanity as well.

LOUPS-GAROUS
—NATSUHIKO KYOGOKU

In the near future, humans will communicate almost exclusively through online networks—face-to-face meetings are rare and the surveillance state nearly all-powerful. So when a serial killer starts slaughtering junior high students, the crackdown is harsh. The killer's latest victim turns out to have been in contact with three young girls: Mio Tsuzuki, a certified prodigy; Hazuki Makino, a quiet but opinionated classmate; and Ayumi Kono, her best friend. And as the girls get caught up in trying to find the killer—who just might be a werewolf—Hazuki learns that there is much more to their monitored communications than meets the eye.

TEN BILLION DAYS AND ONE HUNDRED BILLION NIGHTS
—RYU MITSUSE

Ten billion days—that is how long it will take the philosopher Plato to determine the true systems of the world. One hundred billion nights—that is how far into the future Jesus of Nazareth, Siddhartha, and the demigod Asura will travel to witness the end of all worlds. Named the greatest Japanese science fiction novel of all time, *Ten Billion Days and One Hundred Billion Nights* is an epic eons in the making. Originally published in 1967, the novel was revised by the author in later years and republished in 1973.

THE BOOK OF HEROES
—MIYUKI MIYABE

When her brother Hiroki disappears after a violent altercation with school bullies, Yuriko finds a magical book in his room. The book leads her to another world where she learns that Hiroki has been possessed by a spirit from The Book of Heroes, and that every story ever told has some truth to it and some horrible lie. With the help of the monk Sky, the dictionary-turned-mouse Aju, and the mysterious Man of Ash, Yuriko has to piece together the mystery of her vanished brother and save the world from the evil King in Yellow.

BRAVE STORY
—MIYUKI MIYABE

Young Wataru flees his messed-up life to navigate the magical world of Vision, a land filled with creatures both fierce and friendly. His ultimate destination is the Tower of Destiny where a goddess of fate awaits. Only when he has finished his journey and collected five elusive gemstones will he possess the Demon's Bane—the key that will grant him his most heartfelt wish…the wish to bring his family back together again!

ICO: CASTLE IN THE MIST
—MIYUKI MIYABE

A boy with horns, marked for death. A girl who sleeps in a cage of iron. The Castle in the Mist has called for its sacrifice: a horned child, born once a generation. When, on a single night in his thirteenth year, Ico's horns grow long and curved, he knows his time has come. But why does the Castle in the Mist demand this offering, and what will Ico do with the girl imprisoned within the Castle's walls? Delve into the mysteries of Miyuki Miyabe's grand achievement of imagination, inspired by the award-winning game for the PlayStation® 2 computer entertainment system, now remastered for PlayStation® 3.

ROCKET GIRLS
—HOUSUKE NOJIRI

Yukari Morita is a high school girl on a quest to find her missing father. While searching for him in the Solomon Islands, she receives the offer of a lifetime—she'll get the help she needs to find her father, and all she need do in return is become the world's youngest, lightest astronaut. Yukari and her sister Matsuri, both petite, are the perfect crew for the Solomon Space Association's launches, or will be once they complete their rigorous and sometimes dangerous training.

ROCKET GIRLS: THE LAST PLANET
-HOUSUKE NOJIRI
When the Rocket Girls accidentally splash down in the pond of Yukari Morita's old school, it looks as though their experiment is ruined. Luckily, the geeky Akane is there to save the day. Fitting the profile—she's intelligent, enthusiastic, and petite—Akane is soon recruited by the Solomon Space Association. Yukari and Akane are then given the biggest Rocket Girl mission yet: to do what NASA astronauts cannot and save a probe headed to the minor planet Pluto and the very edge of the solar system.

USURPER OF THE SUN
-HOUSUKE NOJIRI
Aki Shiraishi is a high school student working in the astronomy club and one of the few witnesses to an amazing event—someone is building a tower on the planet Mercury. Soon, the enigmatic Builders have constructed a ring around the sun, and the ecology of Earth is threatened by its immense shadow. Aki is inspired to pursue a career in science, and the truth. She must determine the purpose of the ring and the plans of its creators, as the survival of both species—humanity and the alien Builders—hangs in the balance.

THE LORD OF THE SANDS OF TIME
-ISSUI OGAWA
Sixty-two years after human life on Earth was annihilated by rampaging alien invaders, the enigmatic Messenger O is sent back in time with a mission to unite humanity of past eras—during the Second World War, in ancient Japan, and at the dawn of humanity—to defeat the invasion before it begins. However, in a future shredded by love and genocide, love waits for O. Will O save humanity only to doom himself?

THE NEXT CONTINENT
-ISSUI OGAWA
The year is 2025 and Gotoba General Construction—a firm that has built structures to survive the Antarctic and the Sahara—has received its most daunting challenge yet. Sennosuke Touenji, the chairman of one of the world's largest leisure conglomerates, wants a moon base fit for civilian use, and he wants his granddaughter Taé to be his eyes and ears on the harsh lunar surface. Taé and Gotoba engineer Aomine head to the moon where adventure, trouble, and perhaps romance await.

DRAGON SWORD AND WIND CHILD
—NORIKO OGIWARA

The God of Light and the Goddess of Darkness have waged a ruthless war across the land of Toyoashihara for generations. But for fifteen-year-old Saya, the war is far away—until the day she discovers that she is the reincarnation of the Water Maiden and a princess of the Children of the Dark. Raised to love the Light and detest the Dark, Saya must come to terms with her heritage even as the Light and Dark both seek to claim her, for she is the only mortal who can awaken the legendary Dragon Sword, the weapon destined to bring an end to the war. Can Saya make the choice between the Light and Dark, or is she doomed—like all the Water Maidens who came before her...?

MIRROR SWORD AND SHADOW PRINCE
—NORIKO OGIWARA

When the heir to the empire comes to Mino, the lives of young Oguna and Toko change forever. Oguna is drafted to become a shadow prince, a double trained to take the place of the hunted royal. But soon Oguna is given the Mirror Sword, and his power to wield it threatens the entire nation. Only Toko can stop him, but to do so she needs to gather four magatama, beads with magical powers that can be strung together to form the Misumaru of Death. Toko's journey is one of both adventure and self-discovery, and also brings her face to face with the tragic truth behind Oguna's transformation. A story of two parallel quests, of a pure love tried by the power of fate, the second volume of Tales of the Magatama is as thrilling as *Dragon Sword and Wind Child*.

SUMMER, FIREWORKS AND MY CORPSE
—OTSUICHI

Two short novels, including the title story and *Black Fairy Tale*, plus a bonus short story. *Summer* is a simple story of a nine-year-old girl who dies while on summer vacation. While her youthful killers try to hide her body, she tells us the story—from the point of view of her dead body—of the children's attempt to get away with murder. *Black Fairy Tale* is classic J-horror: a young girl loses an eye in an accident, but receives a transplant. Now she can see again, but what she sees out of her new left eye is the experiences and memories of its previous owner. Its previous *deceased* owner.

ZOO
—OTSUICHI

A man receives a photo of his girlfriend every day in the mail...so that he can keep track of her body's decomposition. A deathtrap that takes a week to kill its victims. Haunted parks and airplanes held in the sky by the power of belief. These are just a few of the stories by Otsuichi, Japan's master of dark fantasy.

ALL YOU NEED IS KILL
-HIROSHI SAKURAZAKA

When the alien Mimics invade, Keiji Kiriya is just one of many recruits shoved into a suit of battle armor called a Jacket and sent out to kill. Keiji dies on the battlefield, only to be reborn each morning to fight and die again and again. On his 158th iteration, he gets a message from a mysterious ally—the female soldier known as the Full Metal Bitch. Is she the key to Keiji's escape or his final death?

SLUM ONLINE
-HIROSHI SAKURAZAKA

Etsuro Sakagami is a college freshman who feels uncomfortable in reality, but when he logs onto the combat MMO *Versus Town*, he becomes "Tetsuo," a karate champ on his way to becoming the most powerful martial artist around. While his relationship with new classmate Fumiko goes nowhere, Etsuro spends his days and nights online in search of the invincible fighter Ganker Jack. Drifting between the virtual and the real, will Etsuro ever be ready to face his most formidable opponent?

BATTLE ROYALE: THE NOVEL
-KOUSHUN TAKAMI

Koushun Takami's notorious high-octane thriller envisions a nightmare scenario: a class of junior high school students is taken to a deserted island where, as part of a ruthless authoritarian program, they are provided arms and forced to kill until only one survivor is left standing. Criticized as violent exploitation when first published in Japan—where it became a runaway best seller—*Battle Royale* is a *Lord of the Flies* for the twenty-first century, a potent allegory of what it means to be young and (barely) alive in a dog-eat-dog world.

MARDOCK SCRAMBLE
-TOW UBUKATA

Why me? It was to be the last thought a young prostitute, Rune-Balot, would ever have...as a human anyway. Taken in by a devious gambler named Shell, she became a slave to his cruel desires and would have been killed by his hand if not for the self-aware Universal Tool (and little yellow mouse) known as Oeufcoque. Now a cyborg, Balot is not only nigh invulnerable, but has the ability to disrupt electrical systems of all sorts. But even these powers may not be enough for Balot to deal with Shell, who offloads his memories to remain above the law, the immense assassin Dimsdale-Boiled, or the neon-noir streets of Mardock City itself.

THE CAGE OF ZEUS
-SAYURI UEDA

The Rounds are humans with the sex organs of both genders. Artificially created to test the limits of the human body in space, they are now a minority, despised and hunted by the terrorist group the Vessel of Life. Aboard Jupiter-I, a space station orbiting the gas giant that shares its name, the Rounds have created their own society with a radically different view of gender and of life itself. Security chief Shirosaki keeps the peace between the Rounds and the typically gendered "Monaurals," but when a terrorist strike hits the station, the balance of power is at risk...and an entire people is targeted for genocide.

MM9
-HIROSHI YAMAMOTO

Japan is beset by natural disasters all the time: typhoons, earthquakes, and...giant monster attacks. A special anti-monster unit called the Meteorological Agency Monsterological Measures Department (MMD) has been formed to deal with natural disasters of high "monster magnitude." The work is challenging, the public is hostile, and the monsters are hungry, but the MMD crew has science, teamwork...and a legendary secret weapon on their side. Together, they can save Japan, and the universe!

THE STORY OF IBIS
-HIROSHI YAMAMOTO

In a world where humans are a minority and androids have created their own civilization, a wandering storyteller meets the beautiful android Ibis. She tells him seven stories of human/android interaction in order to reveal the secret behind humanity's fall. The tales that Ibis tells are science fiction stories about the events surrounding the development of artificial intelligence (AI) in the twentieth and twenty-first centuries. At a glance, these stories do not appear to have any sort of connection, but what is the true meaning behind them? What are Ibis's real intentions?